IN A STUDENT'S COMPANY

A DEBUT NOVEL FROM

D.M. CHADWICK

www.dmchadwick.com

First published in 2019 by D.M. Chadwick
South Australia, Australia

ISBN 978-0-6485209-1-7

This book is for everyone who isn't 100% sure about their next step in life. So everyone.

A HEALTHY SCHOOL

"It's hot," Angus mumbled under the shade of the classroom veranda.

"Welcome to Australian winter," Lucas said through a mouthful of sandwich.

Angus wasn't concerned about his own wellbeing in the heat; he was accustomed to the Australian sun radiating down upon the school yard regardless of season. He was, however, concerned for the welfare of the fifteen chocolate bars in his school bag. Two Waffleos had already melted. The rest of the bars were only holding their shape thanks to the barely-cold ice pack Angus had rented for five dollars from a Year 8 boy with a sprained wrist. The students moved aimlessly along the verandas and under the courtyard shade sails, grazing on whatever they had found in their lunchboxes. All were Angus's potential customers. With a nod, Angus got the attention of a passing Year 10 girl.

"Do you want to buy a chocolate?" he asked quietly. The girl's eyes widened. She looked around for the teacher on recess duty.

"How much?" she asked, fishing in her pocket for coins.

"Four dollars," Angus said, also keeping an eye out for any teachers, staff or untrustworthy students.

The girl found two $2 coins. "What have you got?"

"What do you want?"

"Have you got any Caramilk bars?"

Angus knelt on the pavers and opened his school bag, a navy-blue backpack embroidered with their school's crest. He found a Caramilk bar, revealing it to the girl. They discreetly exchanged money for chocolate, and the girl excitedly went to find a hidden corner to enjoy her illicit treat. Every sale made Angus's heart beat a little faster. He felt a tap on his shoulder.

"Can I have the ice pack back now?" the Year 8 boy asked. "My wrist still hurts."

Angus, never one to wish pain upon anyone, retrieved the ice pack from his lunch box. "Do you see this, Lucas? A sprained wrist. That's the 'healthy school' initiative in action. What does exercise get you?"

"A longer, healthier, more fulfilled life?"

"No... Well, yes. Sure," Angus said. "But exercise that the school encourages, like handball and football, also increases the chance of injuries."

"I hurt my wrist when I fell off my chair in the library," the Year 8 pointed out.

Angus handed the younger boy a complimentary chocolate bar. "I guess chairs will be banned next week. I'll see if I can get some in stock."

The healthy school initiative had been founded at the year's start because one of the school principal's favourite teachers' magazines had claimed that "school children are unable to make healthy choices". One proposed solution was to remove everything from the school canteen that brought students joy. It began innocently with the 600ml iced coffees disappearing in the first week of school, but the healthy canteen regime soon accelerated. The chip bag sizes were halved; the chocolate milk sizes were quartered; the ice creams were taken off sale in favour of sugar-free, flavourless ice blocks; the packets of gummy lollies were replaced with packets of apple slices. The completion of the sugar exodus was announced in assembly on the first day of the second semester.

On the first day of each term, tradition dictated that the school held an assembly to bring the students up to date with any news from the holidays of changes in staff, any education initiatives the school had decided to tack on, and other proclamations the leadership thought important. Assemblies were a great time for the students to catch up through whispers and pokes and jokes and jabs between the rows. The teachers hated assemblies; it was a constant hour of shushing the restless, whispering, poking and jabbing students.

Three days before Angus sold the chocolate bar to a Year 10 girl and borrowed an ice pack from a boy crippled by a new-found appreciation for gravity, he and the rest of the Year 12 cohort walked into the auditorium on the first day of the semester and took their seats in the front row. Angus and Lucas landed nearest to the wall; it was the best place to make running commentary on proceedings without being told off by Mr Fletcher, their homeroom teacher. Both boys wore their school's winter uniform: dark-grey pants, white long-sleeve shirts, navy-blue ties and—once shiny, now scuffed to grey—black shoes. This first day back after the mid-year break, their uniforms were at their neatest. Angus had short, dark brown hair cut so as to spend no time in the mornings styling it. Lucas just let his dirty-blond hair be however it wanted. He only styled it for special occasions, and school was not a special occasion. Neither boy was fat or fit, but it was true that half a year of sitting behind desks and eating junk food for recess and lunch hadn't improved their health.

"How much would you bet I could go the rest of the semester with no sight?" Angus asked.

"As in blindfolded?" Lucas asked.

Angus nodded. "I reckon I could do it. I might need help getting around, but I can type on my laptop without looking. And I'd still be able to hear the teachers."

"I'd bet you two million dollars and fifty percent of all my future earnings as a doctor that you'd fail. I think you'd last for half a day," Lucas said. "But why do you feel the need to do to the semester blind?"

"It doesn't have to be blind—I could try deaf or mute. It's just a thought experiment; I'm thinking of ways to make our final semester of school more interesting."

"You could make school more interesting by doing it well."

"What's the fun in that?" Angus said. "I know how to do school-work well. I don't know how to do school-work blind."

Lucas shook his head. "I know you're joking, but please

message me if you're thinking of wearing a blindfold for the walk to school. It might give me a chance to practice my first-aid training."

After all the high school classes were seated in the auditorium, their principal stepped up to the podium. By all appearances, Mrs Campbell was unexceptional and uninteresting—just a middle-aged woman in an unfailingly green outfit. But seasoned students knew who she really was: their commanding officer. It took a new student but a single exchange with Mrs Campbell to understand the respect she demanded. The littlest first graders acknowledged this demand by crying whenever Mrs Campbell entered their classroom. Older students internalised their tears or claimed their hay fever was acting up. She held the power in the room over every teacher, parent, student and staff member.

"Welcome back," Mrs Campbell said into the microphone, attempting her best smile. "I hope you are all ready for another term of learning."

Her voice carried no enthusiasm; everything she said was purely matter-of-fact. She paused, as if waiting for applause in celebration of learning. There was a shush from a Year 8 teacher trying to settle some girls in her class.

"To begin, I have a number of announcements, so please listen attentively. As you may already know, Mrs Gillian had her baby over the holidays. Isn't that wonderful and precious?"

"Wouldn't know it," Angus whispered to Lucas.

"Please remember," Mrs Campbell continued, "although it is still winter, when it is sunny you will need to be wearing

5

your hats at recess and lunch. We will be cracking down on hat non-compliance this term, and detentions will be given out. We do this because we care about you and your health. Speaking of health, as you know, the school has been working hard this year to provide you with healthy options at the canteen, and I'm excited to let you know there have been some changes to the menu."

"I bet the chocolate bars are gone," Lucas whispered to Angus.

"There are new vegetable chip flavours—beetroot, I believe—vegetable juices have been added to the menu, and we have also removed some less healthy items from the menu, such as chocolate bars."

From the groan that travelled through the audience, one would think Mrs Campbell had just added a mandatory kick in the shin to the daily schedule. The principal, clearly prepared for the backlash, was quick to add: "But you will be happy to know we have added a very tasty alternative."

"I bet it's muesli bars," Angus joked.

"We've added a new range of muesli bars to the menu," Mrs Campbell said proudly. The groan re-echoed through the congregation. Mrs Campbell stopped, staring over the crowd. The students took this as a cue to be quiet or face further consequences. Consequences with Mrs Campbell always started with a "meeting", where she proved neither bark or bite were necessary to frighten a student's soul into submission.

After more announcements and the presentation of awards that held no interest to most of the students, the assembly concluded. Angus and Lucas, friends from the day Lucas had come to the school in Year 9, walked with the crowd of students from the auditorium to the courtyard locker bays.

"I think it's hilarious," Angus said.

"What, the award for most melodramatic poem?" Lucas laughed.

"That poem was deep," Angus said sarcastically. "Comparing life to a piano? It spoke to me. No, I'm talking about the whole 'healthy school' thing. For years the teachers have been saying, 'The canteen is a privilege, not a right' and 'The canteen runs at a loss so don't complain about the prices'. But by removing all the things the students love, like chocolate bars, the canteen will just run at an even bigger loss."

"Since when do you care about the school's finances?" Lucas asked.

"I don't. It's just interesting. I read two business books over the holidays and neither of them said 'Get rid of the products your customers like the most'."

"Are you planning to start a business after Year 12?"

Angus shrugged. "I don't know. Maybe."

They arrived at the locker bays, gently squeezing between other students to reach their lockers.

"I don't think it's bad that they're getting rid of the chocolate bars," Lucas said. "Sugar is very addictive. Some say it's worse than cocaine."

"My point isn't whether chocolate is bad or not," Angus said. "I agree that people should eat more apples than chocolate. My point is that the school is a business. Students—or more accurately parents—are the customers. If a school has no students, it has no money. It makes more sense for the school to introduce *more* varieties of chocolate to the canteen to attract new students."

"You think a canteen filled with chocolate, lollies, chips and soft drink is going to attract more students? Why don't they just sell paintball guns and the answers to maths exams? And flamethrowers?"

"It could be worth a try," Angus said.

They retrieved their laptops and walked across the school grounds to the library.

"What subjects are you doing this semester?" Lucas asked.

Angus pulled out an electives list from his pocket. The list hadn't been unfolded since the final day of last semester. He read out each subject in a grandiose way. "I'm doing Information Communication Technology, English Literary Studies, Mathematical Methods, and Business and Enterprise."

"I'm in business too," Lucas said with a frown.

Angus was surprised. "You've moved into BnE? You have no interest in business."

"It's unfair," Lucas said. "Mr Fletcher didn't tell us last semester that we had to submit elective changes before the end of week 9."

"He did tell us. A number of times."

"Well, I must have missed it every time. I was originally doing Design and Technology, but then I found out that wouldn't give me the ATAR I need to study medicine. Apparently because I didn't submit the form or something, they put me in whatever class had an opening. Now I have to learn how to shake people's hands, or whatever they teach in BnE."

"Business won't be that bad. You might actually have fun."

Lucas didn't agree. "I'm going to ask Mrs Campbell if I can move subjects."

"This is our final semester of school for the rest of our lives!" Angus exclaimed to cheer up his friend. "I'm feeling good; I'm willing to try out your advice. I'll make this semester interesting by doing it well with thirty-thirty vision."

It only took Angus five hours to remember why he detested school so much. The repetitive, monotonous, repetitive, boring, repetitive nature of learning drained his enthusiasm. When the end-of-day bell rang, he was back to how he had felt all year: bored.

Angus and Lucas lived in the same neighbourhood, about a twenty-minute walk from the school. As was their habit, they met up at the school gate after they were dismissed and walked home together. Part of their habit was stopping at the shopping centre; a random assortment of shops including a supermarket, café, jeweller, newsagent and an office supplies store. Every afternoon, Angus and Lucas stopped at the supermarket to browse the junk food on special. They were always hungry after school and knew they wouldn't get to eat until they had finished the walk home and could raid their parents' fridges.

"What are you getting?" Lucas asked as they walked down the confectionery aisle.

"I can't decide." Angus gazed over the brightly coloured chocolates. "I really feel like a Caramilk bar. I don't even really like Caramilks."

"It's because they're now forbidden," Lucas said

dramatically, picking his choice. Then he doubted his choice of a Waffleo bar and put it back. "If you could force the supermarket to sell only one type of chocolate, which would you pick?"

"Probably plain chocolate—the boring one," Angus said. "It's the cheapest and if it was the only type available, no one would really care. People would just buy it because it's chocolate—"

The idea came to Angus in that moment. He looked at Lucas and couldn't help grinning mischievously as he picked up a whole box of *Caramilk* bars from the shelf.

"I've just had an idea." Angus looked up and down the aisle for any teachers or students who had stopped at the supermarket on their way home. "Let's sell chocolate bars to the other kids at school."

"No," Lucas said without hesitation.

"At no point did Mrs Campbell say that students aren't allowed to bring unhealthy snacks to school. We'll be fine if we keep it discreet," Angus explained, already walking to the checkouts.

Lucas knew Angus could be bold, but this was the most audacious his friend had ever been. "Are you serious?"

"Would you at least help me smuggle them into school? You don't need to do the selling," Angus said as they walked home. The box of chocolates bulged in his school bag.

"If you're looking to get expelled, there are cheaper methods than buying twenty dollars' worth of chocolate bars," Lucas said.

Angus looked at him expectantly.

"The answer is definitely no," Lucas said firmly. "I won't be your chocolate mule or even encourage you by suggesting you'll sell a single bar tomorrow. But I'll give you a generous bonus when you become my window washer after you're expelled."

"I'm not trying to get expelled. I won't get expelled," Angus said. "I just want to see if I can do it—sell products. Those business books have given me an urge to at least try."

"I read a book on brain surgery during the holidays," Lucas said. "Shall we go find an operating theatre?"

During the next morning's recess, Angus sat by himself on a courtyard bench. He kept an eye on the Year 6 classroom teacher on yard duty. Lucas had not changed his mind about helping and had gone to play handball on the basketball courts.

Angus opened his backpack and pulled out one of the two chocolate bars he had stowed in the front pocket. The king-sized chocolate emerged from the backpack like a beacon of light. Other students sitting nearby couldn't help but glance. Some gawked; others pretended not to notice as Angus slowly unwrapped the bar. He paused, making sure he had maximum audience attention before taking a dramatic bite from the sweet, gooey, caramel-filled *Caramilk* bar.

His spectators looked at him with a mixture of jealousy and contempt. A group of Year 7 girls whispered to each other. Angus proceeded to eat the rest of the chocolate bar with a distant stare. When he had finished, he looked around the courtyard to see if anyone was still paying attention. He spotted a Year 9 boy, Samuel, sitting alone against some

11

lockers. Samuel looked between the empty Caramilk wrapper in the older boy's hand and the ground. Angus had his first sales lead.

With his schoolbag at his side, Angus walked over and leaned against a locker a little over a meter away from his lead. Samuel looked down at his shoes, flicking his shoelaces.

"I've got another one, you know," Angus announced quietly.

The Year 9 whipped his head up.

"Would you want it?" Angus asked, eyes following the movements of a teacher in the distance.

"Sure." Samuel held out his hand.

Angus frowned. "I'm not giving it away."

Samuel retracted his hand.

"But it is available for sale."

The younger boy slowly looked up again. "How much?"

"Two dollars."

"They only cost one dollar fifty at the canteen."

"They only *costed* one dollar fifty. They're not available anymore." Angus revealed another chocolate bar from his bag.

Samuel was hesitant, but he couldn't stop staring at the treat. After but a moment's hesitation, he ran to his locker and returned with a $2 coin.

Angus was in disbelief that his plan had worked.

"You can't tell the teachers," he said as he handed over the chocolate.

Samuel nodded firmly.

"But do tell your friends. I'll have more bars tomorrow."

Angus brought ten chocolates the next day.

"You're gonna get caught," Lucas warned at recess.

"And what if I do get caught? It's not against school rules to bring chocolate to school, and there's no rule I know of that prohibits things being sold at school. What about *fundraising* chocolates? You can't walk thirty metres without being stopped by someone selling chocolate to raise funds for a dance school or football club."

"Yes, but they're fundraising," Lucas said. "What are you raising funds for?"

"The... 'International Angus Fund'. It helps a Year 12 student buy a new phone," Angus said. He spotted another Year 9 boy trying to get his attention. "I told Samuel to tell all his friends. I bet you at least eight bars will be gone before the end of lunch. Excuse me while I make a sale."

Lucas was baffled when Angus's sale predictions were accurate. He sold three bars at recess and a further six at lunch. Angus made sure he ate one at lunch for quality assurance purposes.

The next few days were success stories, not only for Angus's first business, but also for chocolate sales at the local supermarket. Each morning before school, Angus purchased as many bars as he thought he could sell that day. On Thursday, he made the unfortunate mistake of underestimating the Australian winter sun and at lunchtime found an oily, sticky pile of sugar and plastic wrappers at the bottom of his bag. One of his exercise books had to be thrown out.

On Friday, Angus remembered to bring a heat-proof lunchbox to keep his chocolates solid. The ice packs he brought from home often only lasted half a day. The second half of the day required more creative cooling methods.

Students across the school knew about Angus and his chocolates. Some students, especially in his Year 12 cohort, found it hilarious and liked to hear the sales numbers at the end of each lunchtime. Other students ignored Angus's underground chocolate dispensary, but Angus knew that someone would eventually tell a teacher.

Angus had just finished his transaction with the Year 10 girl and pocketed the four dollars. He knew four dollars was a steep price, but the cost of renting ice packs from injured children helped him justify the price to customers. Although Lucas was now comfortable being in the same vicinity with Angus while he made transactions, he still didn't support the venture. Angus looked around the courtyard for his next customer. He knew his chocolates wouldn't survive long in the heat and needed to be sold quickly.

Sales leads were generally the kids who kept glancing sideways at him; too afraid to approach. Angus spotted a group of Year 11 girls huddled by the lockers, looking down and counting something in their hands. One of the girls waved to Angus.

Angus nodded and began walking over with his bag open in front of him.

"Angus?" a man's voice asked behind him. Angus froze, his hand inside his backpack. He slowly pulled it out and turned to face Mrs Campbell's assistant, Mr Tilley.

"Yes?" Angus zipped up his bag.

"Mrs Campbell would like to see you right away," Mr Tilley

said, looking down at the bright-yellow sticky note on his forefinger.

"As in, right now?" Angus asked, looking for an opportunity to get rid of the contraband. "Can I just put my bag in my locker first?"

Mr Tilley considered the request carefully. "Yes, but quickly."

Angus walked back to his locker, avoiding eye contact with the surrounding students.

Lucas was less than sympathetic as he accompanied Angus to the lockers. "I told you."

"You could have at least warned me," Angus said under his breath.

"I didn't see him," Lucas replied defensively. "I've been no help to you whatsoever."

"I know that."

"Good. Make sure Mrs Campbell knows that."

The crowd watched as their chocolate supplier was marched to the school office. Everyone knew it was over. Angus had been caught, and he would face the consequence: a meeting with Mrs Campbell.

A MEETING WITH MRS. CAMPBELL

Angus felt calm. He sat in a hard, plastic chair provided for students summoned to the front office. He was confident selling chocolates wasn't worthy of a capital punishment like expulsion. Mrs Campbell's office door, which had remained unopened since Angus's arrival, was painted a dreary green. There was no name plate or indication of what a visitor would find inside.

So much for needing to see me right away, Angus thought, staring at a clock on the wall while his precious lunch time slipped away. Mr Tilley, a man only a year Angus's senior, sat at a small desk across from Mrs Campbell's closed office door. His knees banged against the desk every time he repositioned his legs.

"How's your art coming along?" Angus asked Mr Tilley.

"Fine thanks." Mr Tilley was doing his best to sort and re-staple a pile of teacher professional development booklets whose pages had been printed in the wrong order.

Angus had found out, in the few times they had made conversation and from various other sources, that Mr Tilley's dream was not to be a principal's assistant. Mr Tilley had finished dux of his school last year. He assumed achieving dux implied he could pursue any career he desired, and decided to study contemporary art. Although his ATAR had been 99.4, he was rejected from every university to which he applied because his artistic skills were "unique", according to one of the rejection letters. Truth was, his university application portfolio was indistinguishable from a child's work. Mr Tilley's mother, ever supportive of her son, suggested community art classes. Additionally, through family connections she got him a job assisting in the art rooms at Angus's school. After little more than a week, the art teacher, patient as he was, refused to employ Mr Tilley in the art room any longer.

"He gives bad art vibes," the art teacher had told Mrs Campbell. As "bad art vibes" were insufficient grounds for firing, Mr Tilley was given the next vacant administrative position—assistant to Mrs Campbell. Despite the setbacks, he kept a sketch pad and pencil in his desk's top drawer for moments of artistic inspiration and attended numerous art classes a week. Angus admired Mr Tilley not because of his skills, which never seemed to improve, but for his persistence.

"Got any new works?" Angus asked.

Mr Tilley nodded. Ensuring Mrs Campbell's office door was still closed, he pulled out his sketch pad and held up the most recent page. It was a rough pencil sketch of what appeared to be a wonky, broken version of the chair in which Angus sat.

Angus nodded supportively. "I can see what it is."

"Thanks." Mr Tilley smiled. "Still working on the shading."

The office door opened to reveal Mrs Campbell. She wore one of her green blouses with a big silk bow at her midriff. She appeared tranquil, as if she had just woken from a nap. Mr Tilley quickly hid the sketch pad in his lap.

"Mr Tilley, could you please get me a coffee?" Mrs Campbell asked with a smile that didn't quite reach her eyes. Without looking at or acknowledging Angus, the principal closed the door.

Angus didn't consider himself a bad student. He wasn't rude to teachers. He wasn't antagonistic to other students. In his thirteen years of school, he had only received two detentions, both for missed homework in Year 10. As a preventative measure against wasting any more lunch times on being incarcerated, he challenged himself to never receive any more homework-related detentions. When he felt he had mastered that, he increased the difficulty. From the start of Year 11, his challenge was to never again do homework at home. He had read numerous online articles that provided evidence against doing work at home, and strongly agreed with them.

"How do you never have homework?" Lucas would complain. "I always have to spend at least half an hour every night finishing the maths questions."

"Three ways to avoid homework," Angus explained. "One: only do the bare minimum. Two: make homework your priority in free lessons. Three: if the homework is so hard that you can't work it out during your free lessons, leave it and don't stress. Teachers rarely give detentions because you genuinely didn't understand the work. Some do, but that's the risk element. You've got to work smart, not hard."

Angus was succeeding in his challenge, and homework wasn't part of his school life anymore.

Sitting outside Mrs Campbell's office, Angus considered the possibility that his principal had called him in for advice on how to help other kids be more productive with their homework. He would be glad to give his advice on the matter. Mr Tilley returned with a mug of coffee from the staff room. He paused at Mrs Campbell's door and knocked once. The door instantly opened.

"Thank you for the coffee," Mrs Campbell said. She poked her head out the doorway and looked down at Angus.

"Come in, Angus. Sit down."

Angus entered the office. It was sparingly decorated. Family photos of nieces and nephews adorned the filing cabinets, and a framed copy of Mrs Campbell's Master of Education degree hung on the wall. He took a seat in one of the two visitors' chairs. These chairs were cushioned and should have been far more comfortable than the hard plastic one, but nothing at that moment could have made Angus comfortable. His peace had stayed outside.

Mrs Campbell gently placed her coffee onto a hand-painted coaster and looked at the steaming beverage with a caring smile. She didn't say anything for a few moments, leaving Angus to wonder at her thoughts. He fidgeted with a pen in his pocket.

She eventually looked up at him. "Do you drink coffee?"

"I'm fine for the moment, thank you," Angus said politely.

"I'm not offering you a coffee. I'm just asking if you like it."

Angus decided the best strategy was to play along with wherever the conversation was going.

"I don't mind coffee, but I only have it about once a month."

"I really like my coffees," Mrs Campbell said. "Tea is great, but a cappuccino is just wonderful."

"I heard it's quite addictive," Angus added, content with discussing coffee and nothing else.

Mrs Campbell didn't immediately reply. She sat forward in her high-back leather chair, staring at the boy. Angus, unsure where to look, shifted in his chair and gazed out a window facing the oval. In the distance, he could see a Year 9 boy eating a *Waffleo*.

"Coffee *is* quite addictive," Mrs Campbell said finally.

Angus exhaled, without realising he'd been holding his breath.

"I try to not have more than one a day," Mrs Campbell continued, "but I could very well be addicted. You know, I was recently doing some research on the health benefits of coffee. It turns out there are only a few. Do you know what the unhealthiest part of a cappuccino is?"

Angus knew the answer was sugar. He knew Mrs Campbell knew the answer was sugar, so he doubled down on sugar. "I'd say the sugar. It's insane how much sugar people put in their coffee. My uncle puts about three or four teaspoons of sugar in his coffee, and he has at least five coffees a day."

"That's right. Sugar is the unhealthiest part," Mrs Campbell said. She took a sip of her coffee. "In case you were wondering, this coffee is sugar free. And you mentioned coffee is addictive. Do you know what they say is more addictive than coffee?"

Angus paused to emulate a moment of deliberation. "Cocaine?"

"No—sugar," Mrs Campbell corrected. "I'm surprised you didn't know that."

She stood up from her desk and searched for something on the shelf above her desk. "You are a very bright student, Angus. I am sure you'll do many great things after you graduate Year 12. I was wondering if you would be kind enough to give me your opinion on... an idea I have."

Angus felt his heart rate increase as Mrs Campbell found what she was looking for. She placed a *Caramilk* bar in front of him on the desk.

"As you know, at the start of this term—less than two weeks ago—I announced that the canteen would no longer be stocking chocolate bars or any other products with high sugar content. Were you here on that day?"

Angus continued to play along. "Yes, I was."

"Excellent. And do you remember what I said at the start of this year about why we are striving to become a healthier school?"

He was growing tired of the condescension. "You said unhealthy food and drink cause childhood obesity, and the way to solve that is to take away the ability for kids to choose what they eat for lunch?"

"That is a very disrespectful version of what I said, Angus." Mrs Campbell picked up the Caramilk and turned it over in her hands. "I believe kids can choose what they eat, but within reason. Surely you are aware that children need guidance and teaching and support for making healthy food choices."

"High school students? People old enough to have jobs and earn their own money?" Angus said slowly, keeping a measured tone. "I'm sure junior school kids need guidance, but by the time we get to high school, we know that sugar and fatty foods are bad for us."

Mrs Campbell nodded, appearing to listen thoughtfully. Angus had never had this long of a conversation with his principal and wasn't sure if he was crossing a line. His plan was not to provoke her, but he felt any manager, or principal, should be willing to receive feedback.

"My idea that I'd like to run past you is whether we should ban the school canteen completely," she announced.

"Ban the canteen? Why?"

"Because I don't think it's a good use of school resources. All the canteen does is sell food and drink, and most of the food and drink sold in the canteen contains some form of added sugar."

Angus couldn't help but imagine the demand for his contraband goods if the canteen disappeared.

"I think that might work," he concluded.

Mrs Campbell let out a small laugh. "You agree that banning the canteen will help solve child obesity?"

"I don't see why not." Angus shrugged. "Or maybe just remove everything from the canteen but apples and those ham sandwiches."

Mrs Campbell waited until Angus was looking into her

eyes. "Stop selling chocolates."

"As in, stop *selling*? Or stop selling *chocolates*?" Angus asked quietly, taken off guard by the abrupt judgment.

"You are not to sell anything at all," Mrs Campbell said. "If I catch you selling or hear of you selling anything to students in or around school grounds, you will receive a detention and a parent-teacher meeting will be scheduled."

The purpose of a parent-teacher meeting was to allow the teachers and parents to scheme together and come up with punishments for the student that would further erase the division between school and home. Angus's parents, Thomas and Cathy Newman, were kind, caring and supportive. That made the parent-teacher meeting threat hold gravity. Threatening a parent-teacher meeting on a kid with deadbeat, careless parents was as good as threatening a pet dog-teacher meeting.

"What about the kids who sell chocolates for fundraising? Are they allowed to keep selling?" Angus asked, grasping for a loophole.

"This isn't about them—this is about you. You may not sell anything at school. Is that clear?"

Angus had no more arguments and accepted the defeat.

The end of lunch bell rang, and Angus was sent promptly back to class.

———————————————

"It's over?" Lucas asked quietly as he and Angus opened their laptops in the library.

"It's over," Angus confirmed. Nothing felt more humiliating to him than being told to stop what he was doing without a decent reason or explanation.

One of their classmates, Eli, overheard the conversation. "You're not selling chocolates anymore?"

"Mrs Campbell," was all Angus had to say.

Eli understood. "Have you got any left?"

"Half a dozen. Why?"

"Are you going to eat them?"

"I don't know. Probably. I paid for them."

"Can I have one?"

"A free one?"

Eli smiled. "Yes, a free one."

"No."

"Well, I'll buy the rest from you for a discount."

"I'm not allowed to sell any," Angus said. "I'll get in trouble."

Eli nodded toward Lucas. "Then get Lucas to sell them to me. Lucas can give you the money afterward. Did Mrs Campbell say Lucas couldn't sell chocolates?"

Lucas held his hands up defensively. "Don't involve me in your weird, money-laundering chocolate trade."

Peter, who was sitting next to Eli, joined the conversation. "I'll do the trade—for a cut of the profits."

"Wait, now I'm lost," Angus said.

"The deal is, you give me the chocolates," Peter explained. "I'll sell the chocolates to Eli. I'll keep, say, half of the money, and give the rest to you. That way, you haven't technically *sold* anything. You're merely giving me the chocolates out of the goodness of your heart, and I'll give you some money from the goodness of my heart."

"That's literally just me selling you the chocolates for half price," Angus said.

"Or, alternatively," Eli said to Peter, "once you have the chocolates you could agree to charge me a lower price, so Angus receives less money."

"You two are not convincing me that this is a good idea," Angus said.

"It would be a good idea for you all to be quiet and get back to work!" Mrs Van Paul, the librarian, called from her desk.

"Okay, final idea," Eli whispered excitedly. "Angus, you trade six chocolate bars with Peter for, like, six bags of chips. Then it's definitely not a sale—it's a trade. Peter and I will each buy three packets of chips to do the trade with you."

Lucas, although pretending to be working, shook his head. "Six bags of chips for six chocolate bars? That's not a fair trade. Chocolate bars are worth way more than bags of chips."

"Are you kidding? Chips and chocolates always carry the same value in food trades," Eli said.

Angus craned his neck to watch Mrs Van Paul leave the library to visit the bathroom, make a cup of tea or whatever else teachers did when they needed a break each lesson. He picked up his school bag from under his chair and removed the remaining chocolate bars. He held one out to Lucas, who shoved it in his pocket, looking around for any witnesses or cameras. Peter and Eli each received a chocolate like it was gold, making empty promises to pay Angus back. Angus turned to the table next to him, where two of his classmates, Rachael and Brooke, were focused on their work.

"Do you girls want one?" Angus asked, holding up two bars.

Rachael looked up from her maths book. She had been engrossed in her work and hadn't heard any of the boys' conversations. "No thanks. I don't have any money on me."

Angus placed the two chocolates on their desk. "They're free. I'm banned from selling them."

The girls exchanged a surprised glance, then quickly hid the chocolates in their pencil cases. A few minutes later, Mrs Van Paul returned.

Angus walked over to her desk. "Hey, Mrs V. I've got a present."

He presented his last *Caramilk* chocolate bar. Mrs Van Paul, a twenty-plus-year veteran of teaching, waited in anticipation for something to happen. "Is it a joke chocolate?"

"No tricks. It's just a chocolate bar. I had half a dozen spare from a business project. I'm watching my weight. Getting my body ready for the summer," Angus joked, giving his belly a pat.

"Aren't we all," Mrs Van Paul replied. She took the chocolate. "Thank you, Angus. That is very kind. I shall enjoy the sugar rush while I teach the Year 7s in the next lesson."

Angus went back to his desk and slumped into his chair. He was aware his homework-free streak was on the line if he didn't finish his maths questions that lesson, but he couldn't focus.

"Do you know who else is in Business and Enterprise?" Angus asked Lucas.

"I couldn't even tell you who's in the same maths class as me, and that class hasn't changed since the beginning of the year."

26

"Rachael is," Brooke said.

"Really?" Lucas asked.

Rachael sighed. "Yep."

Lucas had never considered that Rachael would be interested in business.

Maybe she's bored of being the best at everything else and looking for a challenge? he wondered.

Rachael Armand had achieved dux of the class in Year 11 and a merit award for all her subjects. There was a running joke among the Year 12s that the day she got a bad grade for an assessment was the day they'd all give up and drop out. She didn't appreciate that joke.

"Did you forget to put your elective preference form in as well?" Lucas asked with a hopeful smile. If the school's star student had messed up, he wondered if he could use that in his negotiations with Mrs Campbell.

"No, there was a subject clash," Rachael said. "I wanted to do Material Products, but to do that, I had to drop Modern History and choose between BnE or Drama."

"And you chose to be in a class with myself and Lucas?" Angus asked in a silly voice. "That's nice of you."

She smiled. It was true there were worse possibilities than having Angus and Lucas as classmates, but she didn't want to give them the satisfaction of knowing that. "I chose the subject, not the classmates."

"Well, there goes my only chance at a merit award," Angus said. Rachael shook her head. "You'll get it. I doubt anyone else in the class has started an actual business before."

"I doubt anyone else in history has been asked to stop

running a business by a principal either," Angus grumbled.

"Paul Jacobs, 2002," Mrs Van Paul said, rearranging some books on a nearby shelf. "He was unlucky Mrs Campbell caught him before the police did. Now settle and do your work or I'll unleash her on you, too."

LESSON ONE:
HOW TO START A BUSINESS

The Business and Enterprise lessons were scheduled on Mondays before recess. Because Monday of Week 1 had been a free day for student, Monday of Week 2 was their first Business and Enterprise lesson. Angus and Lucas walked across the courtyard to the BnE classroom in their ill-fitting school blazers to combat the indecisive weather's cold breeze.

He didn't know what to expect, but Angus was excited. Over the weekend he had calculated his chocolate profits and was quite satisfied with the result of $36. It gave him confidence going into the new subject. Lucas, on the other hand, had spent the weekend dreading BnE and written down more arguments for trying to convince Mrs Campbell to let him switch subjects.

There was only one other student in the classroom. Rachael's back-row desk was hidden beneath a sea of maths homework. She looked up when the boys entered and, relieved it wasn't the teacher, acknowledged them with a smile. Before the boys could smile back, she had put her head back down and resumed solving algebra questions.

Angus closed the classroom door behind him to keep the cold out, but it would be of little help. The shared-use classroom was built a couple of decades ago, and although every new piece of education technology on the market was in the room to assist the student's learning, nothing had been done to update the room's insulation or reglaze the large, thin windows. The linoleum-covered cement floors and the wall heater were at constant war to keep the classroom at a liveable temperature. The walls were painted a soft orange or blue—a colour completely forgettable and only interrupted by science posters left over from a bygone Biology class. There were three rows of two-seater desks for students and a table at the front for the teacher, making the room feel oversized for what appeared to be the smallest class that any of the BnE students had been a part of.

Angus and Lucas took seats in the front row of desks and took out their laptops.

"I wonder if we get to run a business like they did last year?" Angus said quietly, not wanting to disturb Rachael, who looked to be concentrating intensely.

"What do you mean?" Lucas asked.

"Don't you remember? Last year's BnE class sold hot chocolate and donuts."

Lucas laughed. "No chance of that happening again under the healthy school regime."

"But surely if it's for educational purposes, the 'no sugar' rule has leniency."

"I bet you ten dollars the 'no sugar' rule will apply to everything forever and ever."

Angus knew he was right. They went back to their laptops.

Five more minutes passed, and eventually Lucas grew bored browsing through Wikipedia articles on venereal diseases. He looked at the time on his laptop and frowned. "Do you know who the teacher is meant to be?"

"Are you nervous or something?" Angus asked.

"No, not nervous. Just keen to get this subject over and done with. I emailed Mrs Campbell on Friday and asked if I could do anything else besides BnE, but she said no. Because apparently it's 'my fault' for not submitting the form on time."

"It is your fault," Angus said.

Mr Redding burst into the classroom with his backpack, laptop and coat piled in his arms and a full mug of coffee in his hand. "Sorry I'm late!"

Mr Redding was in his early thirties. His brown hair, which was only neat for school photos and graduation assemblies, blended into quite an impressive beard. His daily uniform consisted of plain, pastel business shirts and black slacks.

"Above the neck, outdoor ranger. Below the neck, banking professional," was how he described his look. None of the three students had ever experienced Mr Redding as a teacher before, but his great reputation preceded him.

He carefully placed his steaming mug of coffee on the teacher's desk and let his other belongings flop down next to it. "I got caught up chatting with one of the other teachers in

31

the staff room. If you'll just give me a moment, I'll get organised."

Angus and Lucas closed their laptops and Rachael put her maths homework away. The students waited patiently as Mr Redding plugged in his laptop and handed out three stapled black-and-white booklets, still warm from the photocopier.

"I'm guessing you're Rachael," Mr Redding said rhetorically, surveying the rows of desks that separated her from the rest of the class.

"Yes, that's right." Rachael pushed her maths book farther under her pencil case.

"Did you want to maybe sit in a desk closer to the front?" Mr Redding noticed her hesitation and began manoeuvring between the desks to hand her a booklet. "Don't stress. If you're happy back there, so be it."

He reached over the last row of desks and passed her the booklet with a smile.

Rachael, a little embarrassed at appearing petty for not moving, avoided eye contact.

Angus flicked through his booklet. It was filled with badly photocopied stock photos of cities and people in suits. The text contained business terms like *internal communications* and *contract law*. Beside him, Lucas gave a quiet groan as he read the booklet's content.

Mr Redding made his way back to the front of the class. "Welcome to Business and Enterprise in your final semester of your final year!" he said. "I will admit, I'm quite excited. I love business studies and most things to do with business. I don't think I've taught any of you before, so let me introduce myself. My name is Mr Redding and I've been teaching for ten years—mainly high school specialist topics. As far as BnE goes, I have some experience in business operations. After high school, I went straight to university and became a teacher. I was never interested in business until my brother-in-law started a food wholesaler business about seven years ago. Since then, I've worked for him part-time, learning from him and reading everything I can get my hands on about economics, business and management. BnE is by far my favourite subject to teach."

He looked at the two boys. "Who is Angus and who is Lucas?"

Angus raised his hand. "I'm Angus."

"Great, so in this class we have Angus, Lucas and Rachael? Everyone's here," Mr Redding said. "This is a small class, but that's good for class discussions, which we'll do a lot of. Now, how well do you three know each other?"

The boys both turned their heads as if double-checking to see who Rachael was, even though they had all been in the same classes for years.

"Reasonably well," Angus answered.

Mr Redding nodded. "Good. In this class, you'll get to know each other better than probably any other cohort in any other subject. I'll give more details later, but almost all your assessments are group work. You'll be marked individually, but your grades will benefit from learning each other's strengths and weaknesses and learning to work as a team. You could imagine this class as being a business. I am your CEO and you are the employees. This will be fun!"

The excitement with which Mr Redding spoke was infectious to Angus but daunting to the other two. Rachael was not convinced in the slightest that anything Mr Redding said sounded fun.

"Do we get paid?" Lucas asked.

"No, we don't get paid," Angus said.

"Never say never," Mr Redding said vaguely.

Angus couldn't help gasping. "We get paid? How? When?"

Mr Redding laughed. "That always seems to generate interest. There may be an opportunity to earn a profit when you run a business later this semester. But before we get to any of that, I want to get to know you all." He retrieved a notepad and pen from his backpack and rolled a chair from behind the teacher's desk. He sat in front of the first row of desks facing the students. "Today, we're discussing what a business is, and how companies get started. To start a company, we need employees, and that is why I like to start each new BnE semester with job interviews. Angus, let's begin with you."

Mr Redding signalled for Angus to move down a couple of chairs so he was sitting opposite the teacher. Angus was not expecting to have to do a job interview. He nervously did as instructed.

"Can I please get your full name?" Mr Redding asked, pen poised above the notepad.

"Angus Newton."

"Good to meet you, Angus. What business experience do you have?"

"I worked part time at my uncle's furniture factory during the Christmas holidays. Is that business experience?"

"Absolutely. What did your role at the furniture factory involve?"

It had been a mind-numbing job, but his mum and dad had thought it was a great idea for him to earn some money. He'd finished at the factory as soon as Year 12 started to "focus on his studies".

"I organised deliveries. Sent out replacement parts to the retailers," Angus explained.

Mr Redding took notes, nodding. "Excellent. What would you say is the biggest strength you bring to this class?"

"I'm good at coming up with ideas." Angus figured that was the least egotistical way of saying he believed he was one of the most creative people he knew.

"It's important to have visionaries and creative thinkers in an organisation. And what would you say is your biggest weakness?"

Angus was unaware of any glaring issues in himself. "Maybe I could improve on my... empathy?" The word felt gross and sappy as he said it.

Mr Redding maintained eye contact. "That's definitely a common weakness."

Angus shrugged his shoulders.

"Last question. If you could start a business, what type of business would you start and why?"

Angus thought through numerous ideas he had stored in his imagination. He spoke slowly and carefully. "Well, I have a million ideas for businesses, but If I had to open a new business tomorrow, I would open a store that deals in high-end art."

"Why high-end art?"

"Because art is subjective. I could go find amateur artists and buy their paintings really cheap, then sell them for over a million dollars and customers would assume it's good art because it's expensive."

Mr Redding laughed. "That's a novel idea; I like it. But can you tell me why that might not work as you expect?"

"Because it's not ethical making a large profit off the artists?" Angus guessed.

The teacher leaned back in his chair. "Whether it's ethical or not is a topic for another day. But I wouldn't necessarily call it unethical; almost all businesses need to make profits. A manufacturer produces a product and sells it to the distributor for a profit, the distributor sells the product to a retailer for a profit, and the retailer sells the product to a consumer for a profit."

"Why wouldn't the manufacturer just skip all the middle men and sell the product directly to the consumer to make a bigger profit?" Angus asked.

"Some manufacturers do, but all those stages in the supply chain have differing roles. Do you think it would be better for your uncle's furniture factory to become better at selling and marketing furniture to customers, like a retailer, or should they instead focus their efforts on making furniture more efficiently and of a better quality so they can sell more products to more distributors and retailers?"

Angus saw his point.

"But back to my original question," Mr Redding said. "Why wouldn't it work to open a store that sells high-end art made by amateurs? Who are your customers?"

"People who like art?"

"More accurately for a high-end art store?"

"Rich people who like art," Angus said.

Mr Redding stood up and moved over to the white board. He wrote *branding* with a blue marker. "The reason paintings sell for millions of dollars isn't because of how pretty they are or because of the high price. It's because of the name and prestige attached to them.

"Take the 'Mona Lisa' by Da Vinci. There are other paintings from the 16th century that would be worth tens of thousands, if not just thousands, compared to the millions that a Da Vinci painting could sell for. The paintings are worth lots of money *because* they're a 'Da Vinci'. Branding is one of the most critical aspects of business. Not only in marketing, so that your products are recognisable in the market, but also for creating products that a consumer will trust because they carry your brand."

He wrote *market needs* on the white board. "When thinking of a business idea, you also need to consider whether there is an actual need for it. If you're unsure, do some market research. The biggest businesses on Earth got where they are because they're fulfilling a customer's need. If you see a need that no one else is meeting, start a business and you have greater potential for success. Like that student who started selling chocolate bars at lunchtime. That is an example of someone seeing an opportunity and fulfilling the market's need for sugar."

"That was Angus," Lucas blurted out, pointing at his friend.

Mr Redding raised his eyebrows. "That was you?"

Angus nodded his head proudly.

Mr Redding laughed, but regained composure quickly. "Well, that was very clever of you. It wasn't quite in the spirit of the school's healthy eating initiative, but still quite clever." He paused. "Did you get in trouble in the end?"

"Not at all."

Mr Redding smiled. "Lucky you. But that brings us to the end of our interview. I look forward to working with you, Angus."

Angus vacated the interview chair, and Lucas apprehensively took his place.

"And what is your full name?" Mr Redding asked.

"Lucas Fuselier."

"What is your business experience?"

Lucas shrugged. "None."

"That's all right. Why did you choose to take Business and Enterprise?"

"I didn't. I got placed here because I put my form in late."

Mr Redding smirked, writing down Lucas's response. "I understand that not everyone who joins BnE wants to be here. But I promise it's not a hard subject if you put in effort."

"I'm going to talk to Mrs Campbell and see if I can change into another class."

"That's fine," Mr Redding said. "In the meantime, however, let's complete this interview. What would you say your strength is?"

"I'm smart," Lucas said without hesitation.

"Smart in what sense?"

"Smart as in I'm good at my school subjects."

"And your weakness?"

"I don't think I have any."

"I see," Mr Redding said, continuing to take notes. "That's very brave to admit."

"No, I'm not saying *that's* my weakness. I'm saying I don't have a weakness," Lucas stammered. Mr Redding left his notes as they were.

"I'm not good at being creative," Lucas said quickly. "That's my weakness. A lack of creativity."

Mr Redding conceded and amended Lucas's weakness in his notes.

"Finally, if you could start a business, what business would you start and why?"

"I don't know," Lucas said stubbornly.

"What do you see as your future career?"

"A brain surgeon or psychologist."

"Would you like to start your own practice one day?"

"No."

"That's fair enough. Not everyone wants to be a business owner. If everyone was a business owner, no one would have any employees. Thank you, Lucas. I hope you change your mind and decide to stay. But if not, best of luck with your studies."

Mr Redding signalled for Rachael to come forward. She made her way through the desks to the interview chair. She had prepared answers in her head after hearing the boy's questions.

"Hello, Rachael. Can I please have your full name?" Mr Redding asked.

"Rachael Armand."

"And what is your experience in business?"

"I work at a clothing store at the plaza."

"That will be valuable experience for your assignments. Why did you choose to study BnE?"

Rachael didn't want to sound obnoxious or offensive. "I needed an extra subject, and business studies was the only subject that fit in my timetable."

Mr Redding laughed. "So only one out of three students want to do this class?"

Angus couldn't help but wonder if Business and Enterprise would be the first time he could win a merit award. Maybe Rachael wasn't a threat after all.

"As I said to Lucas, this course can be great fun," Mr Redding said to Rachael. "If you could open any business, what would it be?"

"I guess if I had to, I would open a fitness studio."

"A fitness studio," Mr Redding echoed, nodding approvingly. "What attracts you to opening a fitness studio?"

"Nothing. But it seems to be the easiest way to make money. A gym makes a passive income regardless of whether the customers actually use the facilities."

"You've given this consideration, then?"

Rachael shook her head. "My cousin owns a gym. He's quite successful."

"Ah, I see," Mr Redding said. "Moving on, what would you say is your biggest strength?"

"I get good grades."

"Getting good grades is a result of your strength. Can you

think of what strength would help you achieve good grades?"

Rachael didn't like this level of inward analysis. She was quite happy getting good grades and leaving it at that. "I work hard," she concluded.

Mr Redding wrote it down. "Determination and perseverance are great strengths to have."

Rachael wasn't sure "determination" was correct for her strength, but she let it be.

"And your weakness?" Mr Redding asked.

"I sometimes get distracted," she said quickly. She had decided *distractible* was an easier weakness to confess than a more honest problem like *perfectionist* or *prone to anxiety*.

Mr Redding thanked Rachael, and she returned to her seat.

"I'm excited about this year," Mr Redding said, placing his interview notes in a folder. "We've got a lot of topics to cover, but each topic is very applicable to your practical assignment, so make sure you pay attention, complete the weekly readings and do your best on homework."

He plugged his laptop into the classroom projector and opened a presentation titled "Assignments". The three students prepared to record notes on their laptops.

"In this semester, which is a short semester for you Year 12s, you are going to complete three major assessments. First is an issues report. It's 1,000 words and due before the mid-semester break. The second assignment is a folio, which will be made up of your weekly homework tasks. The third assessment—"

Angus shot up his hand.

"Yes, Angus?"

"What are the weekly tasks we need to do?"

"They vary week to week. I'll give them out at the end of each week's lesson."

"Can we get the tasks ahead of time?"

"No," Mr Redding said. "You'll need to practice time management skills."

Angus had a lot of week-to-week homework already; he was not looking forward to more.

"The third assessment," Mr Redding continued, "is my favourite. It's the practical. You are going to create and run your own small business."

Angus was back at the edge of his seat.

Lucas shook his head at the boy's delight.

"As a group, you will come up with a business idea and run that business during a lunch time in Week 10. You will need to write a business plan utilising everything you learn in this course. If you manage to make a profit, it will be split fifty-fifty between yourselves and a charity of your choice."

Angus shot up his hand again.

Mr Redding smiled. "There are only three of you in the class. You don't need to raise your hand."

Angus put his hand down. "What type of business are we allowed to run?"

"Anything you like. You can sell a product or provide a service."

"Anything we like?" Lucas asked cynically.

"Well, obviously within reason. No alcohol, weapons or kissing booths. By next week's lesson you'll need to have a business idea that you all agree on, and I will make sure it's suitable. But in the time we have left, let's open the handouts. This first section is on businesses' and organisations' role in the community."

Angus gave the teacher his full attention, soaking in everything and yet nothing that lesson. His mind reeled with all the possibilities of the businesses he could run and what he could earn from running two businesses at once. He glanced over his shoulder at Rachael. She was anxiously writing many pages of notes and highlighting foreign terms and concepts she would research later. Lucas, on the other hand, had written one note: *BnE – lots of group* work, and was now browsing the web for the most expensive violins he could find.

It turned out to be a good thing for Angus that Mrs Campbell stopped him from selling chocolates on Friday. By Monday's lunch time, the school yard was a bustling marketplace of students selling chocolate bars, packets of lollies and cans of soft drink to each other. One Year 9 went as far as to bring a box of boxes of chocolate bars from the local discount store, attempting to form a chocolate distribution service. The sellers, having heard about Angus's meeting with Mrs Campbell, claimed their products were for 'fundraising'.

"This is an important notice from Mrs Campbell," the homeroom teachers announced to their classes at the end of the day. "'There is to be no more food or drink sold by anyone, *to* anyone, in the school yard or outside the school gates, at any time, for any reason, including fundraising purposes.

Anyone found possessing more than a single person's requirement for recess and lunch will have their food confiscated and issued a detention. This is a healthy school, not a food festival.'"

The Year 12s laughed as Mr Fletcher read the memo.

"From what I've heard, a few of you need to take special note of that," Mr Fletcher said, looking right at Angus. "Now, before everyone goes, Damien also wishes to make an announcement."

Damien was a good student. His classmates considered him the expert on being good. He always did his homework on time and was the first to offer assistance to a teacher carrying a heavy box or stack of chairs across the school grounds. In the past few years, Damien's goodness had matured through his exposure to philanthropy. Every month he was discovering new charities, and that meant every month he was asking his classmates for donations to numerous local and international charitable causes.

"Hi, everyone," Damien said with a beaming smile, standing at the front of the classroom alongside Mr Fletcher. He held up a pair of colourful socks. "I thought I'd remind you that this week is Be Green Week, so I'll be selling recycled cotton socks to raise money for the Australian Wildlife Rescue Foundation. The socks are only five dollars a pair. I'll be selling them outside the classroom, and I have permission from Mrs Campbell, so they are completely legal to own. Thank you for giving me your time."

"That's all. You're dismissed," Mr Fletcher said.

The students filed from the classroom. No one bought a

pair of socks from Damien, politely making excuses about not having cash on them or that their mum just bought them new socks. Angus watched his classmates closely. Their reactions to the socks were the opposite of their reactions to chocolate bars.

"That's the challenge," he said to Lucas on their walk home.

"What challenge?"

"I need to find a product that will sell as successfully as chocolate bars to students in a healthy school."

"For BnE?" Lucas asked. Angus didn't respond.

Lucas realised Angus wasn't talking about his challenge of getting good grades. "Angus, you need to stop and think about what you're doing. I don't know why you feel the need to do something extra on top of Year 12, but you're going to get in a lot of trouble."

"But I've got proof I can do it. I can sell things! Surely there's something else as mundane and harmless as socks that will sell like chocolate bars."

"But *why*? Why do you need to sell anything at school? Why don't you just wait until you graduate to start a business?"

"What benefit is there to waiting?" Angus said passionately. "The world isn't waiting for me to finish Year 12."

Lucas could think of numerous reasons for waiting, but he didn't have the energy to quarrel on an empty stomach. "You do whatever you want to do—I'm going to focus on finishing Year 12 with perfect grades. Maybe I'll finally beat Rachael for dux of the school."

Both the boys knew no one, especially Lucas, would get dux over Rachael. Lucas's joke diffused the tension.

"Hot chips?" Angus suggested.

"You're going to try selling hot chips?"

Angus paused, considering Lucas's suggestion. "No, I'm just going to eat them today. But good idea. Keep them coming."

"I'm not giving you business ideas."

"What if I offer to buy you hot chips?"

Lucas looked around the carpark of the shopping centre. "Sell cars or shopping trolleys or planes or grocery bags or... bitumen. That's plenty of ideas. I'd like a small chips with chicken salt, please."

MOVING STATIONERY

"I wonder if Mrs Campbell had a bad childhood experience with chocolate?" Angus said as he and Lucas entered the shopping centre.

"I saw her eating a chocolate muesli bar at lunch," Lucas said.

"So, she's a hypocrite!"

Lucas shook his head. "You've got to move on with your life, mate."

"I'm kidding. I have moved on," Angus said. "But you have to admit, I really nailed it with the chocolates. Everyone else started selling chocolates because I did it first. Even Mr Redding thought it was genius!"

"Mr Redding said the idea was clever. The word 'genius' was never mentioned."

Café Olka, located in the heart of the shopping centre, was the destination of choice for many students after a long day of schooling. Lucas's mouth salivated at the thought of a cup of fresh, hot chips—until Angus walked straight past it.

"I thought you said we were getting hot chips from Olka," Lucas said.

Angus didn't slow down. "I need to buy another exercise book for English and then there's brainstorming to do. And, more importantly, I don't have any spare change on me."

"The café should really get an eft-pos machine," Lucas complained, disappointed by the lack of coins in his pockets. "They're missing out on sales."

Moving Stationery was a big-box office supply store and, along with the supermarket, one of the two main destinations of the shopping centre. Moving Stationery was brightly lit with aisles of every type of stationery and office supply imaginable from printers and laptops to desks and paperclips. Decades old pop hits played over the speaker system with an earworm Moving Stationery advertisement thrown in between every song.

The boys wandered the aisles, picking up bits and pieces and giving the products a shake or trying a writing utensil on the pads of test paper. Angus picked up an orange felt-tip pen and wrote *the end of the world* on the paper. For reasons he himself did not understand, Angus always wrote *the end of the world* when testing a writing instrument or laptop keyboard. He leaned back a little and looked at his atrocious handwriting. His handwriting had always been terrible, which he assumed was due to almost all his schoolwork being completed on computers.

"They should invent a pen that writes for you," Angus

pondered as he picked out a blue, 0.5mm ballpoint pen and wrote the end of the world on the test paper as neatly as he could.

"They have. It's called a printer." Lucas drew a cartoon dinosaur with a thick black marker.

Angus nodded. "True, true." He held the blue pen in the air, focusing his eye on the ballpoint.

"What are you doing?"

"Do you think the ink would drip out if you held it upside down long enough?"

"I don't know. Try it." Lucas picked up a red gel pen. "How long do you think you could draw with a pen until it runs out of ink?"

"Depends on what you're drawing."

"Like a straight line," Lucas said, convinced his test was highly scientific. "How long could you draw a straight line before the pen runs out?"

"A hundred kilometres," Angus guessed, still holding his pen upside down.

"A hundred kilometres?" Lucas said in disbelief. "You're out of your mind. I'd say a standard pen could only do three kilometres, tops."

Angus shook his head. "Three kilometres is nothing. That's the distance from school to my house. Test it. See how much ink is in the pen, then draw it back and forth on the paper twenty times and see if it goes down at all. I bet you won't see the ink move even a little."

"How much do you bet?"

"I promise I'll buy you hot chips tomorrow, despite your

49

unhelpful business suggestions."

Lucas, a fan of scientific testing and especially hot chips, began drawing with the red pen rapidly back and forth along the test pad.

"Do either of you need help with your selection?" a woman's firm voice asked.

Lucas froze in the middle of his fifth line. Angus quickly placed the cap back on his pen. They turned their heads to see a young woman dressed in the Moving Stationery blue uniform. She held a clipboard and a frown.

"Hey," Angus said, recognising her. He placed his pen back in the rack. "Sorry. We're just looking, thanks."

"You're Angus," the woman said.

"Yeah," he said. "You're Olivia."

An awkward moment followed. Angus apologised again, and the boys hastily moved into the exercise book aisle.

"Who was that?" Lucas asked. "She looks familiar."

"She used to play tennis at the same club as my brother Quinten," Angus whispered. "But she's also an actress. Do you remember her in that pizza TV ad? Paulo's Pizza, or wherever it was."

"The one where the girl is meant to have eaten three whole pizzas by herself?" Lucas laughed. "That's her?!"

"I also think she's a manager here."

"Tennis player, actress *and* retail manager? I guess it's good to keep your career options open."

Angus picked an exercise book off the shelf and flicked through the empty pages. "I don't know who would want to be a manager of a place like this."

"Why? What's wrong with this place?" Lucas challenged, watching the woman from afar. She only looked a few years older than him.

"Because it's retail," Angus said. "There's no future job prospects if you work in retail."

"Maybe she likes her job here?" Lucas said. "You do know other people enjoy jobs that you don't think are exciting."

"There are universally boring jobs," Angus said. "What about a fast food restaurant? Surely the managers there hate it and have given up on their careers."

"My second cousin works in a fast food restaurant and loves it. He's been there for fifteen years."

"Fifteen years? Is he a manager?"

"Nope. He's a cook. He gets paid almost nothing, but still loves it."

Angus made his selection of a 96-page lined exercise book, feeling bad for offending Lucas's cousin. He changed the subject. "What kind of profit margin do you think exercise books have? They're just paper."

"I think they'd have a big margin," Lucas said. "Are you thinking of selling books for the BnE assignment?"

Angus shook his head. "Definitely not. We're going to sell chocolate bars. As I said, it's a proven success."

"Even if by some miracle Mrs Campbell allowed us to do that, what if Rachael doesn't want to sell chocolates? We all have to agree on the idea."

"I'll convince Rachael."

"You're overly confident in your ability to sell things."

Angus nodded. "Selling things is just matching what you're

trying to sell with what the customer wants."

"I think there's a bit more to it than that."

"No there's not," Angus said. "I bet you I could sell anything in this store to anyone.

"Anything?" Lucas laughed.

"Anything at all."

"How much would you bet?"

"A hundred dollars."

"A hundred dollars?" Lucas repeated. "How do you think I have a hundred dollars for a bet? I'm poor."

"Fine. Twenty dollars. I bet you twenty dollars I can sell anything in this store to anyone, for a profit." Angus held out his hand for Lucas to shake the deal on. Lucas, very happy to take Angus down a notch, shook his friend's hand.

"Fifty dollars," Angus added with a cheeky grin.

Lucas quickly pulled his hand back. "Twenty dollars was the agreed amount."

Angus laughed and watched Lucas walk up and down the aisles. Lucas looked each product over, trying to find something weird or unattractive. At one point, Lucas chose a single A4 sheet of green cardboard. To Angus's relief, Lucas put the cardboard back. For fifteen minutes, Lucas searched and searched. Angus followed him, but by the time they arrived back in the pen aisle, he began to lose interest in the activity.

"Hurry up. I want to get home—I'm hungry," Angus grumbled.

Lucas, determined to earn $20, worked methodically through the pen aisle looking each pen over. At the tenth pen, he stopped. He had found a perfectly unsellable product.

"Sell this pen to one of the Year 10 boys," Lucas said with a mischievous grin. Lucas did not often give mischievous grins, but when he did, Angus knew there was trouble. The pen was a purple, 0.7mm gel-ink pen encased in a pattern of yellow and blue flowers against a bright pink background. On the end of the pen hung two bright purple, fluffy pompoms. It must have been the most feminine pen ever created.

Angus's confidence wavered. "You're not serious."

"I'm deadly serious." Lucas said. "You're touting that you're an amazing salesman and looking down on other people because of their jobs. This is your job—sell this pen."

Angus took the pen and held it in his palm, trying to imagine the pitch he would give to a peer-pleasing, anti-floral Year 10 boy. He knew it was near impossible, but he wasn't going to admit defeat.

"How much is it?" Angus asked, looking at the price ticket. He almost threw the pen at Lucas. "Eight dollars for a pen?! What is this?"

"Designer, apparently," Lucas said with a straight face.

Angus marched up to the front counter with the pen and his exercise book. The checkout assistant, a boy about the same age Angus, gave a smirk as he scanned the pen's barcode.

"It's for my friend," Angus whispered, nodding at Lucas. "He's a little embarrassed to buy it, but he loves pretty pens with flowers that are ridiculously expensive. It's his...*thing*."

PEN FOR SALE

The following day, students meandered around the courtyard, trying to forget about their lessons before recess and dreading the lessons yet to come. The paved courtyard, dotted with garden beds and trees, was surrounded by most of the high school classrooms and students' lockers. The trees in the courtyard had been selected for their "student friendliness"—a fancy way of saying their branches were unattractive to school boys who liked to practice fencing. There were plenty of benches to sit on and a large shade sail hung overhead, making it quite a comfortable spot for one to sit and talk to friends, or for one to sit and stress about the upcoming test one hadn't studied for.

Angus didn't know how to study for his current test. He surveyed the students from a bench on the courtyard's perimeter. There was always a teacher on duty within the courtyard, making it dangerous for illicit dealings, but the teachers were easily distracted. He had the pink, flowery pen wrapped in tissue paper lying on the bench between himself and Lucas.

Lucas, happily eating a packet of cookies, was feeling much more jovial than his friend. "Just clarifying that the twenty dollars will be in cash? I don't accept cheques. If you're really stuck, I could accept a bank deposit, but it may come with a transfer fee."

Angus ignored his friend, crunching away at his carrot sticks. Only half a dozen Year 10 boys were present in the courtyard. Most Year 10s were playing handball on the courts, but he wasn't interested in making a sales pitch to sweaty, competitive Year 10 boys hopped up on adrenaline and surrounded by their peers.

"I think I'll invest the twenty dollars in gold. Do you know if there's a minimum for buying gold?" Lucas asked.

Angus was unsuccessful in tuning Lucas's voice out. "I won't be able to sell the pen if you're with me."

"I'm not going anywhere. How do I know you won't try and rip me off by telling a kid to pretend he bought the pen off you?"

"It'll scare the target if we both approach him. And it would mess up my plan," Angus said, still coming up with a plan. "You'll have to watch from a distance."

Lucas didn't argue further.

Angus focused on a Year 10 boy named Alec. At most lunch times, Alec sat by himself in the courtyard. Angus could see him staring off into space, unmoving.

"Are you thinking about Alec?" Lucas asked. He wanted to watch Angus fail by doing something, not just sitting on the bench.

"I was, but I'd feel bad shaking him out of ten dollars."

"But he always goes to the canteen. I reckon he carries money with him."

Angus shook his head, looking for other prospects.

"What about Riley?" Lucas suggested, pointing to a short boy amongst an entourage of fellow Year 10s. "He's always buying food for his friends."

Angus shook his head. "No, he's with his mates. You're forgetting what I'm trying to sell here."

Lucas smirked. "I know exactly what you're trying to sell here."

Recess slowly ticked on. No other Year 10 boys walked by. The bell finally rang to end the break, and all the students streamed back to their lockers to pick up their belongings for the next lesson.

Angus sighed. "When do I need to sell the pen by?"

"Didn't we say the end of the day?"

"The end of the day?" Angus said. "You never said that!"

"I thought you were the almighty and powerful salesman?" Lucas taunted.

Angus rolled his eyes and watched groups of Year 10 boys return from the courts. Then Angus spotted his best chance at making the sale. He stood with determination on his face, the likes of which Lucas had rarely seen.

"I've won," Angus said quietly as he watched his target rifle through his locker.

"What? Who?" Lucas frowned.

"Just watch," Angus said. He waited for the crowds around the Year 10s' lockers to disperse a little before making his approach. The Year 10s' lockers were in a state of disgust-ingness that only Year 10s can achieve. Every third locker overflowed with printed handouts, school bags, empty food packets and mysterious liquids that ants were vacationing in. Angus weaved between the students. Some gave him funny looks, disconcerted about a Year 12 hanging out by their lockers. Abdul Gilani didn't see Angus coming.

Everyone liked Abdul Gilani. No one knew why, not even Abdul, but everyone from every year level loved saying "Abdul!" and giving the boy a high-five. He was like every-one's younger brother. Abdul and his family immigrated to Australia from Western Asia only a year prior and although he could speak better English than most of his classmates, he was very quiet. He beamed at the attention he received and would return high-fives and reply "Hello!" with as much enthusiasm as those giving it, but no one made further con-versation with him about what his hobbies were or what he did in his spare time. What everybody did know, and what made him Angus's best chance at making the sale, was the boy always had pockets full of money. Every day, without fail, Abdul would buy his recess and lunch from the canteen. There was even a rumour he was related to royalty. Angus could see inside Abdul's locker; it was full of normal, unfemi-nine books. But it was too late to bail now, and time was cer-tainly not on Angus's side.

"Abdul!"

"Hello!" Abdul called back. He instinctively held up his hand to high-five the Year 12.

Angus saw unfamiliarity in the boy's eyes. "It's Angus."

"Yeah, Angus!" Abdul gave one last nod and turned back to his locker.

"Hey, I was wondering if I could ask you something?"

Abdul slowly turned his head, apparently confused as to why the Year 12 was still talking to him. "What about?"

Angus paused; he should have thought further into his sales pitch than just the greeting.

"What lesson do you have next?"

"I have a free lesson." Abdul clutched his pencil case and laptop to his chest.

"Oh, me too! In room R5?"

Abdul nodded cautiously. Angus began to feel more relaxed as the courtyard emptied of potential eavesdroppers. When Abdul began walking across the courtyard to room R5, Angus followed alongside, taking a moment to decide on his sales techniques.

"How are your grades going?"

Abdul shrugged. "Very good."

"That's good. And how are your stationery supplies going?" Angus asked. "Isn't it annoying how the teachers only give you stationery at the start of the year?"

Abdul remained suspicious. "My teacher gave me extra supplies at the start of this semester."

"No way!" Angus feigned amazement. "We didn't get anything extra. What did you get?"

"Do you need a pen or pencil?" Abdul opened the zip of his pencil case.

"No, no. I don't need anything."

"Are you sure? I have thirty spare pens. I'd be happy to

give you one."

An idea finally came to Angus. It was outlandish, but he decided it worth a try.

"I was wondering if you would be willing to help me with an assignment I'm doing?"

Abdul paused under the veranda outside room R5 and turned to face the Year 12. "You want *my* help?"

"Yes, I *need* your help." Angus pulled the pen wrapped in tissue paper from his pocket. He looked over his shoulder to check where Lucas was. Lucas appeared completely out of place in the empty courtyard, loitering next to a nearby tree.

"You see, I have this pen. It's a really cool pen," Angus said. "It was designed by this artist named Alice Verdun, from Italy or France or Peru, I believe, and I want to know what you think of it."

"What I think of it?" Abdul received the packaged pen and carefully unwrapped it. Angus watched the boy's reaction as the pen with giant purple pompoms emerged from the tissue paper. The boy showed no reaction whatsoever. Abdul, apparently unsure how he was expected to evaluate the writing instrument, set his belongings down between his feet and inspected the pen like a jeweller would inspect a watch. He looked the case's design up and down. He slowly removed the cap from the pen, feeling how they clicked when the pen and cap separated. In apparent approval of the pen cap, Abdul focused his eye on the ball point. Angus watched this all take place with fascination. He wondered if Abdul was secretly a pen collector.

"May I write?" Abdul reached down for the exercise book

between his feet.

"By all means." Angus smiled haughtily over at Lucas, who was pretending to tie his shoes. Lucas feigned a yawn in return.

Abdul wrote his name in the back of an exercise book. He wrote his name again, slower than the first time. He looked closely at the ink on the page. Angus tried to spot any emotions on the boy's face.

Abdul gave a small nod and clicked the cap back on. "It's a nice pen."

"You like it?

"Yes. It's a very nice pen."

"Would you like to buy it?"

"Would I like to buy it?" Abdul echoed. "I thought you said it was for an assignment?"

"It is for an assignment, but I'm just noticing how much you like it. I can get another for my assignment."

Abdul, seemingly unsure whether buying the pen would help or hinder Angus's assignment, looked back down at it. "It's a little bit...girly, isn't it?"

"Girly? What do you mean, girly?" Angus laughed, wiping his sweaty palms on his pants.

"It's pink."

"There's no law that says pink is a girl's colour. I think pink is cool!"

"It's covered in tiny flowers."

"Horticulture is very popular at the moment."

"It had pom-poms on the end."

"You can play with them when lessons get boring."

"The label says *Pens by Alice for Her*."

Angus winced. He knew that unremovable label would be his downfall with an eagle-eyed customer. He received the pen back from Abdul and put it in his pocket.

"That's okay." Angus sighed. "Thanks anyway."

Abdul watched as Angus changed from cheery and chatty to dejected.

"Maybe..." Abdul said. "Maybe I could buy it for my sister's birthday next week?"

Angus tried as hard as he could to stay composed and not laugh with joy. He took the pen back out. "Your sister will love the pen! You won't regret your purchase, I can tell you that much. That will just be ten dollars, thanks."

"Sorry, how much?"

"Ten dollars."

Abdul looked between the pen and Angus. "Two."

"Two what?"

"Two dollars."

"Two dollars?!" Angus exclaimed. "This is a designer pen! Designed by the French or Swedish or Japanese designer Alice Verdun! It cost me eight dollars at Moving Stationery."

"Then why would I buy a pen from you for ten dollars when I can buy it for eight dollars at the shop?"

Lucas chuckled from where he pretended to study leaves on a courtyard tree.

Seeing his sale crumbling away, Angus resorted to a compromise. "How about eight dollars for the pen?"

"Four."

"Seven dollars-fifty?"

"Five."

"Six."

"Five-fifty."

Abdul looked at the pen one final time and pulled out his wallet. Angus quickly pushed the boy's wallet back down in a panic. He looked around to see if any teachers were watching over the courtyard.

"Not here," Angus explained. "Pay me after school."

He gave the pen to Abdul and hurried into room R5, where the elderly relief teacher didn't even look up from her tablet computer.

Angus and Lucas found seats in the back row.

"You failed!" Lucas whispered with glee. "You didn't sell the pen for a profit."

"Doesn't matter."

"What do you mean?"

"It was a proof of concept," Angus whispered. "I just sold the most feminine pen to a Year 10 boy for five dollars and fifty cents. If that doesn't prove there's a possible market for pens, like chocolate bars, I don't know what does."

Lucas shook his head. "Don't be delusional—pens aren't chocolate. You got lucky."

Angus's heart was still beating quickly. For once in a long time, he didn't worry about using the free lesson to get his homework finished. He retrieved his laptop from his locker and searched online for the cost of pens and the names of stationery suppliers. He created a spreadsheet with prices and contact emails.

Lucas kept peeking over at Angus's screen, shaking his head at the boy's delusions.

Half an hour later, the relief teacher called out, "Is there a Lucas Fuselier in this class?"

Lucas looked up from his Biology homework. Mr Tilley was standing by the teacher's desk, holding a sticky note on the end of his finger. The Year 12 felt his body heat up as all eyes turned on him.

Mr Tilley walked briskly over. "Lucas, Mrs Campbell would like to see you now."

"Thanks," Lucas squeaked. He looked down at Angus as he followed Mr Tilley out of the room.

Angus shook his head and mouthed, *I don't know.*

Mr Tilley led Lucas to the front office and signalled for him to sit on the chair outside Mrs Campbell's door. Mr Tilley opened the door and let the occupant know that Lucas was waiting.

Lucas began coming up with excuses for his involvement in the pen sale. He didn't really sell anything, but he did encourage Angus and bet him $20, so maybe he was involved—

"Come in, Lucas," Mrs Campbell said from the doorway.

Lucas went into the office and was glad to take another seat; his legs felt stiff. Mrs Campbell sat at her desk and held a subject choice form that all the Year 11 students filled out before Year 12. Lucas could see the form was filled out in his handwriting.

"I received your email requesting I reconsider letting you change courses from Business and Enterprise," Mrs Campbell said. "Why do you want to change?"

Although he appeared to be in the clear for the pen sale,

Lucas began feeling quite warm. He rolled up his sleeves. "I didn't choose BnE. I didn't put in the confirmation form at the end of last semester, so I got put into whatever subject had an open spot."

"Good. So you understand why you have been put into that subject. The coordinators are not great at reading students' minds." She looked at Lucas with concern. "Are you okay? You look quite red."

Lucas nodded. "It's really hot in here."

"Is it?" Mrs Campbell frowned. "The air conditioner is on."

Seeing that pens, Year 10s or expulsion weren't coming up as topics of conversation, Lucas calmed himself by taking a deep breath. "I understand I didn't do the right thing with the electives form, but I am wondering if I could please be moved to a different subject, like Material Design?"

"Unfortunately not. Material Design is full and the materials have already been purchased for their assessments. This is why we asked you many times to ensure you handed up the confirmation slip on time."

Lucas's guilty conscience got the better of him. "Am I in trouble?"

Mrs Campbell furrowed her brow. "Are you in trouble? You've made trouble for yourself by not following instructions, and as a result need to do a non-preferred subject. Do you think you should receive a further consequence?"

Lucas shook his head. "No, no. I don't think so. I think I'm being adequately punished."

Mrs Campbell noticed the boy looking pale. "Is everything okay? Is there something else going on?"

"I'm fine. I'm fine." Lucas tried to regain control of his nerves. "It's just that BnE makes me very nervous."

Mrs Campbell leaned in. "And why does Business and Enterprise make you nervous?"

"Why? Well, it's..." Lucas left his mouth agape, trying to formulate a good reason. "We have to do an assignment where we start a business. I find businesses to be a very cutthroat and consumeristic. They make me worry about the future of society."

"That assignment sounds interesting. I don't quite follow your concern."

"My uncle broke his leg while working at a business."

"You're scared of breaking your leg in Business and Enterprise?"

"It's a... cultural thing. Growing up, I've had negative associations with business. I think my family is related to a branch of the mafia, and I don't want to get a taste of business in case I like it and decide to join that part of the family business."

Mrs Campbell stared at the boy with a look of disappointment and scepticism.

"I have the next seventeen years of my life planned out," Lucas said. "I'm going to go to university and train to become a brain surgeon. I know both BnE and Material Design have little to do with medicine, but at least Material Design involves me using my hands, rather than just my brain. I already know how to use my brain; what I don't know is how to perform a lobotomy, and I think building a coffee table could help with that."

"I know that starting new, unfamiliar subjects can be

scary, but you may find that learning foreign things is good, and sometimes in life we have to adapt our plans because circumstances change. Maybe after a year in university you will change your mind and decide to become an accountant."

Lucas shook his head. "I don't change my mind."

But without any further excuses, Lucas accepted defeat and was sent back to class.

"What happened?" Angus whispered as Lucas sat back down at his desk.

Lucas's face was sullen, and he avoided eye contact. "Mrs Campbell said she would like to see you."

Angus's heart skipped a beat. "Did she say what it's about?"

"She also said to take your bag. And empty your locker."

Angus searched his friend's face for any hint of a joke. "What? How did she find out? Are you in trouble, too? I'll take all the blame."

Lucas faked a sniff. "I told her...I told her everything. I told her your plans to reopen your chocolate business and how you've been talking about opening another business selling bags of sugar to students."

"What? Why did you tell her all that!" Angus exclaimed in a loud whisper.

Lucas smirked.

"You're joking?" Angus asked.

"She told me I couldn't change from BnE."

Angus leaned back in his chair, trying to catch his emotions. "If I wasn't so relieved, I would throw your laptop out the window right now."

"Boys at the back, what's all the fuss about?" the relief teacher called.

"Sorry," Angus called back. "Lucas was just proclaiming his love for you."

The relief teacher shook her head. "Sorry, dear. I'm seventy-three."

"You don't look a day over forty," Angus said.

"What was that?" the relief teacher called, tilting her ear toward the boys. "You'll need to speak up."

"You don't look a day over forty," Lucas repeated loudly.

"Now come," the relief teacher said to Lucas, "you can't be flirting with ladies four times your age."

LESSON TWO:
THE BUSINESS PLAN

It was almost déjà vu.

Lucas and Angus were sitting in the front row of the classroom with their laptops out. Rachael sat in the same third-row seat she had during last week's Business and Enterprise lesson. Several teacherless minutes had passed since their second BnE lesson was scheduled to begin, and all was silent but the sound of the wall heater and the occasional clicking of the boys on their laptops.

Lucas coughed.

Rachael offered only a glance away from the maths problem she was working on.

Angus had been browsing for extraordinarily expensive houses on real estate websites when a banner advertisement for *Businesses for Sale* reminded him of their homework task.

"So, the business idea," Angus said loudly, noticing that both of his classmates were engrossed in their activities. "We need to come up with a business idea for the assignment. Does anyone have any ideas?"

Lucas glanced up from his laptop, but Rachael continued writing in her maths book.

"I haven't given it a single thought," Lucas admitted. He went back to looking at online shoe stores. He didn't really like shoes.

Rachael still didn't respond.

"Well, I have a great idea," Angus said. "Why don't we sell chocolate? Mr Redding thought it was a good idea."

No one acknowledged his suggestion.

Angus sighed. "Fine. Chocolate can be our backup plan."

"It can be in your *why are you even discussing it because it's never going to happen* plan," Lucas replied. "How about you sell carrots?"

"Why do you keep saying 'you'?" Angus asked. "This isn't just me. This is a group assignment. You're in this group."

Lucas, his pen held tightly between his teeth, could not have appeared more bored. He took a deep breath in and closed the shoe store webpages to focus on the task at hand.

"Do you have any ideas, Rachael?" he asked.

"I'm busy." Rachael's focus remained glued to her page.

"Wait, what about instead of selling to the students, we sell to the teachers with something like a car wash?" Angus said. He then considered the logistics and changed his mind. "No, that would require too much labour."

Lucas scrolled through an online list of *50 Business Ideas*. "What about personal training? Mrs Campbell would love that. We could charge students to come to an aerobics class."

"Do you think teens are going to pay to do aerobics with one of us leading the class?" Angus asked. "No offense to any males in this room, but there are no males in this room, myself included, who could run more than a kilometre without dying. Do you know aerobics, Rachael?"

Rachael ignored the boys.

"Rachael?" Angus repeated.

Rachael looked up, thoroughly annoyed by their disruptions. "I'm sorry, but I'm busy."

"*I'm* sorry, but we need to work out what business we're running," Angus insisted.

Rachael pulled out another book from her bag and flicked to a page covered in notes. "I have twenty ideas here, but I need to finish my maths. When Mr Redding arrives, then we can talk about the assignment."

She looked back down and tried to get back into the head space of solving quadratic equations.

Angus and Lucas looked at each other, neither the wiser to Rachael's icy disposition.

"Did I say something?" Angus asked Lucas quietly.

"I think you were sexist to suggest that Rachael knows aerobics."

"How is that sexist?" Angus whispered back. "She said last week she helps out her cousin at a gym."

Rachael put down her pen and sighed. "It wasn't sexist."

She'd noticed the two boys' timidity and realised she may have been too short with them. She began to pack her maths homework away. "Sorry. It's not you guys."

Angus exhaled. "Good. I thought it might have been

because you caught me looking over your shoulder in maths last Friday."

Rachael shook her head. "I wouldn't do that if I were you."

"I don't do it for tests or exams, only classwork," Angus explained. "What did you get for Wednesday's maths test?"

"You can't ask that." Lucas took a swig from his water bottle.

"Mr Bonners gave me a D," Rachael said.

Lucas almost spat the mouthful of water all over his desk. "Are you sick?"

Angus frowned. "You can't ask that."

"I don't mean *sick*...I mean were you unwell when you took the test? I mean, how did that happen? I mean, it could've happened to anyone...I'm just going to shut up now," Lucas stammered.

"What did you get on the test?" Angus asked Lucas, hoping to cheer Rachael up by hearing about Lucas's abysmal performance.

"I got a B," Lucas said defensively. "What did you get?"

Angus looked down, feeling like he was rubbing salt into Rachael's wound. "I got a B as well."

Rachael couldn't believe it. It was the first D she had ever gotten at school, and it came in the last semester of her schooling life. The boys only confirmed what she had feared: she was the only one to blame for the bad grade.

"What if we did a book sale?" Angus suggested, determined to steer the conversation onward.

"Brooke and I came up with some ideas last week," Rachael announced. The two girls had come up with a list of business ideas while sitting in the courtyard, eavesdropping on conversations about other student's hobbies, likes, dislikes and what they spent their money on.

The boys looked at her expectantly.

"We could do a pay-to-play soccer match, with a cash prize for the winning team," she read from her notebook.

Angus thought about it. "That's a good idea, but that would only target students who like playing sport. And this is school, where despite what the PE teachers think and try to promote, not everyone can, or enjoys, playing sport."

"All right, what about selling makeup?" Rachael suggested.

"Once again, that's only targeting half the students," Angus said. "Guys aren't going to buy makeup. We need an idea that targets all the students!"

Rachael stared at Angus with contempt for shooting down her ideas so excitedly.

"Sorry," Angus said, feeling rightly kicked off his high horse.

Mr Redding entered the classroom in a fluster. "Good morning. Sorry I'm late—I just had a quick meeting with Mrs Campbell. How's everyone doing today?"

The students all murmured a greeting back.

"So, what's the business idea?" he asked as he got his belongings organised. None of the students spoke up; they were all unsure how the teacher would react on hearing they had no business idea yet.

"What's the plan for your assignment?" Mr Redding reiterated, handing out another printed booklet.

"We're still deciding," Lucas spoke up.

"You're still deciding?" Mr Redding said calmly. "You've had all week to come up with an idea. Have you at least got a short list? Any favourites?"

"My idea is we could sell chocolate," Angus said.

Mr Redding shook his head. "Unfortunately, that is not going to happen. My meeting with Mrs Campbell was about your assignment, and she explicitly said she doesn't want the business to have anything to do with food or drink."

"But food and drink would be a guaranteed success!" Angus said.

"I know that," Mr Redding said. "But surely you have ideas that don't involve food or drink?"

Rachael held up her notebook. "We were just going through my list of ideas."

Mr Redding signalled with a nod for her to continue.

"Well, another idea would be we could start a dating service."

Lucas gave a nervous laugh that ended in a snort.

"All ideas are worth discussing," Mr Redding said. "What would running a dating service look like? How would it make a revenue?"

"Well, we could charge five dollars for people to sign up, and then they fill out a profile questionnaire—" The more she spoke, the more she realised how absurd it sounded. It made sense when she overhead some Year 11 girls talking about using dating apps on their phones. She quickly moved on. "I had about five ideas that involved food or drink, including milkshakes, cookies and cakes, but I'll skip over them."

"Can we sell healthy foods? Like fruits and vegetables?" Angus asked hopefully. "What about water? Water isn't dangerous or unhealthy."

"It is if you drown in it," Lucas said.

"Well obviously we're not—" Angus didn't dignify Lucas's joke by finishing the sentence.

"Even if Mrs Campbell did say we could sell water, no one is going to want to buy water when they can get it free from the drink fountains," Rachael said.

"And yet..." Angus pointed at the supermarket-bought bottle of water in Lucas's hand.

"That's a really good point you make there, Angus, " Mr Redding said. "Why do people buy a product that they can get for free? Like water?"

"Convenience?" Angus guessed.

"Exactly right. Let's say you were a drinks manufacturer and you wanted to sell water. Lucas, how would you sell water?"

Lucas was blank. "Make it taste nice?"

"Convince people that the water you're selling is better than the water they can get in a tap," Angus added.

"Well, yes. You could try to convince consumers of that. But all that effort and marketing would be wasted if you miss the first step."

"If I was to sell water, I would sell it wherever there are no drink fountains," Rachael said.

Mr Redding pointed at Rachael. "Bingo."

She wasn't sure exactly what she'd said that was *bingo*.

"To sell water, your product needs to be sold where people

would think of buying water, and it needs to be in a packaging size that is convenient for consuming water. A drink fountain is great for when you need a drink right there and then, but what about if you think you're going to need a drink later on? Unless you have an empty bottle with you, that tap quickly loses its value. But bottled water offers value both now and later. You must consider whether the customer just wants water for themselves, or do they need to buy enough water for their family's picnic in the park? This is applicable to all businesses everywhere. You don't need to create the most amazing brand on Earth. You don't need to sell the fanciest product or service. All you need to do is come up with some-thing your customers would be willing to buy, and make sure it's available where and how they want to buy it."

"I don't believe that," Angus said.

"Which part?" Mr Redding asked.

"Surely a business has to convince customers their product is better than everyone else's. That why ads say, 'we have the most refreshing drink or the best burger' or 'the most fu-el-efficient car'. Say I'm going to sell...a pencil," Angus said, making sure to not say pen. "You suggest I sell that pencil without telling the customer about how good the pen is? No one's going to buy my pen—pencil if there's a better one with more features and stuff."

Mr Redding listened thoughtfully. "What you're basically asking is, 'How does marketing work?' I promise we'll look at that when we cover marketing in a couple weeks' time. But I don't want to get ahead of ourselves. For now, we need to focus on simply coming up with a business idea." He sat in the teacher's chair. "I'm going to sit here, and the three of you need to discuss and come up with your idea. If you can't come up with an idea then I'll choose it for you, and it's not going to be a fun idea. It will be selling pens or something like that."

Angus jumped into gear. There was no way he was going to let his pens idea go to waste on school marks. "Rachael, what other ideas do you have on your list?"

Rachael scanned her page. "I have tutoring? We could charge parents of primary school students tutoring by the hour."

"That would be easy," Lucas said.

"I'm not sure parents would be willing to spend more money, on top of their school fees, for a Year 12 student to teach their kids," Angus said.

"The pens idea isn't bad," Rachael suggested.

"The tutoring idea isn't bad," Angus said quickly. "Anything else?"

"The only other usable idea I have is...a movie theatre," Rachael said.

"A movie theatre," Angus repeated to himself. "What would that involve?"

"We could sell tickets to see a movie in the auditorium," Rachael explained. "I originally thought we could sell food for people to eat during the movie, but maybe we can just make money on the tickets."

"That would be easy," Lucas said.

"It could work," Angus said. He didn't know the economics of movie theatres, but he did know they made a lot of their profit from overpriced lollies, chocolates and popcorn.

"Do you think Mrs Campbell would let us sell healthy popcorn?" Angus asked Mr Redding.

The teacher shrugged. "We would need to discuss it with Mrs Campbell."

"You—we—could make the popcorn extra salty, and sell bottles of water as well," Lucas said.

"Are we all in agreement?" Angus asked. "Shall we try and make the movie theatre work?"

Rachael nodded. Lucas nodded. They turned to look at Mr Redding, who was leaning back in his chair. "Diamonds under pressure. I think your idea could work quite well, with or without food. I will go and speak to Mrs Campbell and see if there's any wiggle room for selling healthy popcorn and bottles of water."

Mr Redding wrote *movie theatre* on the whiteboard. Underneath that he wrote *business plan*.

"We have a business idea. Now we need a business plan. In this course, we will be creating a simple business plan, much simpler than what you would need if you were starting a business in the real world. The three sections of your plan will be business, marketing and finance. Lucas, can you give me the name of our business please?"

"We don't have a name," Lucas replied. He looked to Angus for guidance.

"You can name it whatever you want," Mr Redding said.

"Lucas, Angus, Rachael, Films. LARF," Lucas proposed. Mr Redding wrote the name in big letters on the board.

"Great. Now Angus, what products and services are you offering at LARF?"

"We're selling movie tickets and hopefully some kind of snack," Angus said. Mr Redding wrote *movie tickets and snacks* on the board.

"Rachael, who is the target market for LARF?"

"Either girls or boys. School-aged," Rachael said, unsure if she understood the question.

"Let's get specific," Mr Redding said.

"We could try for females between 11 and 17 years of age," Rachael said.

"Couldn't we try going for teenage males *and* females aged between 11 and 17?" Angus asked.

"Let's just aim for the whole human race," Lucas added.

Mr Redding added *human* to the list. "But how would you target such a wide audience? Is a movie that appeals to a Year 7 girl the same as a movie that appeals to a boy in Year 11?"

"We could show one movie that appeals to girls and one that appeals to boys," Rachael suggested.

"We could play ten movies—one for each age group and gender!" Lucas said sarcastically.

"Or we could watch Shrek. Everybody loves Shrek," Angus said.

"I hate Shrek," Lucas said.

"It sounds like some market research is required." Mr Redding wrote and circled *market research* on the board. "And that can be half of your homework this week. You need to find out, with evidence, what movie would get the most interest from the students in the high school. The other part of your homework is working out how much running a movie theatre would cost, and whether it's financially worth pursuing."

Angus couldn't be more excited as Mr Redding closed out the lesson by teaching them how to create a basic survey and how to conduct a cost-benefit analysis for a movie theatre. Angus was beginning to feel ready. Not to start a movie theatre, but to start selling pens.

OUTSIDE THE SCHOOL GATES

The timber slat fence encompassing the retirement village next to the school was tall, with little enclaves every few metres along the main road. These enclaves offered valuable places for students to hide when they wanted to conduct activities out of sight.

"It's cold," Angus mumbled to himself, his backpack against the fence near his feet. Like at the height of his chocolate business, hardly a fortnight ago, his backpack and pockets were filled with products he was looking to—needing to—sell. On the way to school, he had purchased a box of the cheapest pens he could find at Moving Stationery. The box of 100 pens cost him $30. He had made the optimistic calculation that if he could sell the pens for one dollar each, he would only need to sell thirty to break even.

Angus, standing just inside one of the enclaves, had let at least thirty students walk past him. As the students passed by, some appearing to have awoken only minutes earlier, he sized them up as potential customers. On paper, asking a student if they wanted to buy a pen was simple, and he had proven to himself he could do it with his successful sale to Abdul. But he could feel the weight of dozens of pens in his pocket, and making dozens of sales was a daunting task.

"I sold two pens this morning!" was how Angus greeted Lucas half an hour later at their lockers.

"Bull," Lucas greeted back.

Angus pulled a $1 coin and two 50c coins from his pocket. He showed Lucas the money with pride.

"Who bought the pens?" Lucas asked.

"Damien from our class, who maybe thinks I'm homeless, and a girl from Year 9. My plan is working!"

"I wouldn't say your plan is *working* yet," Lucas said sceptically. "Two dollars a day is not a liveable wage."

"I know, I know," Angus said. "But I've proven there's potential for the plan to work. I just need to work out how to sell more pens and make more money."

The next morning, Angus stood in the same enclave outside the retirement village, hoping for lightning to strike twice. He arrived very enthusiastically at 7:45am and leaned casually against the fence, trying to look inconspicuous. With a renewed confidence partly fuelled by a coffee from Café Olka, he asked every passing student if they wanted to buy a pen. In fifteen minutes, only ten students walked by. He made no sales. At around 8am the foot traffic increased, but the sales were stagnant. Disheartened, he stopped asking and wished that people would just come to him and ask if he was selling anything. By 8:20am, Angus was ready to pack up shop and head into school. He began packing his pens into his backpack.

"What are you doing?" Rachael asked. She had spotted Angus from a distance holding large quantities of pens, and her curiosity got the better of her.

"Selling pens," Angus sighed. He held a pen toward her. "Do you want to buy one?"

"Wait," Rachael said. "You took Mr Redding's pen idea? I thought you said selling pens was a bad idea?"

"First of all, I came up with the idea before him. Secondly, I didn't want to sell pens for the assignment because that would be a waste. I'm running a real pen business."

"Why?"

He shrugged. "I think I can make a decent living from selling pens."

Angus picked up his bag and walked with Rachael into the school.

"Why don't you get a job?" she asked.

"This is a job. I'm starting—I've *started* a business."

She smirked and looked at the ground.

"What's so funny?"

"Is your business working?" she asked slowly.

"I've made some sales, but... no, not really."

"Maybe it's because you're selling those pens." She pointed at the blue pen in Angus's hand.

"What's wrong with these pens?"

Rachael didn't want to hurt his feelings but felt the kind

thing to do was to be honest. "Those pens don't work very well most of the time, and they're free at the front office if you say you left your pencil case at home."

Angus's heart sank. He put the pen in his pocket.

"I'm sorry," Rachael said. "Maybe you could find a good pen and try selling that."

Angus forced a smile. "Yeah, we'll see."

Angus's school day was a slow crawl. His mind drifted from dreams of a pen empire to the realities of monotonous lessons, monotonous conversations and the binary weather— too hot or too cold.

———————

Angus arrived home that afternoon in a rut. Not even a bucket of hot chips on the walk home had cheered him up. His parents' home was a suburban, single-story house sporting a large front yard that his mum had filled with raised vegetable gardens. She couldn't put them in the backyard because of the family dog, Mike, who had an affinity for redesignating gardens as mining operations.

He unlocked the house, went to his bedroom and flopped onto the bed. As he had done habitually many times over the past week, he did a web search for pens on his phone and scrolled through dozens of entries for online stationery stores. The colours, shapes and brands of pens appeared countless. It seemed crazy to him that so many pen brands could co-exist. The ink colours and case colours were the obvious differences...

He lost interest and prepared himself a double-stacked peanut butter and jam toasted sandwich.

While the sandwich was in the toastie-maker, his mum arrived home. Cathy Newton worked as an office manager at a finance company. Frankly, Angus had no idea what the company did. Cathy thrived on positivity. She had once said "Thank you, have a wonderful day", to a man who stole her handbag in the shopping centre parking lot. That's not to say she was ditzy; Cathy was whip-smart. She had a degree in office management and could defeat anyone she came across in chess. In high school, she represented the state at the national inter-school chess tournament and had won the championship match. The person she won against was Angus's dad, Tom Newton. Tom had initially claimed he'd let Cathy win because she was so pretty, but very soon after admitted that Cathy had beaten him fair and square.

Tom was also smart, but in entirely different ways from his wife. He could build almost anything out of almost anything. Tom had built the house they lived in by his own hand in less than five months. He only borrowed Angus's uncle Phil, also a builder, when four hands were needed to hold things up. The final day of the fifth month after the land was cleared, Cathy and Tom Newton plonked down on the bed in their new, finished house and went to sleep, because it was midnight and they had just arrived home from their wedding.

Angus had grown up in a middle-class, modest family who could afford everything they wanted because they were content with what they had. Thanks to Cathy's stringent budgeting, there was always money in an emergency fund to replace a broken fridge or repair a car. There was always money set aside to go on annual holidays, because their holidays were down to the coast, not flying to exotic destinations.

Cathy put her bag down by the front door and gave Angus a hug. "Good afternoon."

Angus gave a smile when she finally released him. "Hey."

"How was school?"

"Yeah, fine."

Cathy opened the fridge. "I'm about to head to the shops. Is there anything you need?"

"No, I'm fine, thanks." He was distracted by a gold pen sitting on the kitchen bench. "Hey Mum, if you were looking for a pen to buy for your office, what would you look for?"

"I don't look for new pens anymore," Cathy said. "The ones I buy took two years to find, and they're the most perfect pens ever manufactured."

"What's so good about them?"

"Well, they write smoothly, they're comfortable to hold and they last for a long time. If you need I can buy some for you, but I thought you bought a box of pens yesterday?"

Angus shook his head. "They're not good enough. Too cheap."

He hadn't told his parents about his business. It wasn't that he didn't trust them, but Angus wasn't even sure if what he was doing was legal. He resolved he would tell them after he was successful.

"How much are these perfect pens you buy for the office?"

Cathy paused with her head in the pantry. "Oh, less than six dollars each."

"Six dollars?" Angus exclaimed.

"They're very nice pens, and when you work in an office, it's better to have nice pens that cost a little more over cheap pens that break after a day or two," Cathy explained. "What's gotten you so interested in pens?"

"It's for an assignment," Angus said quickly. He rescued his burning afternoon tea from the toastie-maker and headed back to his room. He loaded up his desktop computer and once again did a web search for pens. This time, however, he sorted the products by high to low prices. He skimmed past the unnecessarily expensive diamond-encrusted fountain pens and one-off commemorative pens used for signing historical things.

A picture of a pile of pens caught his eye. This particular product listing had a price of $1,000 and said *Best Cheap Pens*. Angus, feeling curious, clicked on the product. He was taken to a website that had to have been created before the turn of the 21st century. Angus couldn't help but laugh at the design; the wallpaper was baby-blue with little animated GIFs of pens dancing across the webpage. The title at the top of the page was written in a late '90s *Microsoft Text-Art* font. It read *Pentastic Importers*.

He scrolled down the web page. It listed generically-branded pen and pencil products in bulk quantities. Angus, feeling like he was becoming an expert in pen prices, sensed the prices were far too cheap to be legitimate. The $1,000 offer he had initially clicked on was for an order of ten thousand pens.

He was about to click back to the search engine, already fearing the viruses the website might be sending out, when he saw a phone number. It was local.

If Angus had come across this website a couple days earlier, he would have excitedly created another spread sheet and conducted a cost-benefit analysis for the pen listings. But he didn't feel excitement anymore. He felt out of his depth.

Feeling he had nothing to lose, Angus dialled the number into his phone. He didn't know what he was going to ask for. He certainly didn't have more than a couple of hundred dollars in his bank account to make an order. The phone rang only twice.

"Hello," a man's voice said with speed and a hint of annoyance.

"Hello, sorry," Angus said. "I'm just looking at the prices of pens."

"Called?"

"Angus."

"We don't carry those."

"No, that's my name. Angus Newton."

"Good to know," the man said. "Which company are you with?"

"Uh, private sale," Angus answered, as if it was a secret code to gain access to information.

The man gave a raspy cough. "What pens do you want, and how many do you need?"

"I'm just looking for prices at the moment."

"Prices for what?"

"For pens."

"Which pens?"

"What pens have you got?"

"What pens have I got? I guarantee you, if it's a brand of

pen, I sell it. I can't spend all day going through all the pens I've *got*."

Acknowledging that the conversation was going nowhere, Angus hung up the phone. He sat still at his desk, feeling like he had just talked with a drug dealer.

His phone began vibrating, listing a private number.

"Hello, this is Angus," he answered cautiously.

"This is Doug Fox from Pentastic Importers. The phone line cut out. I understand you're in need of pens. How many?"

"I'm not sure. I'm looking at starting to sell pens," Angus said in a panic, realising this stranger had his phone number. He wanted to make it very clear it was just pens he was after.

"What's your budget?"

"Uh, a thousand?" Angus said, picking the number out of thin air.

"Come to my shop. Nine-eight-nine Frome Road in the city. I'm open until five on weeknights."

"Oh, okay. I'll see if I can make it," Angus said. The call was abruptly ended with a "goodbye" from both parties. Angus was once again left sitting at his desk, stunned.

"You're going to go where and do what?" Lucas asked when Angus called him to explain the plan.

"This guy has really cheap pens," Angus said. "If he's legit and I can order from him, I'll be able to make serious profits!"

"And if he's a serial killer?"

"He's not a serial killer. He sells pens." But Angus was fully aware serial killing could be a pen seller's hobby.

"What if he's doing shady dealings, and pens are a cover

for drugs? What if 'pens' is just a code word?"

"If that's the case, I'll just say no thanks and walk away," Angus said. "I need a supplier if I'm going to make a profit from selling pens. I can't keep buying them from Moving Stationery—the profit margins are too low. And I know what you're thinking—"

"Whether you've left anything in your will for me?"

"You're thinking 'Where is Angus going to get the money to order pens in bulk?'"

"I was actually thinking about how you're going to cart boxes and boxes of pens home if you catch the bus to see this dealer, as I doubt you're going to ask your mum to drive you to a business meeting."

Angus considered his answer for a beat. "Well, to answer your first query, I'm not going to order any pens straight away. I'm just going to go and look. As for the second question..."

Angus couldn't think of any way not to embarrass himself.

Lucas could tell what he was thinking.

"You're going to get your mum to drive you to a meeting with a supplier?" He cracked up laughing.

"Why not?" Angus said. "You don't see me laughing when your mum has to drive you to the dentist."

"Lame," Lucas sang. "'Hello, I would like to buy thousands of dollars of pens. By the way, this is my business associate, my mother.' Have you asked her yet? Because I can't guess what she's going to think when you say you want to meet a stranger in the middle of the city to discuss buying thousands of dollars of pens."

"I'm glad this is all so comedic for you," Angus said.

"You want to go where and do what?" Cathy asked.

Angus finished his mouthful of apricot chicken. "I'm doing research on pen products for that school assignment, and I was wondering if you could drive me there sometime after school."

"Why don't you look up the prices online?"

"I already have looked them up online, and now I need to go check them out in person. It's an important assignment."

"I've never heard of this store before. 'Pentastic Importers'?"

"They're not a retail store. They're a supplier."

"Grab the bus into town," Tom Newman suggested.

Cathy gave her husband a stern glance. "I don't want him catching the bus into that part of town."

"Why not?" Angus frowned.

"Why not?" Tom shrugged his shoulders.

Cathy tilted her head. "You know that part of town isn't safe. There's all sorts of unsavoury characters there."

"He'll be fine," Tom said. He turned to Angus. "What do you do if some bloke comes up to you and asks you for money?"

"I'd ask him what he wants it for," Angus said.

Cathy shook her head. "No—"

"What if he starts getting agitated and asks again for money?" Tom continued.

"I'd tell him that money doesn't buy happiness," Angus said, just to see his mother's reaction.

"Are you joking?" Cathy asked. "I hope you're joking.

That's how you get hurt."

"Of course I'm kidding," Angus said. "If a man asked me for money I'd give him all the money I had on me, and then take him to the closest ATM and empty my bank account for him as well."

"I think you could claim it as an education expense," Tom said.

"You can't claim being robbed as an education expense," Cathy tutted.

"Well I'd learn not to go back into that part of town," Angus said.

"Look, I don't mind driving you in—and after this conversation I'd prefer to—but it's going to need to wait until next week," Cathy said. "I can't leave work early until probably next Tuesday. Is that okay?"

Angus agreed to his mum's terms. In the meantime, he had 95 pens from his old stock he needed to get rid of.

LESSON THREE:
FINANCIAL PLANNING

"Still selling the pens?" Lucas asked Angus as they walked across the courtyard to their Week 4 Business and Enterprise class.

"Nope. They're in my desk drawer at home," Angus said. "Rachael was right—those pens were cheap and rubbish. Did you want some?"

"They could be fun to light on fire," Lucas suggested.

"Light them on fire?" Angus said. "Why?"

"The might make cool colours when they burn." Lucas had spent hours over the weekend watching online pyrotechnic videos while procrastinating his business studies homework.

"You're the last person I'd expect to suggest that burning inks and plastic would be a good idea."

"Safety first, of course, but I find fire fascinating. I saw this video last night where this guy had potassium nitrate and—"

Lucas stopped mid-sentence. Both the boys were

surprised, not only to find Mr Redding on time to class and waiting in the classroom, but also to see a visitor sitting in the teacher's chair.

"Good morning, boys," Mrs Campbell said cheerfully, but without actually smiling. She twirled a pen in her fingers.

Angus had to fight the urge to turn on his heels and power walk out of the classroom. Rachael was seated at her desk without any maths books open before her. She had been equally surprised to find Mrs Campbell waiting in the classroom and had figured if anyone was going to tell her off for doing maths during a business studies lesson, it would be the principal.

The boys sat in the second row of desks.

Mr Redding was standing with his arms crossed, his face stern. He talked quickly, as if talking was a painful necessity. "All right, good morning everyone. Mrs Campbell and I were having a talk about the practical assignment, and she has requested—"

"If I might interrupt, Mr Redding," Mrs Campbell said. She looked at the students. "Mr Redding and I were having a conversation about how we could use this assignment in business studies to address current issues in the school. Now, I must say you are a very bright group of kids—some of the brightest in the school—and I love the movie theatre idea. I absolutely love it. My only issue with the idea is movie theatres don't promote some of the initiatives our school has, including healthy eating and exercise."

Angus tensed up. He didn't know exactly what Mrs Campbell was about to suggest, but whatever it was, it wasn't going to be good or profitable.

In a demeanour the students occasionally saw at school assemblies, Mrs Campbell stood up and began to talk excitedly. "I was thinking, maybe there is a way that we could promote our healthy-school policies in your assignment? Do any of you have any ideas how we could do this?"

The students were silent. Even Lucas, who somewhat agreed with the healthy school agenda, wasn't particularly interested in changing their movie theatre idea.

"Any ideas for promoting a healthy school?" Mrs Campbell repeated. She took the cap off a whiteboard marker, ready to record ideas.

Mr Redding avoided anyone's eye contact, looking just as defeated as the kids felt.

Angus hid his disbelief behind confusion. "So you're saying we can't do the movie theatre idea?"

"That's correct, Angus," Mrs Campbell said shortly. "As I said, the movie theatre doesn't align with the school's principles."

Angus tried to swallow his frustration. "Is one of the school's principles to restrict learning?"

Mrs Campbell gave him her signature stare. "Angus, you are being very disrespectful. You will not pass this assignment unless you can come up with some business ideas that promote healthfulness. Rachael, do you have some ideas?"

Rachael was just as annoyed as her classmates that their idea was being crushed underfoot, but it wasn't in her nature, nor did she think it wise, to argue with her principal.

"Maybe we could show a movie like Chariots of Fire or

Cool Runnings. A movie that promotes physical fitness?" she suggested.

Mrs Campbell's face contorted as though trying to read whether the girl's suggestion was a display of defiance.

Mr Redding stepped forward to break the tension. "It is all right if I speak to you in private, Mrs Campbell?"

Mrs Campbell sent the three students outside the class-room, closing the door behind them. As much as Angus strained to hear the conversation inside, he couldn't hear a thing.

"Can you believe her?" he whispered, leaning against the veranda pole facing away from the classroom so that Mrs Campbell couldn't read his lips through the window. "She's like a dinosaur trying whatever techniques and policies she read in the latest teachers' magazine to survive extinction!"

"Do they have actual teachers' magazines?" Lucas asked.

"I'm sure they do."

"What, with articles like 'Bachelor Teacher of the Year'?"

"Probably. And maybe a section called 'Ten Easy Steps to Avoid Extra Work'."

"Mr Bonners wrote that section," Rachael added. The boys looked up at her. They had never heard Rachael talk bad about a teacher.

"To be fair to Mr Bonners, you always finish the given maths questions too quickly and, he just refuses to give you extra work," Angus said. "You can't blame him for doing his job correctly."

"I can when I get a D for a maths test."

"You've got to work smart, not hard," Angus said.

95

Rachael held her tongue. She wasn't going to take advice from Angus, whom she knew almost always got worse grades than her in every subject.

"If you want extra work, you can swim my two-hundred metre freestyle at the swimming carnival at the end of the year," Lucas suggested to Rachael.

Rachael smirked. "And how would that work?

"I'm no expert," Lucas said, "but I'm pretty sure you just flail your arms around until you start going forward through the water. Again, no expert."

Angus turned his head quickly to glimpse through the window. Mr Redding was standing with his arms folded, calmly explaining something to Mrs Campbell. The principal, on the other hand, was frowning, fidgeting with the white-board marker. He sighed. "If Mrs Campbell does get her way and we have to do some hippie-time health business, what do you think we should do?"

"The aerobics class would fit the bill," Lucas said. The boys looked hopefully at Rachael, the only one of them with any fitness experience.

She started to shake her head but realised their options could be very limited. "I would be willing to do an aerobics class, but only for girls. I wouldn't want any guys in the room."

"Then we're only targeting half the market," Angus said.

"The market we can target is going to be tiny anyway," Rachael said. "A healthy business with no food or drink just leaves physical education options. Either we do a pay-to-play soccer game, a basketball game, aerobics or we...dunk a teacher in sunscreen to teach students about sun safety."

Angus began considering the logistics behind dunking a teacher under a bucket of sunscreen. The classroom door reopened, and Mr Redding signalled for the students to return. The white board had *market orientation* written in Mr Redding's handwriting.

Mrs Campbell was now the one with her arms crossed.

She switched eye contact between the three students as she spoke. "Mr Redding has put forth a proposal, and I have decided to leave this assignment in his hands."

The three students didn't relax. They were waiting for the "but".

"But, I do have conditions," Mrs Campbell added. "Rachael, your idea is good. You need to choose a film that promotes health and fitness. Also, you may sell healthy snacks, but *only* healthy snacks. No added sugar or salt or fats."

Lucas raised his hand. The fact that Mrs Campbell silently rested her gaze on him for an uncomfortably long time made him feel he had permission to speak.

"There is no evidence that a little bit of fat leads to health issues. That is largely based on un-replicated studies from the early '90s supported by the sugar industry, to avert consumers gaze from the health problems of...sugar." Lucas's voice trailed off at the end.

Angus wished he could smother Lucas with his pencil case.

Mrs Campbell looked at Lucas with what could have been a similar desire. "No added fats."

She tried to pick up the pieces of her smile as she closed

out her visit. "Thank you for your time, and I look forward to one of you coming and presenting your movie and snack selections for my approval at my earliest convenience."

She gave a nod to Mr Redding and closed the classroom door as softly as she could behind her. The students watched her walk across the courtyard back to the front office building.

"What was that?" Angus blurted.

"Mrs Campbell just wanted to give a few suggestions," Mr Redding said diplomatically. "Her role as the principal is to look at the school on a macro level, not at the individual lessons or assignments. She saw an opportunity on the micro level that could benefit the macro level."

"What did you say to change her mind?" Lucas asked.

"I simply gave her more information on the assignment, and what factors would help it succeed." Mr Redding paused with his mouth agape. "I implore all three of you to try to be in Mrs Campbell's good books. There is nothing to stop her from returning and shutting this assignment down. I know any business you three attempt will be successful, including a healthy school idea, but it would be a real setback to be forced to change your business after planning has been completed."

The students understood what Mr Redding was saying, but it was Angus who everyone was worried about. Angus knew he was in Mrs Campbell's bad books and would need to tread lightly. He didn't want to mess up the assignment for the other students.

Mr Redding rubbed *market orientation* from the white board and wrote up *financial planning*. "Okay, let's start on today's topic, financial planning. It was your homework to estimate the expenses of running a movie theatre. Angus, how did it go?"

Doing his best to hide his panic, Angus opened his laptop, turning it slightly so Lucas couldn't see the screen, and pretended to open his completed homework, which in reality had barely been started.

"Sorry, one moment. My computer is taking its time," Angus bluffed. "Maybe start with Lucas?"

"Lucas, how did your numbers look?" Mr Redding poised the whiteboard marker at the board.

Lucas, unlike Angus, had actually done his homework. He had used the very basic cost-benefit analysis template Mr Redding had taught them last week and had filled it in as best as he could with information found online.

"Well, to play a movie there's apparently no upfront costs," Lucas explained. "We just need to pay sixty percent of the ticket sales in the film's opening week, and that amount will decrease over the weeks that we show the movie."

"I'm not sure that's quite correct," Mr Redding said. "We're not a movie theatre showing new films. We're looking for the cost of licencing a film in a ticketed venue. But great research all the same, especially if the business decides to expand in the future."

Rachael raised her hand.

"No need for hands. What have you got, Rachael?"

Rachael looked down at the beautifully set out and organised table she had drawn into a grid exercise book. "I found information saying a licence will depend on the film and the distributor, but it seems in most cases there is an upfront fee, and the film distributor gets a percentage of the ticket sales. The upfront fee could be between one hundred and two thousand dollars, and we can't estimate the ticket cut, because we don't know how many tickets we'll sell."

"We can make pretty good estimates of ticket sales," Mr Redding said. "Let's estimate that the film will cost one thousand dollars upfront and fifteen percent of the ticket sales will go to the distributor. The auditorium, when full, can seat about three hundred students. Let's say you run the most amazing marketing campaign ever and three hundred students buy tickets. What will the ticket costs be?"

Lucas's brain checked out and went on holidays.

Rachael was already typing the math into her graphics calculator. "One thousand dollars divided by three students is three dollars and thirty-three cents per ticket."

Mr Redding laughed. "I should have guessed that. Lucas, how much have you written down we should charge per ticket?"

"I was going to charge fifteen dollars."

"Fifteen dollars?" Angus chuckled. He gave up pretending to have done his homework. "That's what it costs to see a new movie in a real theatre."

"Yes, but we're offering convenience, and we need to make a profit," Lucas replied.

"I was thinking we could charge eight dollars," Rachael said.

Angus shook his head. "I still think eight dollars is too high a price. I would say five dollars a ticket."

"Why?" Mr Redding challenged.

"The only real value we're offering students is they get to sit inside and watch a movie. The movie probably won't even be that good."

Rachael and Lucas didn't argue Angus's price, so Mr Redding wrote *Ticket price - $5* on the board.

Rachael did another calculation and announced that once the 15% ticket cut was considered, the total profit per ticket would only be—

"Ninety-two cents?" Lucas exclaimed. "Is that it? I was planning on at least five dollars profit per ticket."

"And now you can see why movie theatres sell snacks at ridiculous prices," Mr Redding said. "Speaking of snacks— Angus, what profit margins did you come up with for the food and drink items?"

Angus quickly opened a web browser and found an online supermarket. "Well, I was having a think this week about what we could sell..." He clicked on the 'health foods' section. "And there are prunes that sell for three dollars for half a kilo."

"You're going to sell prunes to teenagers?" Mr Redding asked. "Is that being market orientated?"

Angus quickly scrolled to another product. "We could, of course, get popcorn. You can get the packets that air cook in a microwave."

"Very good. How much are they, and what will you sell them for?"

"Well, they're a dollar a packet. One packet could serve at least two kids; we could sell one serve for two dollars. That's one-dollar fifty profit per serve."

"Popcorn with no flavouring is like eating...grain," Rachael said.

"It's literally eating grain," Lucas agreed.

Angus rolled his eyes. He kept scrolling thought the supermarket website, but failed to immediately find anything else that would be attractive to students.

"Rachael, you seem to have all the answers today," Mr Redding said. "What foods would you suggest?"

Rachael smiled proudly and looked around the near-empty classroom for inspiration. A giant poster on the wall showed the germination stages of an apple tree. "Fruit smoothies are trendy at the moment. I'm sure we can get bananas and berries at a good price if we buy them in bulk."

"Yes! Well done." Mr Redding enthusiastically wrote *Smoothies* in giant letters on the board. Angus wished he had thought of smoothies.

"I'd estimate smoothies could bring in about three dollars of profit," she added.

Mr Redding stood back and looked at the whiteboard. "I think this is looking like a good plan so far."

"Wait! We haven't gotten to my other ideas for food yet," Angus said.

"What food ideas do you have?" Mr Redding asked.

"Well, I also think smoothies are a great idea." Angus pointed at his screen, pretending he had the idea recorded on his laptop. "But I think another good idea would be burritos. Everyone loves burritos!"

"My mum doesn't like burritos," Mr Redding said.

"Everyone but Mr Redding's mum likes burritos," Angus

said. "And they fit into Mrs Campbell's dictatorial agenda for healthiness. If we sell them for about six dollars each, we could make a profit of about three dollars fifty per burrito."

Mr Redding recorded the information on the whiteboard. "We have three products and three profit margins. How many of each do you think we can sell? Lucas?"

"Two hundred movie tickets, two hundred smoothies and three hundred burritos," Lucas guessed wildly.

"You think that almost every single high school student is going to buy a burrito for six dollars each?" Angus asked.

"I'm optimistic."

"Speaking from experience," Angus said, "few students have excessive amounts of money to spend. Most students get money from their parents. It's highly unlikely that a parent will give sixteen dollars to their child to spend on food and a movie at school. My guess is we'll sell one hundred tickets, one hundred smoothies and maybe one hundred and fifty burritos."

Rachael said she agreed with Angus. The class arrived at their total theoretical profit figures: $92 for the tickets, $300 for the smoothies and $350 for the burritos.

"Seven hundred and forty-two dollars profit. Three hundred and seventy-one after half goes to charity," Lucas gushed. "One hundred and twenty-three dollars profit each!"

"A hundred and twenty-three each isn't too bad." Angus wondered how many pens that could buy.

"That would be a successful profit, but let's not lose sight that you might not reach it. You might even make a loss," Mr Redding warned. "But that's business. You can create plans, shop around for the best prices and conduct thorough market research, but due to an external force, you might just fail. Those who succeed in business are those who are able to pick themselves up after they fail and try again."

PENTASTIC IMPORTERS

On the drive into the city the next evening, Cathy tried to get more information about her son's assignment. "I thought you said you were running a movie theatre for your business assignment? What does that have to do with pens?"

Angus sat in the front passenger seat wearing jeans and a black V-neck t-shirt. He wanted to look as professional as he could without raising his parents' suspicion.

"This is for a different assignment," he said. He didn't like lying to his mum, but he justified it in his conscience that selling pens would help him learn skills for the school assignment. The justification had helped him finally get to sleep the night before.

Cathy pulled to the curb of the near-deserted city street where Angus directed her. She looked out the window. "Is this the right address?"

Angus double checked the map on his phone. The GPS

showed they were at the correct location. They were parked in front of a dull-grey building which, other than the paint colour, had no descriptive features. This nondescript building stood next to another forgettable building, which sat next to another forgettable building. The only informative shop front on the whole street, which could also be described as an alleyway, was a Vietnamese café whose sign claimed they had the best Banh Mi in the southern hemisphere. The windows to the grey building were frosted and secured by a grid of iron bars. The door was similarly secured, but with the pleats of a scrim visible on the other side of the glass.

"Maybe I should come inside with you," Cathy said.

"No, that's fine."

Angus saw the concern on his mother's face. As derelict as the environment was, he didn't feel apprehensive. The building looked exactly like how he'd expected it to look. He assumed international importers kept their prices low by not wasting money on fancy shop fronts.

"If it doesn't seem safe in there, I want you to come back to the car straight away."

"Mum. I'm seventeen," Angus said. "I'll be fine. If it's not the right place, I'll come back straight away. But just in case I am kidnapped, how much spare money do you and Dad have to pay the ransom?"

"That's not funny, Angus."

"I'm kidding." Angus undid his seat belt. He had a moment's hesitation as his hand rested on the door handle. "I shouldn't be more than ten minutes."

He got out of the car and heard his mum activate the

central locking. Feeling excited about what he would find inside, he walked quickly across the footpath to the shop door. He pushed at the door; it didn't budge. He gripped the metal door handle and gave it an extra-strong push, but it didn't help. He looked back at his mum, feeling embarrassed. Maybe he did get the wrong address after all.

Cathy looked back at him with apparent relief that the door hadn't opened.

Angus tried to peer through the glass door. He couldn't see past the scrim, but could tell there was a light on inside.

The door opened with Angus's face still between the iron bars.

"Can I help you?" the man standing inside asked abruptly.

"Sorry." Angus stepped back. "Are you open?"

"Yes, I am open," the man said. Angus recognised the voice as Doug Fox, the same man he had spoken to on the phone the week prior.

"The door was locked," Angus said.

"No it wasn't."

"I couldn't get in."

"That doesn't mean the door was locked."

Angus wondered if this low-level customer service was given to everyone. He gave his best confident smile to his mum as he entered the shop.

The shop looked like it had only been moved in that morning. There were no shelving units or products on show. There was no advertising or price tickets. What the shop did have was boxes—piles and piles of boxes upon boxes. Some boxes were open, but most were as sealed as the day they left the factory. In one corner of the shop, on a makeshift desk constructed from more boxes, lay a laptop and a notepad. An open doorway in the rear appeared to lead to another room where Angus glimpsed more boxes, probably more than what occupied the front room.

Angus stood awkwardly in the middle of the room with his hands in his pockets, waiting for the man to make some introduction or sales pitch.

Fox, who appeared in his late thirties, sat down on a box behind his makeshift desk and peered under his glasses at his laptop.

"How long have you been here for?" Angus asked to break the silence.

Fox mumbled something incomprehensible.

Angus didn't sense an introduction would come from the man. "My name's Angus. I called up about a week ago—"

Fox looked up from his laptop. "You're after pens?"

"Yes."

"Which ones?"

"I don't know yet. Do you have samples I can see?"

Fox looked the boy up and down. After a moment of consideration, he stood back up and began moving about the shop. He stacked three large boxes together in the middle of the room to create another makeshift table. Angus watched as the man opened a box, pulled out a pen and laid it on the makeshift table. He continued this, red pen after green pen after blue pen after black pen. Although the boxes were labelled, the man never stopped to check them. He seemed to know exactly where everything was. Angus recognised some of the pens' brands as they were placed before him. Some were labelled in foreign languages, while others had no labels at all.

Apparently satisfied with the selection, Fox stopped on the opposite side of the makeshift table which was now adorned with over a dozen pens.

"How much do you know about pens?"

"Nothing," Angus admitted. To anyone else, he would have said he was an expert.

Fox picked up a clear-plastic, blue-ink pen which Angus was very familiar with. He had dozens of them, unsold, sitting in his desk drawer.

"This is a common ballpoint pen. It takes D-type refills. Really cheap to produce, and that's why everyone buys them. You can buy expensive D-type ballpoint pens, but it's the cases that make them expensive. Inside is still going to be the cheap, oil-based ink and the ballpoint tip."

He picked up a glittery purple pen. "This is a rollerball pen. Think ballpoint, but with much thinner ink. The thinner ink makes them smoother to write with. Although they're nicer to write with, rollerballs will smudge easily and bleed through paper. If you leave a rollerball uncapped in your pocket, be prepared to spend the night scrubbing the stains. But if you're selling the pens, the rollerball is much better than the ballpoint because it will run out of ink quicker. That means more sales for you."

Angus only understood fragments of the man's rapid pitch, but the last sentence was as clear as day.

Fox picked up a gold-nibbed, blue-cased fountain pen.

"This is a fountain pen. They're the original modern writing instrument but offer no benefit over a ballpoint or rollerball. They leak easily and run out of ink quickly but sell incredibly well because everyone thinks they're fancy."

"So fountain pens run out of ink quickly, meaning I can sell more. And people think they're fancy, meaning I can sell them for a higher price?" Angus clarified.

The man grabbed a selection of pens he hadn't looked at yet and shoved them into his pocket.

"What were they?" Angus asked.

"Felt tips. You don't want felt tips."

"Why not?"

"You're looking for a writing pen. Felt tips are not writing pens. Unless you're wanting to draw a smiley face on your pet rocks, you don't want a felt tip pen."

Angus picked up the blue fountain pen and asked if there was a piece of paper he could test it on. The man got his notepad and placed it on the makeshift table. Angus had never used a fountain pen before; he had always used cheap ballpoints at school and slightly nicer gel pens at home that his mum procured as promotional gifts from suppliers and clients. He wrote *the end of the world* on the paper.

"How old are you?" Fox asked.

Angus's face got hot. He certainly looked older than he was and could have lied about his age, but he didn't see any benefit. "Seventeen."

Fox nodded.

"I'm looking to start a business selling pens," Angus explained. The man's face remained expressionless, and Angus feared he was beginning to lose the confidence of his potential supplier.

"Is that okay?"

"Is what okay?"

"Me, starting a business." Angus didn't know why he was asking this stranger's permission.

"How much would one hundred of these pens be?" he asked quickly.

"They're three dollars each." Fox placed the purple glittery pen back in its box.

"What about for a thousand?"

Fox paused. "A thousand of the Flyrite fountain pens would be about three thousand dollars."

Angus had no idea where he could get that amount of money. "Any further discount on ten thousand pens?" he bluffed.

"I can sell you a million pens with a good discount, but I'd need some proof that you have that kind of money to spend."

"Well, I need proof that your pens are worth spending that kind of money on," Angus replied, crossing his arms. "I'll admit I'm new to this business. But if you can offer me the right product, I'll find the money to pay for it."

Angus's intensity was a gamble. He didn't know if the man could see right through him, and the way Fox looked at him with one eyebrow raised made him feel powerless.

The man's face eventually softened. He put out his hand. "I'm Doug Fox."

"Angus," Angus said. They shook hands.

"Who are you planning on selling the pens to?" Fox asked.

111

"Students."

Fox shook his head. "Don't bother. Schools don't want to buy anything except the cheapest pens they can find. I'm the supplier to several schools and they'll switch pen brands if it saves their whole budget a dollar a year."

That was not what Angus wanted to hear. "That sounds right, but I think I know what schools want more than cheap pens. They want students to get good grades."

Fox snorted. "Unless schools have changed dramatically since I was in one, they don't give a damn about students. Whether a student stays in school or not is just a question of whether the kid's parents can afford to pay the fees."

"I think they have changed over the years," Angus said defensively, though he was unsure if he believed it himself.

"You're going to try and convince schools to buy pens because it will make their students smarter?"

"No, I'm going to sell the pens to students by convincing them the pens will help them get better grades."

Without another word, Fox disappeared into the back room.

The front door creaked opened and Cathy poked her head in. She looked around the box-filled room and noticed her son was alone. "What is going on?"

"He's just going to look for a pen," Angus guessed, giving his mum a reassuring smile. "It's all fine. I'll only be another couple of minutes." He held up the blue fountain pen to show her it was really pens they were dealing in.

Cathy reluctantly stepped outside the store and closed the door.

112

Fox returned holding a large box, which thudded as he placed it on the wood-panelled floor. He opened what seemed to be a babushka of boxes until he finally pulled out the most unique pen that Angus had ever seen. From the nib, Angus could see it was clearly a fountain pen. The casing was black and triangular with a soft rubber grip. Fox handed Angus the pen. It was perfectly comfortable in Angus's fingers.

"That is the Prince 994," Fox announced. Angus wrote *the end of the world* in large letters on the pad of paper. The pen glided across the page, and Angus couldn't help but smile as he wrote *the end of the world* again and again on the page.

"That pen is what you're looking for," Fox continued. "It's cheap—really cheap. Only thirty cents per pen. It uses a unique oil-based ink formula that writes as smooth as water-based fountain pens but doesn't run out as quickly. It's not available anywhere else in the country except through me."

Although it was clearly a nice pen, Angus didn't feel entirely convinced a fountain pen would be attractive to the common student. "Any other pens you can show me? Maybe one of the rollerballs would be better."

Doug shook his head. "No, that's it."

"You have no other pens?" Angus asked rhetorically.

"The Prince 994 is the only pen I have to sell to you."

"But I want to buy a different pen!"

"Well then you'll have to go somewhere else."

"You can't not sell me a different pen. That's illegal."

"No it's not. It's my shop. I can do as I like," Fox said. "In my professional opinion, the Prince 994 is the pen you need.

113

Any other pen would be unsuitable."

Angus looked at the Prince 994 again, meticulously searching for a flaw that could persuade him to leave. He liked the pen and he was a student. He wondered if because he liked the pen, the other students at his school would like the pen.

"How much would one thousand pens be?" Angus asked.

"Five hundred dollars."

"I thought you said they were thirty cents each."

"They are, but this isn't a charity. I have a profit to make as well."

"I'll give you four hundred for one thousand."

Fox chuckled. "That's not how this works. The cost is five hundred dollars for one thousand pens."

Angus didn't have that kind of money. "I'll need to go away and think about it."

He went to hand the pen back, but Fox didn't accept it. "You keep that one. I can have them custom branded and shipped within a week when you're ready to buy."

"Custom branded?" Angus hadn't considered that he'd need a brand, but the thought of having his own brand name and logo excited him.

"You pick the case colour and logo and whatever else you want. The factory produces it however you want," Fox explained. "Give me a call when you want to order."

Fox closed the conversation by sitting back down at his laptop and seemingly ignoring Angus's very existence.

Angus wasn't ready to leave. He felt impulsive. Impulsivity in that moment looked like Angus reaching into his pocket and pulling out $300 cash. It was all the money he had left from working in his uncle's furniture factory. He held the $300 in the air feeling like a powerful man. "How many pens will three-hundred dollars get me?"

"That would get you six hundred pens." Fox's said eyes never left his screen. A printer hidden underneath Fox's makeshift desk whirred to life and spat out a piece of paper. Fox handed the printed invoice to Angus. "Email me your brand logo tomorrow. TIFF format. Single colour only. My email is on the invoice."

Angus nodded, pretending to know what a TIFF format was.

"How did it go?" Cathy asked as Angus got into the passenger seat. She quickly relocked the doors.

"Yeah, good," Angus said excitedly. The invoice was hidden in his pocket. He realised going on a research trip for a school assignment wasn't something one would normally be excited about, so he tried to play it cool. "He gave me a free pen."

"That was nice of him," Cathy said. "And you got all the information you needed for your assignment? You won't need to come back here again?"

Angus gave an affirmative "Mm-hm."

The whole ride home, his mum cheerfully talked about ideas for her garden and new crops she wanted to plant now that spring was coming, but Angus wasn't listening. He was thinking about names for his pen company.

Exponential Growth

"Hey, your name is Karen, isn't it?" Angus asked a Year 10 girl on her way to school. "Do you want to see something cool?"

Three days after meeting Doug Fox at Pentastic Importers, Angus felt a sense of déjà vu as he stood by the retirement village's fence with a backpack full of pens. Only this time, Angus felt confident. He was prepared with a sales pitch and a one-of-a-kind pen. A student could not get a better free one from the office.

He didn't know how Doug Fox had managed to get him a few boxes of pens in such a short amount of time, but on Wednesday morning he had emailed Fox his crudely created new branding logo, and by Thursday night he had a package of pens delivered to his house. Thankfully he was able to receive and hide the package before his parents got home. He figured the factory must have been somewhere local, but that part of the process wasn't his job. His job was to sell the things.

He felt his sales pitch was foolproof:

"Do you want to see something cool?" he'd say.

"Sure! What is it?" they'd say.

"It's an incredible new pen the likes of which you've never seen before!"

"What makes it so incredible?"

"Well," he'd say, presenting them with one of his bright orange pens, "it's a fountain pen, which is super fun and smooth to write with, but this pen contains a new, secret ink formula that makes it last for ages!"

"Wow, that *is* incredible!" his potential customer would say.

"I purchased a couple of boxes because I think they're really good, but I'd be happy to give you one, if you give me two dollars."

"Two dollars! That's really cheap!" they'd exclaim. "I'll buy two, please."

Two pens would be exchanged for four dollars, and the satisfied parties would part ways.

Karen—the Year 10 girl whose name was actually Sharon— apparently didn't read the script and walked straight past Angus, keeping her eyes averted to avoid any more attention.

Angus shook off the rejection and moved onto the next student, then the next, then the next.

"What are you wanting to show?" Damien asked with a caring smile. Damien himself was on a mission that Friday morning, handing out flyers at the school gate promoting a charity dinner for dogs. Whether the dogs were the recipients of the dinner or the money raised, Angus didn't ask, but he

117

did know Damien was asking about his business out of pity.

"Nothing," Angus said.

"No, I want to see it. You're asking everyone that walks past." Damien tilted his head like a clinical psychologist. "Is it another pen?" he asked gently.

Angus, unable to escape Damien's attention, opened his hand to show a bright-orange pen.

"Oh, that looks interesting," Damien said. "What is it?"

"It's an incredible new pen," Angus said with little enthusiasm.

"What makes it incredible?" Damien asked, not really paying attention to the pen.

Angus sighed and handed Damien the pen. "It's a fountain pen with a new type of ink that makes it last for a long time."

"Wow, that *is* incredible. I think that's really cool."

He examined the pen closely, reading the name on the side. "What's an Inkda?"

"That's the name of the pen."

"Oh. That's an interesting name."

There was a moment of silence between them before Damien asked, "What are you doing with them?"

Angus didn't want another pity sale but couldn't think of an explanation that would make Damien leave him alone. "I bought a bunch and am seeing if anyone wants to buy one from me."

Damien could not have appeared keener. "How much?"

Angus resigned himself to selling pens to the philanthropic boy. "Two dollars each."

"Two dollars? That's really cheap. How many do you have?"

"Only about a dozen," Angus lied. Damien opened his backpack and found his leather wallet. He searched and found a $20 note, which he held out.

"I'd like to buy ten, please."

On one hand, Angus wanted to assert that he was running a business, not a charity, and he was not looking for handouts. On the other hand, this was a paying customer. He didn't feel it was his place to judge the motivations of his customers.

Angus handed Damien a box of ten pens from his backpack and received the $20 bill.

"Thank you so much for these pens," Damien said, walking away with a big smile.

Angus placed the twenty dollars in his pocket and realised the large transaction had attracted attention from other students passing by. He couldn't help but smile; the pity sale had created something very valuable: publicity.

Angus met eyes with a Year 11 boy. The boy, walking much slower than the other students, appeared at war with himself over approaching Angus to see what was being sold.

"Do you want to see something cool?" Angus asked with reinvigorated self-assurance.

"Are you selling chocolate bars again?" the Year 11 asked.

Angus shook his head. "No, but I've got something even cooler."

He pulled a pen from his pocket and showed it to the boy. "This is an Inkda, one of the newest pens on the market. And as you just saw, it's really popular."

"The Ink-what?"

"Ink-da."

"Oh. That's a weird name."

"Yes, well…" Angus frowned, quite happy with the name he had come up with.

The Year 11 prided himself on being an early adopter of new technologies, games and gadgets. If something was growing in popularity, he wanted it. He fished in his pocket for money. "How much?"

"But I haven't even told you why it's so incredible."

The boy paused, suddenly becoming aware of his actions. "Why *is* it so incredible?"

"It writes well and has a good design," Angus said quickly, his attention on the $10 note the boy had found.

"Cool," the boy said, holding his money out. "How much?"

The boy purchased two pens.

Angus was over the moon with his morning sales. A dozen pens in less than five minutes. Although he was tempted to keep going, he didn't want to push his luck by becoming too popular. There were still untrustworthy students about. He packed up shop and joined the crowd of students walking onto the school grounds.

Ahead, Rachael walked amongst the crowd, her plaited hair bouncing. He sped up until he was beside her. They exchanged a smile.

"Oh, by the way," Angus said, as if they were continuing a long conversation, "I've got something to show you."

He pulled an Inkda from his pocket and gave it to her.

"What's this?"

"It's a good pen."

Rachael connected the dots. "You're still trying your pen business idea?"

120

"Yep, and it's working. I sold twelve pens this morning."

Rachael was genuinely shocked. "That's impressive. Well done." She looked at the foreign word on the pen's casing. "What's Inkda?"

Angus couldn't believe everyone was asking. "It's the name of the pen."

"Oh. That's a curious name."

"It's not *that* bad, is it?" Angus wondered if he had made a terrible branding mistake. He had spent nine hours trying to come up with a name. After trying all the obvious names that came to mind—which were either taken or uninteresting—he arrived at Inkda. He felt it was unique.

"No, I don't think it's a bad name," Rachael said gently. "I just think it's...unique."

Rachael went to hand the pen back.

"You can keep that one," Angus said.

"I've already got a pen, thanks."

Angus refused to accept the pen back. "Try it out and let me know what you think, for research purposes. Besides, you were the one who suggested I should look for better pens to sell. Inkdas are way better than the ones you can get in the office."

Rachael thanked him and put the pen in her dress pocket.

The Year 12s arrived at their classroom for morning homeroom. Angus found a seat next to Lucas, who looked like he hadn't slept at all the night before.

"Hey," the boys greeted each other.

"You looked wrecked," Angus pointed out as only a good friend can.

Lucas yawned. "I *am* wrecked. I was finishing my English assignment until two in the morning."

Daniel Pajero, their classmate and a boy easily distracted, overheard Lucas. "Which assignment?" he asked.

"The five-hundred-word character analysis," Lucas said.

"I thought it wasn't due until next week." Daniel looked at the other students for confirmation.

Now Lucas was confused. Maybe he had got the date wrong. He turned to Abigail, one of the girls who was known for being highly organised. "Hey Abby, the character analysis is due today, isn't it?"

Abigail nodded. The nod of her head made Daniel almost pass out.

"You were practicing basketball, weren't you?" Alan, one of their classmates, laughed.

"I can't fail," Daniel said. He ran to the back of the classroom and found a disowned notepad on the bookshelf. He rummaged around his backpack for a pen. The rest of the class watched this show of desperation and didn't dare laugh at their classmate's distress. "Does anyone have a pen I can borrow?" Daniel cried.

"Heads up!" Damien said from the other side of the room. He chucked a bright-orange pen through the air. In an impressive display of skill that could only be attributed to Daniel's basketball skills, he caught the atrociously inaccurate throw and began scribbling his homework onto the page.

The rest of the class applauded politely at the catch.

"Anyone else want a pen?" Damien asked. There was something irresistible about free things to high school students.

Eight students spoke up and received an Inkda, tossed into or near their outstretched hands.

Laina Michaels held the pen as if it might explode. "What's an Inkda?"

"It's the name of the pen," Damien pointed out.

"Oh. That's a dumb name," Laina said. She opened the back of an exercise book and gave the pen a scribble. Her face contorted from judgement to appreciation. "It's kind of cool. I like fountain pens."

The rest of the class with Inkdas followed suit and gave their pens various levels of scribbles on pieces of paper.

Angus apprehensively watched this all take place. As much as he was interested in selling more pens, he was very uninterested in being labelled by his peers as "that weird kid trying to sell weird pens".

"Where are these pens from?" Nigel Lawrence asked.

"I bought them from Angus."

Every head in the room except Daniel's turned to look at Angus. He felt like a deer in the headlights.

"Are you selling things again?" Alan's eyebrows raised in a mixture of fear and hope. Fear for the boy's future, and hope for more chocolate.

Angus didn't want to make a public announcement about his business. There were kids in his class that he didn't know if he could trust. He picked his words carefully. "I have come into...possession of a number of really cool pens. And because I don't need them all, I am offering them to other students."

"How much?" Alan pulled out his wallet.

Angus looked around at the other students, searching for

signs of distress. Erin, the one girl he was most concerned would go and tell a teacher, held one of the free pens in her hand. Angus hoped having possession of an Inkda would make her feel guilty enough to not snitch.

"Two dollars each," Angus said.

Alan retrieved a $2 coin from his wallet and held it out.

The classroom door opened. Everyone hid their pens in bags, shirt sleeves and under desks. They didn't know if they were holding illicit goods.

Mr Fletcher paused in the doorway, wondering what he had just missed. The students all silently pretended to do nothing, which was as abnormal as a group of high school kids could be. Mr Fletcher, experienced in pretending to not notice things, began the day with announcements. He even pretended to not see Alan walk past Angus's desk and leave something behind, followed by Angus walking past Alan's desk and leaving something else behind.

Angus wished he knew how what happened next actually happened. He had four students from four different year levels come to him during his free lesson after recess in the library and ask to buy a pen.

He later put together all the pieces.

Alan had a little sister in Year 9 named Paige, who had left her pencil case at home. Alan gave her his Inkda to use. Paige, quite fond of stationery, asked her older brother where the pen had come from. Paige also showed the pen to her friends, fellow lovers of stationery, who all then wanted an Inkda for themselves. In the second lesson of the day, three of the Year 12 students who received free pens were helping struggling

Year 10 students in the Student Buddy program, and two of the three accidentally left their Inkdas behind. Two of the Year 10s picked up the pens and used them at recess as bets for a game of Texas Hold'em. The pens were won by a Year 11 boy. This Year 11 boy subsequently gifted one pen each to two girls he was interested in.

After recess, Angus grew very uncomfortable with the attention he was getting. Every ten minutes, a random student came to him and asked to buy a pen.

Lucas, who sat next to him, shook his head in disbelief. "You're going to get caught."

"I know," Angus whispered frantically, keeping his head down.

"Then stop selling them."

"Stop? I just got started." But he knew Lucas was right. It was impossible to continue selling pens without word getting back to Mrs Campbell by the end of the day. He had to stop.

A Year 8 boy pretended to peruse a bookshelf nearby. Angus had done enough transactions to know the student wanted something. He caught the boy's attention and whispered, "I'm sold out."

The boy nodded and quickly left the library to return to class.

"What do I do?" Angus quietly asked Lucas.

"Give the money back and stop jiggling your leg. It's moving the table."

"Why would I give the money back?"

"If you give the money back to those who bought pens, then you haven't sold anything. You've merely given the pens away."

"But I need the money to pay for the pens. I can't just be giving away free pens!"

"Okay," Lucas said, "I'll send you an invite to my graduation ceremony."

———————————

It was very confusing to the customers when Angus found their classes and covertly handed back their money.

"No, it's fine," Damien insisted as they stood by the drink fountain.

Angus, who'd already had the conversation five times in the past few hours, rolled his eyes. "Look, right now it's important that my business remains in the pre-selling stage."

"But I like the pens."

"You can keep the pens."

"Well then, it's only fair for me to have paid for them."

"They're unfit for sale. They're still in the design and testing phase."

"Should I stop using them? Are they dangerous?"

"No, they're not dangerous." Angus sighed. "I just still need to make sure they're perfect. I'm a perfectionist."

"I think you've done an excellent job."

"Exactly," Angus said. "And excellent isn't perfect."

Damien reluctantly accepted the money back, vowing to donate it to the local dog charity in Angus's name.

———————————

By lunch time, Angus was back to where he'd been that morning, minus two dozen pens. He sat in the Year 12 common room thinking deeply about his situation while eating a ham-and-tomato-sauce sandwich. The afternoon sun meant all jumpers and blazers were off, and the students had turned the air conditioner on full-blast.

"People bought the pens and liked the pens. Did they not?" Angus asked Lucas. "I didn't force anyone to buy the pens."

"Uh-huh." Lucas was preoccupied on his laptop, researching a new, expensive MRI machine he could never afford.

"But here I am, too scared to do anything with them because of Mrs Campbell."

"That sounds right."

"I really should have thought about this before I bought six hundred pens."

"They say thinking is smart," Lucas said.

Angus threw his sandwich wrapper across the room, missing the bin by metres. He rose from the couch with a loud groan and picked up his litter.

"I mean, they're just pens," Angus said. "What would Mrs Campbell have against me selling pens? They're helpful. Yes, I can see why she had a problem with the chocolates, but pens are good! I'm helping the school, in a way. If I had access to a freezer, I know I could make a killing selling ice cream in this weather, but I feel like I'm taking an honourable path to making money."

Rachael, who was working with Brooke on their maths assignments, couldn't concentrate past Angus's voice any longer. "Can you please justify your actions a little quieter? We're trying to focus."

"Sorry," Angus said. "But the school's job is to teach us, isn't it?"

"Yes."

"So aren't I learning by starting a business?"

Rachael shrugged. "Maybe you're learning that you need to learn *before* starting a business."

"That doesn't make any sense." Angus slumped back down onto the couch. "What do you think, Lucas?"

"Whatever Rachael said was probably right." Lucas closed his laptop. "Hey, can you lend me any money for an ice cream from the canteen?"

"Have you paid attention to anything I've said in the last fifteen minutes?" Angus asked.

Lucas gave a blank stare. "All I heard was ice cream."

LESSON FOUR: MARKETING

By Monday morning of Week 5, the students were well and truly back in the routine of school, though most had started counting the five weeks until their mid-semester break, when a little bit of freedom would be returned to them. Angus struggled to imagine what freedom would be like after Year 12; no more regimented early mornings, no stringent schedules to follow and no principals telling him what he could and couldn't do.

The three Business and Enterprise students entered the classroom they had come to know so well. Even Lucas had to admit that out of all his classes, BnE was one of the most relaxed environments. *Marketing* had been written on the whiteboard in thick, red letters. Mr Redding sat at the teacher's desk, reading an email he had printed out.

Rachael, seeing that Mr Redding was on time and she wasn't going to have time to work on other subjects, took a seat in the middle row behind Lucas and Angus.

"Morning, all," Mr Redding said without looking up. "Welcome to another week of business."

Angus could tell there was something occupying the teacher's mind.

Mr Redding put down the piece of paper. "How are you all progressing with the movie theatre? Do you have an accurate financial plan?"

Rachael, who had unanimously been appointed head of finance, had spent the previous night formatting their financial plan into a presentable format. It had been the most fun homework she had completed for the subject so far. She produced printed copies from her folder and passed one each to the boys and one to the teacher. Mr Redding appeared genuinely impressed as he flicked through the document's pages. "This looks excellent, Rachael. Well done."

"Thanks." Rachael smiled; she was proud of herself. Although a lot of the business concepts were still unfamiliar to her, budgeting was a topic she excelled at.

Mr Redding flicked back and forth between the pages. "I hate to be the bearer of bad news, but you've missed a section."

Rachael's smile disappeared. "What section?"

Mr Redding pointed at the whiteboard. "Marketing. Probably one of the most important expense items. But don't stress—what you've done so far is really excellent. Adding in the numbers for marketing expenses shouldn't take long."

Rachael slumped in her chair. She didn't have time to make continual adjustments to her work.

130

"I would have forgotten to add marketing costs as well," Angus admitted, sensing Rachael's frustration.

"I forgot that marketing was even a thing," Lucas said.

Rachael appreciated the boys' empathy.

"Marketing is most definitely a 'thing'," Mr Redding said. "So much so that we're going to spend a whole lesson discussing it. Marketing is probably my favourite topic in this whole course because it's the factor that will either make or break your brand." He looked down at the email he'd been reading earlier. "And, as we'll discuss in just a moment, you'll get a lot of marketing experience in the coming weeks, so be sure to listen and take notes. Lucas, how would you define marketing?"

"Advertising?" Lucas suggested.

"Yes, that's correct. Rachael, is there anything you could add?"

Rachael didn't know how to articulate her thoughts. "Marketing is a thing you do. Marketing is the process of...putting things in a market? I don't know how else to describe it."

"It is hard to describe, but you're certainly on the right track. A concise definition of marketing will vary between sources, but marketing is, as Rachael has said, the process of bringing goods and services to a market. The American Marketing Association defines marketing as 'the activity, set of institutions, and processes for creating, communicating, delivering, and exchanging offerings that have value for customers, clients, partners, and society at large'."

Mr Redding smiled at the students' blank expressions. "You can see that giving marketing a single definition is almost impossible, because marketing involves many different facets. Let's explain marketing using an example." He picked up the printed email. "We're going to discuss marketing in terms of this."

"Paper?" Lucas asked.

"No, it's an email," Mr Redding said.

"I don't think email needs much marketing," Angus said.

Mr Redding shook his head. "No, I'm talking about the content of this email from Mrs Campbell."

The name of their principal caused the students to sit up straight.

"She can't keep changing her mind!" Lucas exclaimed. "It's not fair."

"Mrs Campbell hasn't changed her mind," Mr Redding said. "She seems to be quite happy with the movie theatre idea. But in order to get her support, a deal had to be made. For her support for the movie theatre, I told her we would use this week's topic, marketing, to promote a cause of her choice at our school."

Angus immediately assumed the cause would be anti-sugar, but asked the question all the same. "What are we promoting?"

"Well, summer is coming up," Mr Redding said. "And she thought it would be a great idea for the three of you to come up with a marketing plan, and execute that plan, to promote—"

"Hats." Angus finished the sentence in unison with the teacher.

Australian schools were obsessed with hats. The students

were trained, from the day they began school, to surgically glue their hats to their heads during every recess and lunch. Even if a student was under the shade of a tree or veranda, they still needed to wear a hat. The punishment of choice for not wearing a hat at Angus's school was detention. He understood the obsession; the teachers had grown up in an era blissfully unaware of the sun's harm and were developing cancerous sun spots all over their bodies. The teachers didn't want the students to suffer the same fate. But the hat rules were legalistically enforced. It made the school yard a war zone of hatless students dodging the teacher-on-duty's line of sight.

Lucas was relieved. "Promoting hats will be easy."

"That's all—promote hats? No further catches?" Angus asked Mr Redding sceptically.

"No further catches," Mr Redding said. "But what will your approach be? You're advertising something intangible. You're promoting the idea that the individual and community will benefit from everyone making the healthy choice to wear a hat to help prevent skin cancer."

"It's like those anti-smoking and safe driving ads that the government creates," Angus said.

"Exactly right," Mr Redding said. "You don't have to worry about a product or distribution for this campaign. The only concern is the actual communication. Rachael, if this campaign is successful, what would you expect the outcome to be?"

"Everyone will wear their hats."

"Correct. So what message would we want to communicate

to students that will encourage them to regularly wear their hats?"

"That wearing a hat is better than not wearing a hat?" Rachael guessed, feeling like she was stating the obvious.

"That's right—but now the tricky part: how do we make sure that students *remember* the message we're communicating?"

None of the students had an answer.

Mr Redding wrote a word on the board: *associations*. "What we need to create is associations. We will use our advertising to create associations with hats in each student's memory."

Knowing that his students would continue with their blank stares, Mr Redding picked up a bottle of water from the teacher's desk. "Let's say you're a marketing officer for a bottled water company. You take an excursion to the local supermarket and stand next to the drinks fridge. If you were to ask each customer who purchased a drink why they wanted to buy that drink, what do you think their response would be?"

"They were thirsty?" Angus suggested.

"Why else would someone buy a specific drink?"

"Because it might be a cheaper option?" Rachael suggested.

"The taste?" Lucas added.

"Yes, all correct," Mr Redding said excitedly. "Let's say those three factors—thirst, taste and cost—were the main reasons why a customer would want to buy a drink. As the marketing officer at the bottled water company, what three things do you want your ads to tell your customers?"

Angus took a stab in the dark. "That our drinks are cheap, will quench your thirst and taste good?"

Mr Redding nodded. "These are the associations you would want to make with your water. When a customer is looking at the drinks fridge and deciding what to buy, you want your brand to be the first to come to mind when they think about those things: price, thirst and taste. When customers think to themselves 'I'd like a drink to quench my thirst', you want them to think of your water before they think of any other brand of drink."

Angus couldn't make the connection. "So, we need to advertise associations between hats and water?"

"No," Mr Redding said. "You need your advertising to create associations between something students already think about and hats. What associations would you want to make with hats in this campaign?"

"The sun," Rachael said.

"Yes, good." Mr Redding wrote *sun* on the whiteboard. "It would be good to create an association between the sun and hats, so that when students think of the sun, they will remember they should be wearing their hats. Another idea, off the top of my head, is hats are required at recess and lunch when students eat food. Could food and hats be a good association? Can we make it so that when students think of getting food from their backpack, they also think about getting their hat?"

"Like sombreros and burritos," Lucas said.

"That's racist," Angus said.

"No, it's not," Lucas replied. "They're both Mexican. When

135

I think of sombreros, I often think of burritos."

"I associate you with food," Angus retorted.

"You want to eat me?"

"No, as in you *eating* food. I associate you with eating food."

"Fair enough," Lucas said with a shrug.

"Any other ideas for your campaign?" Mr Redding asked, attempting to steer the conversation back on course.

"Death," Lucas said.

Mr Redding paused. "Death?"

"When students think about death, like from the sun, we'll make them think about hats. Then when students want to avoid death, they'll put on their hats."

"Why don't we instead create the less morbid association between *healthiness* and hats?" Mr Redding suggested. "When students think about being healthy, we want them to think about wearing a hat."

"I once thought about being healthy," Angus said.

"Yes," Mr Redding said. "And what was the first thing you thought about?"

"I thought of all the effort that would require, and so I purchased a Caramilk."

"Why did you choose a Caramilk?"

Angus laughed. "That was a joke."

"Yes, but why did you say Caramilk?"

"Because that was the first unhealthy food that popped into my head."

Rachael, who had been listening quietly, finally got it. She spoke quickly and enthusiastically. "So just like a Caramilk

136

was the first thing that popped into Angus's head when he thought about unhealthy foods, we want hats to be the first thing that pops into students' heads when they think about going outside!"

"Yes! I couldn't have put it better myself," Mr Redding said. "Now, we've established that associations will form the underlying strategy for the campaign. What types of media could be used to communicate our message with the students?"

"We could do a presentation in assembly," Angus said. "And while everyone's in assembly, we could stick posters all over the school."

"We could burn a hatless scarecrow on the oval?" Lucas suggested.

"Let's not do that," Rachael said.

Angus smirked. "We could steal all the hats from the students' lockers, then force the students to sit in the middle of the oval on a forty-degree day. That would teach them about sun safety."

"You propose we burn students to teach them about not getting burned?" Rachael asked.

"That's called negative reinforcement," Lucas said. "It could theoretically work."

Mr Redding laughed. "I think that's called a bad, unethical idea. I'm sure the three of you will be able to come up with a great campaign together. But please, boys, be sensible."

The boys both looked at each other and laughed, wildly inappropriate campaign ideas running through their imaginations.

"Rachael, please make sure the boys are sensible," Mr Redding said.

Rachael had little faith in her ability to do that. As much as she dreaded the extra work Mrs Campbell had assigned them, she was more relieved to finally understand a business topic. Understanding the minds of her two classmates was work for another day.

NEW ZEALAND BURRITOS

It had taken the three students a single lunch hour to come up with a marketing campaign to promote sun safety. They met in the library at Wednesday lunch time and brainstormed all the ways they could tell the students to wear hats. None of them were particularly enthusiastic about their ideas, and so in the end settled on the campaign ideas which seemed easiest to produce. Rachael had taken on the role of recording the group's ideas in her notebook, both for the sun safety campaign and their movie theatre project. As they sat on a courtyard table, she also began creating poster mock-ups on her laptop. She didn't consider herself a great graphic designer, but both boys seemed quite pleased with what she was making.

"Who's going to go and talk to Mrs Campbell?" Rachael asked.

"About what?" Angus said.

"She wants to check all our ideas."

The end-of-lunch bell rang. Rachael closed her notebook and held it toward Lucas.

"Why am I doing it?" Lucas had no interest in being in a room with Mrs Campbell any more than necessary.

"I'll do it," Angus said eagerly.

"Is that the best idea?" Rachael asked. "It doesn't appear that you and Mrs Campbell get along."

"No, we're great buddies, Mrs Campbell and me," Angus said. "I don't think you two are able to handle Mrs Campbell like I can. Interacting with her involves a level of diplomacy—"

"That's exactly why I suggested Lucas," Rachael said.

"And I think the best approach would be to tell Mrs Campbell as little as possible," Angus continued. "She seems to enjoy saying 'no', so the less she can say no to, the easier for us."

Lucas and Rachael still weren't convinced Angus was the person for the job, but neither of them wanted to do it, so Rachael handed the notebook to Angus.

———

The following day, during a free lesson after recess, Angus went to the front office with Rachael's notebook full of neatly written lists pertaining to their Business and Enterprise projects. He decided to be as professional as he could and represent his classmates well. He even tucked his shirt in as he walked up to Mr Tilley's desk.

"I'm here to see Mrs Campbell," Angus said confidently.

Mr Tilley opened a calendar on his computer. "Do you

have an appointment?"

Angus shook his head. "I don't. She asked for one of us BnE students to come and seek her approval for a project."

Mr Tilley, seeing an empty period in the calendar, went to Mrs Campbell's office door and gave a timid knock. After a few moments, Mrs Campbell opened her door.

"I have Angus here to see you," Mr Tilley announced.

"Did Angus make an appointment?" Mrs Campbell ignored the presence of the student standing only meters away.

"No, he didn't. He said you asked him to come."

Mrs Campbell looked at Angus, who stood pretending to be interested in a Year 10's abysmal painting of a fish hanging on the wall.

"Angus." Mrs Campbell beckoned him to the office with a wave of her hand.

It was then that Angus saw a small orange object on Mr Tilley's desk. It was an Inkda. He'd been so distracted by his BnE assignment that he'd forgotten about his pens. He had no idea how one of his Inkdas had come into Mr Tilley's possession, but he no longer wanted to be anywhere near the principal. As he entered her office, all he could do was pray that Mrs Campbell was still oblivious to his extra-curricular activities.

Mrs Campbell closed the door behind him. "How are you today, Angus?"

Angus sat on the edge of the visitor's chair. He wasn't planning on staying long.

"Good, thanks." He spoke quickly. "I'm here to discuss the Business and Enterprise project."

Mrs Campbell appeared to genuinely smile. "The sun safety campaign! I can't wait to hear what you have planned."

"Actually, I'm here to talk about the movie theatre project. You asked one of us to come and present our plan for your opinion."

"For my approval. Not my opinion," Mrs Campbell corrected. "But before we talk about that, has Mr Redding talked to you about the sun safety campaign?"

"Yes, Mr Redding told us about your idea on Monday, and we started coming up with ideas for the campaign today."

"Great. What are they?" Mrs Campbell leaned forward in her chair.

Angus realised he should have known Mrs Campbell would have wanted to be involved in that project as well. "I don't have any materials to show at the moment. I just came to talk about the movie theatre."

"That is fine, I just want to hear what ideas you have for promoting sun safety."

Angus sighed loudly, but quickly turned the sigh into clearing his throat. "Well, we're thinking of doing a presentation in assembly and creating posters to be placed around the school."

Mrs Campbell nodded thoughtfully. She turned in her ergonomic desk chair and looked out the window across the oval. "Do you know what would be a wonderful idea? A consequence chart."

"A what?"

"A consequence chart," Mrs Campbell repeated. "As I'm sure you are aware, a student without a hat receives a detention. If they are a repeat offender, they will eventually receive a suspension and a parent-teacher meeting. Don't you think it would be excellent to create a poster with that information so that students will be able to see how much trouble they will be in if they forget their hats?"

Mrs Campbell, looking out the window, missed Angus shaking his head in disbelief.

"I'm not sure that would work."

Mrs Campbell turned back. "Why not?"

"Students already know there will be trouble if they forget their hats," Angus explained. "A poster with that information isn't informative. Mr Redding has just been teaching us about associations in marketing. We're going use the campaign to create associations, for example, between the sun and hats or lunch and hats. That way, when students think about lunch time, or see the sun, they'll remember their hats."

Angus could see Mrs Campbell didn't comprehend a thing he was saying.

"That's a nice idea," she said, "but I think punishment as a deterrent would be the best approach to this problem."

"If you're wanting to do 'punishment as a deterrent', we could make the kids with detentions stand on a table in the middle of the courtyard as a warning to other students," Angus said dryly.

Angus could swear he saw the idea flash across Mrs Campbell's eyes as a possibility.

"Angus, you're being silly," Mrs Campbell huffed. "If you could do an example of a consequence chart and email it to me, that would be fantastic."

143

"But we don't have time to do extra posters," Angus complained. "We've got a lot of other work to do."

"It's not extra posters. Just do less of your other designs," Mrs Campbell said, clearly not understanding the complaint.

"Sure," Angus mumbled, writing down *consequence chart* at the bottom of a page in Rachael's notebook. He didn't expect Rachael to be too pleased with the additional work.

"Now, you mentioned you have ideas for the movie theatre?"

Angus didn't even bother hiding a sigh. "The two things you wanted to know about were the food and the movie. For food, we'll be doing burritos and smoothies. For the movie, we're planning on—"

"Slow down. One thing at a time," Mrs Campbell interrupted. "Burritos. The Mexican ones?"

"Yes, Mexican burritos. We're also thinking about the possibility of New Zealand burritos."

Mrs Campbell raised her eyebrows. "New Zealand burritos? I have never heard of them in my life. What do they have in them?"

Angus realised he had dug himself into a hole. "I believe New Zealand burritos have lamb in them."

"Oh. Like Greek yiros?"

"Yes. Very similar to Greek yiros."

"That sounds very interesting. I might like to try that," Mrs Campbell said. "Do burritos have any added sugars or fats?"

Angus shook his head. "Nope. Our Mexican burritos will not have any added sugars or fats."

"And the New Zealand burritos?"

144

"I'll need to double-check the ingredients for the New Zealand burritos, but I believe they're also healthy."

"Okay," Mrs Campbell said, making a note for herself. "Be sure to find out and let me know."

"The other food will be smoothies," Angus continued. "We haven't completely decided what we'll put in the smoothies, but they'll be very healthy."

"Smoothies have milk, don't they?"

"I believe most smoothies contain milk. Milk is healthy, though."

"Is it?"

Angus had no idea. "Milk is natural."

Mrs Campbell made another note. "Could you please do some research and let me know if milk is healthy?"

"Why don't we just do smoothies without milk?" he asked as politely as he could, but it didn't really work. "Would that be okay with you?"

"It's not about me being pleased, Angus," Mrs Campbell said calmly. "It's about ensuring the health and well-being of your generation. Did you know, if we are able to eliminate obesity in the current cohort of students, there will be significant savings in the public health system? I'm trying to save you money on your future taxes, Angus."

"That's very kind of you," Angus said, "but I don't think half a cup of milk will be the tipping point of childhood obesity."

"You're willing to bet your future prosperity on having milk in smoothies for one school project?"

"Yes. Yes I am." Angus took his principal's silence as

approval of their food options. He moved on quickly before she changed her mind. "We've discussed a number of films to show, including Chariots of Fire, Cool Runnings and The Rookie."

Mrs Campbell grimaced. "They're all quite old movies, aren't they? Why did you pick those?"

"Because you asked us to pick a sports movie," Angus said. "All the sports movies that exist are either inappropriate, old or cheesy."

Mrs Campbell stared at the wall of her office. "What about Shrek?"

"Shrek? What does Shrek have to do with sport?"

"I was watching Shrek during the holidays with my grand-daughter, and I thought it was quite funny. Have you seen Shrek?"

"Yes, I've seen Shrek," Angus said. "Are you saying you want us to show Shrek?"

"No, if you feel that one of those old sports movies are better, you can choose one of them."

Angus wrote SHREK in big letters in Rachael's notebook. "I'll report your recommendations to the others. I better get going to my next class." He rose from his chair.

"Just one moment, Angus. There is something else I'd like to discuss with you."

Angus was thankful he was still next to the chair so he could lean against it without losing his balance.

Mrs Campbell looked intently up at the boy from her seat. "Do you remember when we had a discussion about chocolate bars, Angus?"

He nodded. "Yes, I remember."

"Good. Great. I'm glad," she said slowly. "Could you give me a summary of that conversation?"

"You said you thought that chocolate is unhealthy and has too much sugar."

"And?"

"I think you also mentioned you were thankful the canteen doesn't sell cocaine."

"I'm referring to what I said about your actions," Mrs Campbell said. "What did I say about your actions and chocolate bars?"

Angus felt the guillotine rising above his neck. "You said I'm not allowed to sell any more chocolate bars to students."

"I said you are not allowed to sell *anything* to students. Do you remember that?"

"Yes, I do recall that." Angus met Mrs Campbell's eyes as much as he dared.

"Good. Very good. Excellent," she said slowly.

Angus, trying to appear casual leaning against the chair, waited for what would come next. There was no certainty in his mind that she was aware of the Inkdas.

Mrs Campbell stood up. "I do everything for the benefit of the students in this school. There is nothing I wouldn't do for the benefit of the students in this school. Even if that means asking...unbeneficial students to leave this school. Are you at this moment, Angus, being beneficial or unbeneficial to the school?"

Angus felt genuinely afraid. "Beneficial," was all he could say.

Mrs Campbell walked briskly past Angus to the office door and held it open with a smile. "That is fantastic to hear. I can't wait to see the consequence chart posters and try a New Zealand burrito."

THE INVESTOR

The meeting with Mrs Campbell had unnerved Angus. He couldn't focus on any of his lessons for the rest of the day.

At lunch time, Alan and a few other Year 12 boys commandeered the common room projector and speakers and were watching online thrash metal videos. Angus and Lucas sat at one of the aluminium tables in the quieter courtyard, where Angus recounted his meeting with Mrs Campbell.

"She sounds like a lunatic," was Lucas's response.

"I think she sincerely believes that her way of doing things is always right, and anyone else's way is wrong."

"Sounds like someone else," Lucas scoffed.

"Who?"

"You."

Angus turned quickly to face his friend. "What do you mean?"

"I mean, and don't take offense to this, you're always bent

on being in control. It's your way or the highway."

Angus felt offended. "The movie theatre idea was Rachael's. The food ideas were Rachael's. How have I been controlling?"

"Yes, they may have been her ideas," Lucas said, "but it was you who was the most vocal about agreeing."

"That's because I thought they were good ideas!" Angus said. "Are you saying I'm bossy because I agreed with her? That doesn't make any sense."

"No, I'm saying that if you came up with another idea, you would try to convince us it's better. As much as you think this has been a group assignment, you've been calling the final shots."

Angus picked at a piece of bark on the tree. "Whatever you say, man. I'm just trying to ensure that our assignment is the best it can be. Right now, I'd much rather my pen business becomes successful. I've had some new ideas for marketing campaigns, I just need more money."

"Don't we all," Lucas mumbled.

"I've spent all my savings. If I could get five hundred dollars, that would buy me an extra one thousand pens to sell."

Angus didn't ask the question outright, but Lucas still shook his head. "I am not giving you any money for this. I'm saving up for my university textbooks. And besides, you couldn't sell a thousand pens."

"I could sell five thousand pens."

Lucas sighed, almost worried about his friend's imagination. "How are you planning on selling five thousand pens?"

"I've already said—and Mr Redding has said it as well—I'll be successful by being market orientated."

"Thanks for that completely vague answer," Lucas said. "There's not even five hundred kids who go to our high school."

"Who said anything about limiting myself to just our school? I'll sell to students at other schools."

Lucas shook his head. "You're going to end up with a bedroom full of Inkwads or whatever they're called, hundreds if not thousands of dollars in debt, and weeks of your life wasted."

"They're called Inkdas." Angus took one of his pens from his pocket. He imagined the speaking tours he would go on, telling other students how he became a self-made millionaire before he turned 18.

Lucas wasn't sure if he had taken the teasing too far. "Look man, I'm sure you'll succeed in the end. Just don't get disappointed if you don't succeed straight away. You still have your whole life ahead of you."

Angus pretended not to hear. "I looked online at angel investing sites and crowdfunding, but they look far too complicated and take too long."

"Do you have any rich grandparents?"

"Nope. Family is out. I want this to be kept as low-key as possible. My parents will think I'm foolish."

"I think you're foolish."

"Exactly. So imagine what they'd think."

"So, you're looking for someone just as foolish as yourself, who is willing to give you hundreds—"

"Thousands," Angus corrected.

"Sorry, *thousands* of dollars with no evidence that your business actually works?"

"No—I have evidence. I have spreadsheets."

"Theoretical spreadsheets."

"Abdul!" a Year 10 girl called, walking past the Year 9 boy and giving him a high-five.

"Abdul," Angus said, the idea growing into a smile.

Lucas couldn't help but laugh. "You're going from foolish to idiotic if you think Abdul has thousands of dollars to invest in your business. He's fifteen—"

Angus was already walking away. "Abdul!"

"Angus!" Abdul called back, looking up from the book he was reading.

Angus sat down next to the boy on a bench overlooking the courtyard. "How did your sister like the pen?"

"She thought it was very pretty." Abdul looked back down at his book. "But I don't want to buy any more pens at the moment, thank you."

"No, I'm not here to sell you any pens." Angus's smile, and his hope for an investment, were already dwindling. "I'm just here to see how you're doing."

"Fine, thank you."

Angus nodded. "That's great. Great to hear. Really random question, but what does your dad do for a living?"

"He's a doctor."

"A doctor?" Angus repeated. "There are rumours going around that your dad is actually a billionaire oil tycoon."

"That's my uncle," Abdul said, somewhat sadly. "We

152

don't see him."

Angus stopped smiling and pulled at a loose thread in his shirt. "I don't know if you know, but I've grown my pen business."

"I'm not interested in buying pens, thank you."

"I know. But I was wondering if you would be interested in investing in my business?"

"What?"

Angus knew he was clutching at straws. "You were my first customer, and I think it's only fair that I allow you to invest in my business."

Abdul frowned at the ground. Angus realised the poor boy had no idea what investing was. Abdul closed his book and walked away from the bench.

Angus was left sitting by himself, truly feeling like a fool. He had genuinely hoped that Abdul would leap up and run to his locker, where there was a secret compartment filled with thousands of dollars.

Lucas had witnessed the meeting from afar. He couldn't understand what was driving his friend. He was sure there was a psychological reason and decided to do some research during the next study period on what drove desperate behaviour.

He took a seat next to Angus on the bench. "You know what you might need for your pen business?"

"What?"

"Help. Advice from someone with experience."

"No," Angus said quickly. "I need money, not help. Once I have money to pay for my products and marketing, then I can start finding help."

Lucas sat at his bedroom desk that evening, playing a computer game instead of doing his English homework.

His phone rang. He was surprised to see the caller ID was Angus. Although the two boys messaged frequently, they had only spoken on the phone to each other maybe twice in their lifetimes. They both felt it was awkward and weird.

Lucas answered the phone. "Wassup."

"Guess what." Angus's voice was high-pitched with excitement.

"What?"

"I have an investor."

"No you don't."

"Well, I have a meeting with an investor. Luke Pilcher."

"Who's that?"

"I found his website this afternoon. He says he's looking for any and all investment opportunities. I called him, and he wants to meet tomorrow morning!"

"I can't tell if you're joking."

"I am definitely not joking."

"Well then, you're going to get murdered by a random guy tomorrow morning."

"Nah, I'll be alright," Angus said. "I'm meeting him before school at Café Olka."

Lucas sighed. "Angus, seriously. First the pen supplier, and now this guy. You can't just keep finding random strangers and meeting with them. That's how you end up in ties with the mafia."

"You sound like my mum."

"You should listen to your mum."

"I can tell very quickly who's legit and who's not. You said I need outside help. I'm being proactive and getting help."

"This isn't the help I was..." Lucas saw no point in trying to talk Angus out of it. "If any police are listening back to this conversation after Angus has gone missing, I would like to put on record that I did *not* say he should meet with this guy."

The time was 6:01am when Angus entered the shopping centre the next morning, ready to meet this investor who had sounded so keen on the phone.

The shopping centre was almost deserted, apart from maintenance workers and some staff late to their shifts at the supermarket. Most of the stores wouldn't open for a couple more hours. Angus, wearing a hoodie over his school uniform and his backpack full of sample Inkda pens, walked past a tired cleaner who looked like she had woken only minutes before, leading Angus to wonder whether mall cleaners slept in a back room overnight.

Angus felt energised. The coffee he had chugged at home was partly to blame, but the other part was the sense that his life could change this morning. He had a plan for his pen business; all he needed was the money.

Café Olka was a classic middle-of-the-mall café, where the regular patrons were old people having their morning tea and coffees. They typically read *The Vine*, the local daily newspaper, while riff-raff flowed in and out of the mall, children cried in the distance, and busy people rushed in and out of shops like their lives depended on it.

On this morning, Angus was the first customer of the day. Behind the counter, an old woman was placing cakes and pastries into the glass display fridge. She looked up and frowned as Angus sat down at one of the tables.

"What can I do for you, son?"

"I'm just waiting for my meeting," Angus called back. The lady, although suspicious of the boy so early in the morning, shook her head and continued setting up shop.

Angus had no idea what the man he was meeting looked like. On the phone, the investor had a deep but loud voice—

"Angus?" the voice asked behind him.

Angus turned around to see a man in his late fifties with a short white beard, and only a wisp of white hair remaining on his head. He stood up. "Yes, that's me."

The man, a head taller than Angus, looked down at the boy in confusion. After a moment of awkward silence, the man put out his hand. "Mr Luke Pilcher is my name. Have you ordered anything yet?"

"No, I haven't." Angus smiled, shaking the man's hand.

Pilcher pulled out a thick wallet from his black overcoat. "What would you like? A coffee? Breakfast?"

Although Angus had never taken part in a business meeting before, he felt sure that he, as the business asking for investment, was supposed to be the one to pay for coffee. "Oh no, that's fine. I can pay. What would you like?"

The man laughed loudly. "No, I have more money than you. I insist."

To not appear impolite, Angus asked for a black coffee and sat back down at the table as Pilcher made their order over at

156

the counter. After Pilcher had a loud, meaningless conversation with the old woman about the cold weather, he returned to the table, but his attention was distracted by something across the mall.

Angus turned in his chair to see what the man was looking at. There was nothing of interest—just an empty shop with a For Lease sign taped to the front window.

"I wonder how much a shop would cost to lease here," Pilcher said.

"I come here almost every day. It's quite popular, but there are a number of empty shops. I'd say they're on the cheap end," Angus said, trying to sound knowledgeable.

Pilcher nodded, but was already looking at something else farther down the mall. "That's an interesting sign. 'Sale: Gold Rings 50% off'."

Angus couldn't see a single interesting thing about it. "What makes the sign interesting?"

"Well, If the rings are fifty percent off, it means they're putting at least a 50% markup on their products," Pilcher explained. "When you know how much a store is willing to discount their products, you know how much bargaining power you have when negotiating prices."

"Yes, that is quite interesting," Angus lied. Anxious to talk about pens instead of rings, he placed a crisp, freshly printed document from his stuffed bag in front of the prospective investor. He had rehearsed their meeting late into last night.

"Thank you for agreeing to meet with me today," Angus began. "I have put together a feasibility report with projected earnings for you to look over."

Pilcher glanced down at the document. The man's expression made Angus feel very inadequate, as if he had just passed across a primitive crayon drawing as though it was fine art.

"What year are you in?" the man asked.

Angus had gotten away many times with looking like a university student; he had a face that made him look far older than he really was. He had hoped the hoodie would have hidden his uniform, but it was a thin disguise, especially since he had his schoolbag.

"I graduate Year 12 in a couple months' time," Angus said. "But I can assure you that if you read through the feasibility plan, you will see this is a great investment."

Pilcher still didn't open the document. He turned and watched a supermarket worker walk briskly down the mall, apparently late for his shift. "I wonder how much they earn working at the supermarket these days?"

"Probably about 25 dollars an hour," Angus guessed. He reached into his bag. "Did you want to see the product?"

Pilcher kept watching the worker. "Not particularly."

Angus, growing quite irritated and confused by the man's disinterest, left the pens in his bag and fidgeted with a packet of sugar from the condiments holder. The waitress brought their coffees over. Pilcher had also ordered a giant triple-chocolate muffin.

"This is breakfast and morning tea," Pilcher said with a smile. He cut himself a piece of the muffin with a dessert fork. He placed the morsel into his mouth and chewed it dramatically. "This muffin is excellent!" Pilcher exclaimed across the café to the waitress.

"Thank you!" the lady called back. "I baked them fresh this morning."

Pilcher turned his whole body away from Angus to talk to the woman. "Is there a secret ingredient?"

Angus sat staring at the man's back, wondering if any of this was the way in which "business" was normally conducted.

"No, not a secret ingredient," the lady responded, enjoying the praise. "But it is a secret method."

Pilcher spoke in a flirty tone. "And would you be willing to share the secret method with me?"

The lady laughed and shook her head.

"Ah, come on," Pilcher coaxed. "I won't tell anyone."

The lady continued shaking her head. "No, but I promise it's not that interesting."

Pilcher feigned a sigh. With a wink to Angus, he took out his wallet and casually extracted five $100 bills. "Would five hundred dollars help change your mind?" He held the bills in the air.

"Sorry, what?" the lady asked.

"I said, will you tell me your secret muffin method for five hundred dollars?"

The lady and Angus stared at the money in shock.

"Well," the lady stuttered, "I'm not sure the secret is worth five hundred dollars. If you really want to know, I can just tell you."

Pilcher walked over to the counter and placed the $500 in front of the woman. The woman looked between Pilcher and the money, taking a moment to comprehend whether this man was seriously about to give her a large sum of money for such a small secret. Pilcher placed his hands in his pockets and stepped back. The lady looked around and, seeing that there were no other witnesses beside Angus to this dubious transaction, took the money and placed it in her pocket. She leaned forward over the bench. Pilcher also leaned forward. The woman whispered something. Pilcher nodded as he listened, smiling and raising his eyebrows.

"Well, I'd say that's interesting," Pilcher concluded when the lady had finished her explanation. The lady shrugged and quickly disappeared into the café's kitchen to secure the money in her handbag.

Pilcher sat back down at the table.

"That was not worth five hundred dollars, I can tell you that," he said quietly, giving his coffee a stir.

"What was the secret?" Angus asked with piqued curiosity.

Pilcher frowned. "That secret cost me five hundred dollars. I'm not going to give it out for free."

"But you just said it wasn't worth the money you paid for it."

"Yes, true," Pilcher said. "So I would only charge you four hundred dollars for the secret."

Angus looked down at his own coffee, wondering if it was even worth bringing up the pens anymore. He resolved to politely finish the coffee and leave.

"Ah, excuse me!" Pilcher called out to another supermarket employee power walking past.

"Yes?" The young man looked flustered and aware of how late he was.

"I was wondering how much you get paid an hour?"

"I don't know. Like twenty-five an hour?" the man answered without slowing.

"Thank you."

The young man shot off down the mall toward the supermarket.

"It turns out you were right," Pilcher said. "Do you work at a supermarket?"

"No. At the moment I'm focusing my efforts on my business, which I'd like to hear your opinion on," Angus said, giving one last attempt to start the conversation.

"You'd like to hear my opinion?" Pilcher asked. "But we've only just met."

"It said on your website you've had a lot of business experience and have invested in many companies."

Pilcher nodded. "Yes, that is true. What would you like my opinion on again?"

Angus sat up straight. After fifteen minutes of wasted time, they could now start the conversation he had gotten up in the freezing cold at 5:30am to discuss. "I have a supplier who was able to get me some truly unique pens that—"

"Sorry, I'll just stop you there," Pilcher interrupted.

"Yes?"

"I'm not interested today." Pilcher cut himself another piece of muffin.

Angus stared at the man in bewilderment. "But you haven't looked at the information yet. Have a look in my feasibility report and you'll see—"

"I like your initiative with your feasibility report, but I'm not going to invest."

"Can I please ask why?"

Pilcher looked over Angus's shoulder to the digital advertisement. "That fifty percent off sign. Do you remember what I said that means about their products?"

"They have a big markup on their products."

Pilcher nodded. "That means I am going to ask for sixty percent off if I want to buy a gold ring."

"What does that have to do with anything here?" Angus asked bluntly, tired of the old man's flightiness.

Pilcher leaned to look in Angus's open backpack on the floor. "You're a fifteen-year-old boy with a schoolbag full of pens."

"I'm seventeen," Angus corrected. His correction made him feel even younger.

Pilcher put another piece of muffin into his mouth with his fingers, giving up on the fork. "I gave the waitress five hundred dollars because she had something I wanted—the secret to making these great muffins. Those kids working in the supermarket make twenty-five dollars an hour because they have something their manager wants—hands and feet and the willingness to do whatever is required of them to keep their jobs."

"Well, I'm willing to do whatever it takes to sell pens." Angus failed to keep his voice from wavering as his confidence dissipated.

"I'm sure you are," Pilcher said. "I'm sure you're the smartest lad in your school. But I think you should stick to your studies, go to university, and find a career that way.

Starting a business requires work and determination."

"You don't know me." Angus had to consciously keep his tone from rising. "You don't know how much determination I have."

Pilcher laughed in a way that crushed Angus's self-confidence. "You're selling pens. That must be one of the silliest ideas I've ever heard. People don't care about pens anymore, they care about technology. Yes, people still use pens, but they don't care about a pen's make or model or whatever else it has going for it. People care about getting done what needs to be done in the cheapest, easiest way possible."

Angus knew the man was wrong, but there was no use arguing.

"I can see there's no convincing you. Thank you for your time." Angus pulled out his phone to check the time. It was only 6:30am.

"If you find success, you call me and ask me again. You never know," Pilcher said. "So what subjects are you doing at school today?"

"I have to go now," Angus said with a failed attempt at a smile.

Pilcher appeared surprised the meeting had ended. "Oh, okay. I hope my advice was helpful."

Angus left a five-dollar note on the table to pay for his untouched coffee.

HELP

The meeting with the prospective investor had finished so early that Angus walked home again. He had a burning desire to prove Pilcher wrong. Angus imagined the man picking up a Moving Stationery catalogue, seeing Inkdas on the front page, and realising he had been wrong to dismiss the boy. But as he took the boxes of Inkdas out of his backpack, he wondered if this was the end. He couldn't get financing to sell to students at other schools, and he couldn't sell the pens he did have to his fellow students, not with the risk of expulsion. He didn't trust himself to resist the temptation of making an easy sale if he took the pens to school. Students were still approaching him sporadically and asking for Inkdas and chocolates.

Cathy Newton burst into his bedroom just as Angus was sliding the box of Inkdas under his bed. "Are you okay?"

"Yes, I'm fine." Angus laughed as his mum looked him up and down.

"I am not okay that you went to this meeting with a stranger without asking my permission."

"I asked Dad's permission."

"I know. I am not okay that he gave you permission to meet with this stranger."

"Once again: Mum, I'm seventeen. I can handle myself. If it makes you feel any better, I had the police on speed dial."

"Why would it make me feel better that you felt the need to have the police on speed dial?"

Angus decided it best not to mention the ornamental letter opener he had packed in his bag during a last-minute lapse of confidence before the meeting.

His mum fussed with retrieving dirty clothes from his laundry hamper. "What was he? A financer?"

"Yeah, something like that."

"Did he give you the information you needed for your assignment?"

"He taught me how *not* to run a business."

"What do you mean?"

Angus sat down on his desk chair. "He was just an obnoxious old rich guy with too much money. I once thought it would be nice to be rich and retire at thirty, but if being rich means you turn out like him? That doesn't sound fun."

Cathy nodded. "As someone who works with incredibly rich people day in and day out, let me assure you: there comes a point where money becomes meaningless numbers. And although these people have numbers listed in their bank accounts bigger than the worth of everything I'll own in my lifetime, you know what they want?"

"Happiness?"

"No. They want to see a bigger number."

Angus sat in the school library staring at the wall. His computer was open to his English assignment, but not a word had been typed in the last fifteen minutes.

"What's the point of school?" Angus asked aloud.

Rachael, who was working on her laptop to Angus's right, looked to see who he was talking to. They were sitting at a row of desks along the wall, and there was no one to Angus's left.

"To learn," she said, hoping Angus would take the hint.

"Teachers tell us that we need to achieve good grades to get into uni. It's almost like they all think there's no life after Year 12 apart from university."

"That's probably because all teachers went to university. That's what they know."

"Are you going to uni?" Angus asked.

"I hope to." She sighed, thinking back to the D she'd gotten on the maths test. "I was going to apply for an engineering degree, but I think it might be too much work. My dad's an engineer, but he's incredibly smart."

"Engineering would be cool." Angus wondered if he would be any good at building bridges.

In Year 11, the students had to do a big assignment on what career they wanted to pursue after graduation. It was, in theory, a way for students to explore possible career paths. Many students in Angus's cohort were becoming serious about their futures and used the assignment to explore careers such as medicine, accounting and software developing. Other students, aware of opportunities outside of university, looked at careers such as the army, police force, or in the trades.

Angus did his assignment on pursuing a career as a mime artist. On the day the students presented their career research to the rest of the class, Angus attempted to present all his information through mime, until their teacher demanded that the presentation be done with words. He still got a B for the assignment.

Over the past two years, Angus had considered twenty-six different careers. He had considered for weeks at a time, though sometimes for just a fleeting moment, pursuing a career as a police officer, a teacher, a brain surgeon, a musician, a mime artist, a book writer, a fashion designer, an electronics importer, a retail manager, a musical instrument builder, a language professor, a translator, a politician, an electrician, a director, a producer, a videographer, a customer service representative, a millionaire, a philosopher, a painter, a software developer, a game designer, a food scientist, a confectionery salesman, or a stationery salesman.

As Angus sat in the library staring at the wall, where a lady bug sticker had been left over from book week, he didn't know what he wanted to do. Selling pens had been the closest he had felt to succeeding in his life, and that dream was all but finished.

"Did you do question four?" Rachael quietly asked Brooke at the next table over.

I wonder if Rachael has ever worried about what she's going to do with her life, he thought. *She'll succeed. She'll be one of those success stories who succeeds in everything she*

*does. She works really hard, even if it's more than she needs
to. I think I should start writing a list of all the hard-work-
ing people I meet that I could hire one day for a business. I
don't know what that business will be, but I wonder if she'd
be willing to do an internship—*

Angus realised he was staring at Rachael. She was looking
back at him expectantly.

"I think I need your help," Angus said. Saying the phrase
out loud felt like a burden lifting from his shoulders, but he
said the phrase with such serious conviction that it made
Rachael feel uncomfortable.

"What with?"

"Inkdas," Angus said. "Selling pens."

"I'm not going to buy any pens from you." Rachael turned
her attention back to her laptop.

"I'm not asking you to buy any pens. I need your help with
selling pens."

The last thing Rachael desired was another project. Every
single day of the week from the moment she woke until the
moment she went to sleep, schoolwork was on her mind. She
couldn't fathom how Angus was able to do all his schoolwork
as well as try to start a business.

"You're smart," Angus said. "All the ideas you've given in
BnE have been really good ideas. I need your advice."

"I'm flattered you want my advice," Rachael said. "But
I don't know how I can help you. I feel like the best way
I can help you is by encouraging you to stop with your pen
business. Didn't you say Mrs Campbell is very close to sus-
pending you?"

168

"She mentioned it as a possibility."

Rachael gave a nervous laugh, lowering her voice. "I'm struggling to keep my head above water, and you want my help with something that could potentially get me suspended? I can't get suspended."

Angus lowered his voice as well. "I don't want to get expelled, either. That's why I'm asking you. What would you do if you were in my shoes? Selling pens here at school is ruled out. I can't get any money to buy more pens or market my pens to other schools. What would you do if you were in my shoes?"

"I'd go back to studying and figure it out once I've graduated."

"Yes, but I mean if you were in *my* shoes. I don't give up."

Angus looked sincere and helpless. Rachael wanted to help him. She tried to empathise with her classmate, but didn't understand the attraction of starting a business before finishing high school. They were so close to graduation. Why put all that at risk?

Mrs Campbell pushed the library door open with her hip and entered holding a heavy load of textbooks. She loudly dumped the pile of textbooks onto the librarian's desk, making no attempt to conform to the 'quiet zone' library policy.

"Just pop them here," she said to Mr Tilley, who followed behind with an even bigger armful of textbooks.

"Katherine?" Mrs Campbell poked her head into the librarian's office. She looked around the desk area. "Has anyone seen Mrs Van Paul?"

169

The students present dutifully shook their heads. Mrs Campbell looked to Rachael. "Rachael, when she returns, can you please let Mrs Van Paul know I'm looking for her? I need to give her the invoice for these textbooks."

Rachael smiled and nodded.

Angus, who was ensuring he didn't make eye contact with his principal, had typed *English* twenty times in a row into his homework document.

The principal and her assistant left the library.

"Mrs Campbell," Rachael whispered to Angus. "*Angus*," she repeated louder.

Angus looked up.

"Mrs Campbell."

"What about her?"

"Sell the pens to the principal."

"Very funny."

"I'm serious," Rachael said. "Why sell a couple of pens to the students when you can sell heaps of them to a whole school?"

Rachael watched Angus's face slowly change from confusion to surprise.

Her words ran over and over in his head. *Why sell a couple of pens when you can sell heaps of them?*

He let out an involuntary laugh.

"You...you're a genius!" Angus whispered loudly. He couldn't stop smiling.

Rachael gave a thin-mouthed smile back, unsure if she was now an accomplice to his activities. She also didn't want to be responsible for him getting expelled.

170

"And if I could get an advance payment for an order, then I don't need money upfront," Angus said.

Rachael quickly came up with a way to protect him. "You would obviously need to find a different school principal."

"Why? What's wrong with Mrs Campbell?"

"Because you'd be expelled instantly if you tried to sell pens to her."

"But I *know* Mrs Campbell. I don't know other principals like I know Mrs Campbell."

Rachael looked at Angus sternly. "It's your prerogative what you do, but I'm not interested in helping any further. You cannot get me in trouble."

"Come on, we're on the same team," Angus said, trying to assure her of his confidentiality.

"We're most definitely not a team."

"Mrs Campbell." Angus leaned back in his chair. "Why didn't I think of that?"

Rachael smirked and resumed her work. "Because you're not a genius."

———

"If Rachael hadn't come up with it, I would call that the dumbest idea I've ever heard," Lucas said at recess. "There's no way you can do it."

"I know I can't do it." Angus held an apple to his forehead as if it would help him think better. The initial thrill of the idea had given way to the reality of a stunt as precarious as selling pens incognito to his own school. "Would you be willing to do it in disguise?" Angus asked. "I could tell you what to say."

"Would you be willing to pay me a million dollars?"

"Mrs Campbell likes Rachael. I wonder if I could convince her to do it." The apple wasn't helping him think sitting next to his head, so he took a bite.

"Do you really see a student at any school walking into their own principal's office and selling them something?" Lucas asked. "Be realistic. It's not going to work."

"We need an adult."

"You need one preferably with a counselling degree."

Angus sat up straight. He knew the perfect adult candidate. "We need one with stationery experience."

"Start from the beginning again," Olivia said on the phone.

The boys stood behind the toilet building at lunch time, huddled around Angus's phone. Angus hadn't had much difficulty finding the contact number of the girl from Moving Stationery, since she used to play tennis with his older brother, Quinten. Quinten had pointed out how random the request was when he received Angus's text asking for the number of a girl he had played tennis with years ago. But he still happened to have Olivia's number and sent it through.

Angus had never spoken to Olivia apart from their chance encounter at Moving Stationery, so it took a couple of minutes to bring the confused woman up to speed with the out-of-the-blue request.

"We need an actress with stationery experience to help us with our project," Angus explained.

"An actress?" Olivia laughed. "I'm not an actress."

"Weren't you in a commercial?"

172

"I did a couple of acting courses in high school and one commercial for Paulo's Pizza before I realised that acting was a dead end. How do you remember me?"

"I thought you were famous," Angus admitted. "I almost asked for your autograph once."

He heard Olivia laugh.

"You know how to act, and you work in a stationery store. You're exactly who we're looking for," Angus said. In his mind, Olivia was the perfect candidate not because of her experience, but because she had no connection to anyone who could out him as the real pen seller.

"Just because I work at Moving Stationery doesn't mean I have much experience with stationery. I mostly work in the checkouts and print section."

"I'm sure you're being modest."

"And your project is selling pens to your own school?" Olivia clarified.

"Yes, that's right."

There was silence on the line as Olivia mulled over what they were asking of her. "I'm not sure. This doesn't even sound like acting. This sounds more like a sales job. I'm not interested in working in sales."

"This is exactly acting," Angus said. "It's just like doing a commercial, but only one person will ever see it. You are playing a role—in this case, a salesperson—and your role is to convince our principal, convincingly, that you are a salesperson and you believe these Inkda-branded pens are going to be the best thing to arrive at their school since computers."

"Sorry, what were the pens called?"

"Inkdas."

"Oh. That's a peculiar name," Olivia said. "I don't know. I wouldn't know what to say."

"Don't worry. We're going to train you."

"Who's we?"

"Me and my associate, Lucas."

The look Lucas gave Angus was frightful. This had not been discussed. Lucas shook his head adamantly.

Angus signalled with his hand for Lucas to just wait.

"So will you do it?" he asked Olivia. The long silence made Angus very unconfident that Olivia would agree to take the job, so he offered what he hoped he wouldn't have to offer. "It's a paying job."

"Were you expecting me to do it for free?"

"No, of course not," Angus said quickly.

"How much?"

Angus didn't know the going rate for actors and made a stab in the dark. "Three hundred dollars?"

"I'll do it," Olivia said quickly.

"I mean one hundred dollars," Angus said, realising he might have overshot the price.

"I'll take the three hundred, thanks."

"I can only pay you three hundred if this plan works and you make the sale," Angus said desperately. "This is to get an advance order."

There was silence on the line again. Angus was convinced he had blown it.

Olivia finally said, "One-fifty before, and one-fifty after."

"Deal." Angus exhaled. He catalogued in his mind all the

174

things he owned and what he could sell online that could earn him $150. He thanked Olivia and said he would text her the time and location for the training. He hung up the phone, bracing himself for Lucas's onslaught.

"Since when am I helping you with your business?" Lucas asked.

"You're not going to get suspended."

"I'm not scared of getting suspended. I've been suspended before. It's not a big deal," Lucas said. "I just don't like people telling me what I'm doing without me having a say. I have a two-year plan. This year I'm going to get good grades and next year I'm going to medical school."

"Can't you amend your plans?"

"Not easily, and certainly not by someone else's hand," Lucas said. "I like my plan, and I'm sticking with it. Your pen business is not going in my plans."

"Fine," Angus said. "I don't want to mess up your plans. Rachael's help will probably be better anyway."

"No," Rachael said at her locker.

"I told you she'd say no," Lucas said.

"Please?" Angus begged.

"No," Rachael said.

Angus searched Rachael's eyes for any signs of a yes, but he only saw a lot of stubborn *no*.

"So you give me this great idea, but you're not willing to help any further? What about just to see how your idea turns out?" Angus pleaded, trying to not draw too much attention from the other students at their lockers.

"I already told you, I have too much work to worry about

getting in trouble for your side project," Rachael said. "I'm sorry. I want to help you, but I must say no."

"I promise, with absolute sincerity, that no one will know you're involved. And you need to remember: this isn't illegal. We're not selling drugs. We're not even selling chocolate bars, which I will now agree is possibly on the edge—hardly the edge, but it could be argued is somewhere in the vicinity— of being unethical. This is just pens we're talking about. Little pieces of plastic with ink inside that millions of people use every day."

"You're not listening. It's not the product," Rachael said firmly. She closed her locker and glared at Angus. He was quite used to being glared at by Lucas, Mrs Campbell and his mum, but Rachael's glare made him step back. "I'm failing maths. If I get lower than a C, I've failed. I'm really sorry, but if I take on any extra work—" She shook her head, unable to describe the anxiety she felt.

Angus took a deep breath and spoke gently. "All we're asking—"

"*Angus* is asking," Lucas interjected.

"All I'm asking," Angus continued, "is that you come for a couple of hours and play the role of Mrs Campbell for Olivia to train with."

Rachael couldn't believe the boy's determination. "And you seriously think I'm the only one who can help you with this?"

"I don't want anyone else to get involved who isn't already in the know. The fewer people who know, the better."

Rachael couldn't help but be impressed with Angus's

176

passion. In a strange way, his enthusiasm was slightly infectious. She hadn't given herself time for hobbies or fun all year, and she could not classify her schoolwork as *fun*. She decided to give one final push to see just how serious Angus was. She had been told this salesperson, Olivia, was getting paid by Angus, and he didn't seem enthusiastic about it.

"How much are you willing to pay me?" Rachael asked.

"Why is this business all about money to everyone?" Angus asked. "If it works, I promise I'll pay you a hundred dollars. That's all I can afford."

The end-of-lunch bell rang.

"Fine," Rachael said.

"Fine?" Angus repeated in disbelief.

"I'm not free any night of the week but Tuesday and Wednesday," she said. "And only for two hours. No more."

"That's very convenient, because we're doing it next Wednesday night," Angus said, making the decision there and then.

Rachael watched Angus try to walk away without skipping giddily like a little boy.

Lucas also had not expected Rachael to agree to participate. He wondered what he was missing if Rachael, the smartest girl in their year, was willing to help. Maybe Angus was onto something with his business that he couldn't see?

"Hey, Angus," Lucas began as they gathered their laptops from their lockers. "I'm noticing that a lot of people are getting paid for this exercise of yours. How much would I be compensated if I agreed to help?"

Angus thought money might pique his friends interest, but was hoping his participation wouldn't require that incentive. "Lucas Fuselier, as my friend, will you please help me with training Olivia for the pitch to Mrs Campbell?"

Lucas hummed. "Can we negotiate a fee?"

"Okay," Angus said. "Lucas, what business experience and or expertise would you bring to this venture?"

Lucas wasn't willing to let condescending questions faze him. "I have experience cooking noodles in the microwave."

"What are you talking about?"

"I think running a business is just as easy."

"Really?" Angus shot back. "You think running a business is as easy as cooking noodles in a microwave? Man, don't even worry about helping. Rachael and I can do it on our own."

"I'm not trying to offend you and your interests," Lucas said. "But seriously, compared to all my other subjects, Business and Enterprise is like a Year 9 subject."

"That's because at school it's highly theoretical," Angus said. "Applying the stuff in the real world is really hard."

"Yeah, I don't think it is."

"How much do you want to bet?"

"You want to turn this into a bet?" Lucas laughed.

"Yes, I do. If you think business is so easy, come and help me out with Inkdas. For every box of pens you help sell, I'll give you an additional zero-point-one percent ownership of the business."

"Really?" Lucas asked. He did the calculation quickly in his head. "So, all I have to do is sell a thousand boxes of pens, and I'll completely own your business?"

"Up to thirty three percent ownership," Angus added. He saw it as a win-win scenario. Having Lucas on board with a personal motivation to sell could only help the business grow.

"Ah, so you think there's a chance I could actually succeed in selling thousands of pens and take your company away from you?" Lucas said.

"No," Angus said. "I think you'll struggle to sell two boxes. I know you like to succeed, but you can't succeed in everything all the time."

Lucas stuck out his hand. "I'm happy with the thirty-three percent, but you are so wrong."

"You better add paying attention in BnE to your plans," Angus said.

The two boys shook hands.

"I have no idea what I'm doing," Lucas realised out loud.

"We've created a company," Angus said. "Now we need to convince the world that this isn't just a student's company."

SALES TRAINING

Angus constructed a replica of Mrs Campbell's office in his dad's shed. Angus imagined himself to be an army commander assembling the training grounds for his troops before a dangerous mission. Just with less at stake than death, and more Tim Tams to snack on.

The visits Angus had made to the principal's office allowed him to quite accurately replicate the layout, adding as much detail as he could using the bits and pieces lying around the well-stocked shed. Where the walls of the real office were made of gyprock, the walls of the set were made of bed sheets pegged to the roof beams. Where there was the office door, Angus put up a dividing screen. For Mrs Campbell's desk, Angus used an old ironing board his Dad had stored away in the shed "just in case".

As he assembled the set, he ran through the scenario in his mind to foresee all possible outcomes. Mrs Campbell could be very friendly to Olivia but not stay on topic, or she could be resistant or even hostile. As he felt any decent army commander or film director would do, Angus procured a packet of Tim Tams and a few bottles of water from the kitchen. He checked in the kitchen cupboards to make sure there was plenty of tea and coffee supplies in case it was a late night.

"Angus, remember you're on dishes tonight. You can't use the homework excuse every night." Cathy Newton watched him pull out glasses and mugs from the cupboard and line them up on the bench. "What are you needing so many cups for?"

Angus's heart skipped a beat. In his rush and excitement, he had forgotten to tell someone about the training. "Oh, sorry. Didn't I mention I'm having some friends over tonight? To work on our BnE assignment?"

"No, you have not mentioned that!" Cathy exclaimed. "I haven't cleaned the house. You need to give me warning if people are coming over."

"The house is fine." Angus looked around at what he thought was a perfectly clean house. "And we're only going to be working in the shed."

"The shed? What are you doing in the shed?"

"Working on the assignment. I thought you said you didn't mind if I invite people over."

"I don't mind at all, but you need to still communicate with me." Cathy moved quickly around the house, straightening cushions in the living room and gathering up the washing she had been folding. "What time are they coming?"

"In about fifteen minutes."

"And are they staying for dinner?"

"We don't need dinner, thanks."

"What time are they staying until?"

"Probably seven or eight or nine."

"And you're not providing dinner for them?"

Angus hadn't considered dinner. "I've got a packet of Tim Tams."

Cathy shook her head. "Angus, you really need to think these things through."

She graciously offered to order some pizzas for Angus and his friends.

Lucas was the first to arrive. He looked around the shed at the makeshift office, complete with a waiting room and a desk in the same position as Mr Tilley's. Lucas had only been in Mrs Campbell's real office the one time, but he could recognise all the components Angus had set up.

"You're going to be Mr Tilley," Angus explained as they waited for the girls.

"Mr Tilley? I thought I was going to be helping consult and make suggestions," Lucas complained. "I've been doing some research about sales, and it all looks straightforward. I think I'll be able to give great advice."

"You still can make suggestions, but I need someone to play Mr Tilley. He'll be the first person Olivia will need to approach when she goes to the school office for the sales pitch."

"But I don't know a single thing about the guy."

"He's definitely a people pleaser," Angus said, thinking up the best way to describe him. "He wants to be an artist, but is scared of taking the leap and following his passion. I think he thinks Mrs Campbell is his ticket to satisfying his parents."

"What are you? His psychologist?"

Angus shrugged.

"People pleaser. Mrs Campbell-pleaser. Got it." Lucas lowered his vocal tone. "Hello, my name is Mr Tilley."

"What's your name?" Angus asked.

"I'm Mr Tilley," Lucas repeated in his low voice.

"What's your name, Lucas?"

Lucas paused, unsure why Angus was asking. "Lucas?"

"You answer that your name is Lucas. Why would Mr Tilley answer that his name is 'Mr Tilley'?"

"What's his real name?"

Angus opened his mouth to say a name but realised he didn't know what it was. Everyone, including Mrs Campbell, called him Mr Tilley.

"Matthew?" Lucas suggested.

"Arnold?" Angus suggested.

"Rachael," Lucas said.

"I don't think it's 'Rachael'."

Lucas nodded toward the house. "No, I'm saying Rachael is here."

They could hear Cathy greeting Rachael loudly and enthusiastically. Cathy didn't know Rachael personally, but Angus had noticed Cathy was very enthusiastic whenever there was a whiff of a girl being in his life. Rachael eventually made her way out the back door to the shed. The pleasant interaction with Cathy meant that Rachael entered the shed with a smile.

"Hello." She put her handbag down by the door.

"Hey, Rachael," the boys greeted back.

"Do you know Mr Tilley's real name?" Angus asked her.

"Mr Tilley in the front office?"

"Yeah."

"Isn't it Drew?"

"Drew?" the boys repeated in unison.

"It's something like that." Rachael shrugged.

Rachael marvelled at the effort Angus had gone to in constructing the office set, but it didn't make her feel any better about what she was getting involved in. She had felt anxious for the last couple of days about tonight. She had researched state and federal legislative websites to ensure there weren't any laws against anonymous selling. She had physics homework due in a couple of days' time that would have provided a perfect excuse for cancelling. The homework was finished, but she didn't feel 100% confident with the work and wanted to have extra time to go over her results again. But the boys clearly valued her input, and she valued that they valued her input. She didn't want to disappoint the others by bailing.

"Did you bring homework with you?" Lucas laughed, seeing a graph pad poking out of Rachael's handbag.

"I did bring something just in case there was an opportunity."

Angus shook his head. "You can't do homework while you're on my payroll. You've got to get keen for business."

"I am keen about business," Rachael said unenthusiastically. "On the drive here, I listened to all the advertising on commercial radio and looked at all the billboards outside and got excited about business."

"Well, that's a start," Angus said. He straightened a pad of paper he had placed on Mrs Campbell's ironing board. It was awkward, the three of them standing silently together in a messy shed.

"There's Tim Tams, if anyone wants one," Angus said to break the silence. "And there's bottles of water on the work bench if you need a drink."

Rachael gave a thin-lipped smile and said thanks. Lucas joyfully took a Tim Tam. The crunch of the chocolate-covered biscuit echoed through the tin shed.

"Also, my Mum's going to order some pizzas," Angus added.

"Nice," Lucas said between bites.

They heard Cathy enthusiastically greeting someone else. Angus's mum knew Olivia from his older brother's tennis days. The students in the rumpus room could overhear Cathy catching up on the past five years of Olivia's life, asking Olivia what she did for a living, how her parents were, and whether there was a man in her life yet.

After a couple minutes of conversation, Cathy finally said, "Well, I won't keep you any longer, Olivia. It's very good of you to be helping the kids with their school assignment."

Olivia entered the shed looking very disorientated. She glanced around at the training set, not expecting to see such elaborately placed junk.

"Welcome, Olivia," Angus said warmly.

"This is all for a school assignment?" Olivia asked. "I thought you were running a business."

"Ah, sort of," Angus said. "We're still in the planning

stages of our business, so we're keeping our activities incognito." He changed subjects quickly. "This is Rachael. She's a secret genius and is going to help us plan the meeting."

"Nice to meet you," Olivia said with a smile.

"Likewise," Rachael said. She noticed how strikingly beautiful Olivia was and wished she had put more effort into her own appearance than a pair of jeans and a hoodie.

"And this is Lucas," Angus continued. "A business associate."

"I don't get a mention about my level of genius?" Lucas waited for Olivia to start laughing. He was disappointed.

"Hello, Lucas," Olivia said, shaking the boy's hand. Both of their hands were sweaty. Olivia frowned as she tried to make sense of her surroundings. "I assume this is meant to be an office?"

Angus nodded proudly. "Yes. This is an exact replica of Mrs Campbell's office. Mrs Campbell is our principal you'll be pitching the pens to."

"But she obviously won't have an ironing board in her office," Lucas added with a chuckle. Olivia gave a sympathetic smirk. Rachael and Angus exchanged knowing, disappointed glances. Lucas was clearly infatuated with the actress.

"I do need to say," Olivia said slowly, "I'm still unsure about this job. I'm not a business person, and I studied acting a long time ago."

"Don't worry about it," Angus said. "By the time we're done tonight, you'll know exactly what to say or do, no matter what happens."

Angus was desperate to make this work. Olivia was plan A.

There was no plan B.

"Okay, if everyone wants to get into their positions," he began. He pointed Olivia to the corner of the shed where the front door to the office building would be. She ran her sweaty hands down her skirt as she watched Angus direct Lucas to sit behind Mr Tilley's desk, which was a pile of boxes, and showed Rachael to the dining chair behind Mrs Campbell's ironing board.

Angus turned back to Olivia. "Lucas will be playing Mr Tilley, Mrs Campbell's assistant. He's the first person you'll meet when you arrive. I've already emailed him and booked the meeting from the Inkda web domain I purchased. Mr Tilley is a few years younger than you. He's a people pleaser, from what I know, so just, you know, be nice to him and he won't give any pushback. Rachael will be playing Mrs Campbell."

Angus showed Olivia a photo of Mrs Campbell on his phone, taken from the leadership staff's photos on the school's website. "Mrs Campbell can be legalistic, as long as it suits her, and will be probably be difficult to sell to. She holds the power to approve and choose the high school's stationery purchases. We are hoping for a pen order for the beginning of next year or earlier, if we can. If you can convince her to buy five thousand pens for next year, that would meet my goal."

"Five thousand pens?" Rachael cut in. She was seated on a foldout chair behind the ironing board. "There are only five hundred students in our school. You expect them all to use ten pens in one year?"

"Yes I do. And don't forget teachers and staff," Angus said.

"Unlike you, most students and teachers lose their pens, chew them, or lend them to others, which is as good as losing them."

"I have used at least thirty pens this year so far," Lucas said.

"You could label your things," Rachael suggested.

"I know," Lucas said, "but I see labelling a pen like labelling something you know you're going to lose. You don't want to name a roast chicken 'Owen' just before you pop it in the oven."

Rachael sighed. "You label them with your own name."

Lucas shrugged his shoulders. "Once again, I don't name my beef casserole 'Lucas' before popping it in my mouth."

"A beef casserole would have better logic than Lucas," Angus said to Rachael. "But, as Lucas proves, I think five thousand pens for the high school is a very reasonable sales target."

Olivia, doing due diligence, had taken out a notepad and pen from her bag and started writing notes. "So, do the pens have features or special things? What's my pitch?"

"We'll get there," Angus said. "I think we should run through the scenario, and as we go through each scene we'll improvise and plan at the same time."

Olivia was not a fan of improvisation.

"To begin, you'll come through the door and speak to Mr Tilley first. And go."

Angus stood back with his arms folded, watching intently to see what would happen.

Olivia, thrown off by the vague directions, took an

awkward step forward to the cardboard box desk.

"Hello," Lucas said, sitting up straight and proper. "My name is Mr Tilley. What is your name?"

"We went through this," Angus interrupted. "Mr Tilley isn't going to say his name is 'Mr Tilley'—"

"Hello there, good morning," Lucas said loudly over Angus. "My name is Drew Tilley, assistant to Mrs Campbell, amateur artist and people pleaser, esquire. I have not seen you before. How may I help you today?"

Angus gave Lucas a contemptuous stare, but let the scene continue.

Olivia turned on her smile. "Hello, Drew. My name is Olivia from..."

"Inkda Pens," Angus assisted.

"Olivia from Inkda Pens, and I have booked a meeting to see Mrs Campbell."

"Oh, is that so?" Lucas asked, remembering to lower his voice. "Don't mind me for one minute, I'll just need to double check Mrs Campbell's diary."

Lucas dramatically typed away on an invisible keyboard, staring at an invisible screen. He occasionally bounced a cheesy smile to Olivia, who gave a pained smile in return.

"Ah yes, I see. Olivia from Winkma Pens?"

"Yes, that's right."

"*Bellisima*," Lucas said. "Have you signed in?"

"No?" Olivia looked to Angus for direction, who allowed Lucas to have the time of his life miming away.

Lucas activated an invisible sign-in tablet. "I'll just get you to write your name and company in this space here."

189

Olivia played along.

"Excellent, thank you." Lucas smiled. "Now, we need to ask: Do you have a current police clearance?"

Olivia briskly turned to Angus, seeing a way out of the whole project. "I don't have a current police clearance."

"Lucas, she doesn't need a police clearance. She's not interacting with kids," Angus said.

"Hey, I'm just doing my job to protect the safety of the students and my boss," Lucas said defensively. "Do you have any weapons on you?"

"No," Olivia answered.

"Do you have any aerosol cans?"

"No."

"Gaming devices?"

"No."

"Music playing devices?"

"No."

"Magazines with questionable material?"

"No."

"Fictional novels that depict sex or violence or use strong language?"

"No."

"Peanuts? Walnuts? Macadamias?"

"No."

"Earrings that are more than just a simple stud?"

"No."

"Well I think you're all good, then. If you could just take a seat, I'll alert Mrs Campbell that you have arrived."

Olivia sat down on the camping stool which represented

the waiting room chair. Lucas approached the dividing screen and mimed knocking on the door. Rachael, much less enthusiastic about miming her part, got up from her chair and receded the screen. "Yes?"

"Your four o'clock appointment is waiting. I've asked her to sit on a chair until you are ready."

"Thank you," Rachael said. She turned to Olivia. "Please come in."

Angus made a loud popping sound with his lips which caused everyone to pause and look at him. "I don't think Mrs Campbell would immediately invite Olivia in. It's one of her power play things."

"For the purposes of this rehearsal, I think we can skip waiting," Rachael said.

"I'm actually hoping that Mrs Campbell doesn't invite Olivia in straight away," Angus said. "Olivia—at this point, if for some reason Mrs Campbell does invite you in straight away, just roll with it. But if you're made to wait, that's a prime opportunity to work on Mr Tilley. Sell the benefits of the pen to him first, give him a free one if you need to, so that if Mrs Campbell asks for his opinion, he'll be on our side."

"Oh, okay," Olivia said.

Rachael sighed and sat back down at the ironing board. She wondered if it was a good time to retrieve her homework.

Olivia sat forward in the camping stool, waiting for the right moment to pitch the pen to Lucas.

"I'm playing solitaire," Lucas announced, typing away with exaggerated movements at his imaginary computer.

"Oh, do you like solitaire?" Olivia asked.

"What? Yeah, it's all right," Lucas replied, waiting for the rehearsal to continue. "I don't play it much. It's a bit old."

"She's talking to Mr Tilley," Angus said.

Lucas straightened up, resuming his low voice. "Oh, well yes, I love solitaire. It's what gets me up in the morning."

"Very cool," Olivia said with a smile. Angus began to see glimmers of Olivia getting comfortable with her role.

"What other hobbies do you have?" she asked.

"Well, I like to go...skiing. And I like art. And I like...hats?" Lucas said unconfidently.

"You look like someone who likes art."

"Thank you?" Lucas replied, unsure what made him look like an art lover.

"My guess is you're an artist, as well."

"Well, yes, a little," Lucas replied, his voice losing its depth. "I've done a couple of drawings here and there, but I'm not very good."

"That's interesting! What do you draw?"

"Mostly shoelaces."

Rachael laughed involuntarily. "Sorry."

"That's really unique," Olivia said with a smile. "So if you like to draw shoelaces, you'd know great shoelaces."

"Well," Lucas said, "the ones I buy are pretty boring, but there are some great shoelaces out there with stripes and other patterns that I like."

Angus interrupted what he could only see as a digressive conversation. "Let's move on to the selling—"

Olivia raised her hand to shut Angus up. He did as he was told.

192

"Do you know which shoelace brands are good quality?" Olivia asked.

Lucas had completely forgotten the character her was meant to be playing and enjoyed the attention he was receiving from Olivia. "Well, I mean you've got cheap, department-store laces. They're not good quality. There's this website I go on called Tied Up where their laces are only a bit more expensive but way more durable."

"That's really cool that you're so passionate about something like shoelaces," Olivia said. "And I'm sure you'd be able to tell which shoelaces are good just by looking at them."

Lucas leaned back. "Yeah, I probably could."

Olivia stepped closer to the desk and revealed an Inkda that Angus had handed to her. "I might ask, because this is what *I'm* passionate about, do you know a good pen when you see it?"

"No," Lucas said honestly.

"Well, neither do I," Olivia said, breaking the sales pitch to look to Angus for help.

Angus shook his head out of the same astonishment Lucas was experiencing.

"That was incredible!" Angus said. "And you said you're no good at sales."

"I haven't sold anything yet," Olivia said. "You still haven't told me the selling points of the pen."

Angus picked up another Inkda from the workbench. "Get ready to take notes."

Olivia flipped her notepad to the next page.

"This is an Inkda, one of the most unique pens on the

market. It's an incredibly smooth fountain-tip pen which allows you to spend more time getting your ideas onto paper, and less time waiting for the pen to work. Not only does it write smoothly, but it uses a one-of-a-kind ink formula that reduces the chance of leakage, and the slightly thicker ink won't run out as quickly as a standard fountain pen. The case design is modern. It has a triangular grip, meaning it's comfortable to hold for long periods of time. No more hand cramps when you want to write your next great novel or exam. But the best thing about the Inkda is the cost. An Inkda doesn't have fancy gadgets and gizmos and parts that are there just to look good. No, instead the pen is made from just sturdy, quality plastic that makes it a long lasting, hardy pen."

Olivia, writing notes as fast as she could, only managed to get down: *Inkda – unique – smooth – stylish – one of a kind ink – won't run out – triangular grip – no fancy gadgets – quality plastic.*

With her notes at hand, she turned to Lucas and began her pitch. "So this pen is called the 'Inkdas'—I mean 'Inkda', and it's really great and unique... It uses a one of a kind smooth ink that doesn't run out?"

"It never runs out?" Lucas asked in faux amazement.

"Well, you know," Olivia said, rereading her notes, "it does run out eventually, but it lasts a long time. And it's got a tri-angular grip...and no fancy gadgets."

Lucas was completely uncharmed by Olivia's stammering sales pitch.

Olivia slapped her notebook against her leg. "You see, I'm

no good at this!"

"You were doing really well," Rachael encouraged. "No one expects you to be an instant expert."

"Is it all right if I use the bathroom?" Olivia asked. Angus gave her directions to the bathroom.

"I don't think it's going to work," Lucas said after she had left the shed. Rachael silently agreed.

"We don't have a choice," Angus said.

"Can't you just hire some random actor off the internet?" Lucas asked.

"I don't think Olivia's the problem," Rachael said. "You're expecting far too much of her, Angus."

"What if you hire an actual salesman?" Lucas suggested.

Angus shook his head. "The fewer people who know about this, the better. Olivia can do it."

He was paranoid about more people finding out about him and the business. He wanted everyone to know about the Inkda pens, but didn't want anyone, for the time being, to know he was behind them. He opened a bottle of water. "I'm sure she'll get more confident as we continue rehearsals."

"Maybe you could go in with a fake moustache and wig?" Lucas said. "If you could do a New Zealand accent, you could distract her with New Zealand burritos while you pitch the pens."

Lucas stopped his joking around when Olivia returned. He watched as Olivia and Rachael had their meeting, offering serious suggestions where he could.

Angus allowed Rachael, as Mrs Campbell, to be far more accommodating to Olivia than he knew the real principal

195

would be. At one point, the roles appeared to reverse and Rachael was selling the pens to Olivia. This shot Olivia's confidence to pieces. After another hour and two pizzas, they reached a point where everyone but Angus felt they could go no further. Angus was determined not to give up.

Olivia shook her head. "It's not going to happen. You'll to need to find someone else."

"No, you're doing well." Angus smiled. He could see with every passing moment that Olivia was getting more and more frustrated.

"It's getting late," Rachael said, checking the time on her phone to see it was nearly 8:30pm. "I need to get home." She figured if she drove home quickly, she could squeeze in a couple of hours of homework before bed.

Angus watched Rachael begin texting rapidly into her phone to tell her parents she was on her way home. An idea came to Angus in his exhausted state. Once he thought of it, it seemed like the only possible answer.

"I know how we can do it," he said, very unsure whether the others would go along with his far-fetched plan. He pointed to Rachael's phone.

"We'll do the sales pitch over the phone?" Lucas asked.

THE SALES PITCH

Lucas had been on board with Angus's idea straight away. It took Olivia and Rachael half an hour to come around to what sounded like the plot from a spy film.

"...it can't fail!" Angus concluded after explaining the plan for the third time.

"I can see a million ways it could fail!" Rachael said.

"I'll only do it if Rachael's helping," Olivia said. Olivia didn't know the younger girl very well, but Rachael appeared vehemently uninterested in the plan and Olivia saw her as an easy way out.

Rachael looked around the shed at the three people waiting for her decision. She felt the pressure. She could have walked out of the shed there and then and never have worried about Inkdas or Angus's business ever again. She couldn't comprehend why these three people wanted her help with something she felt she had very limited knowledge of. But their votes of confidence in her abilities were enough to entice her.

"You boys are very bad influences on me," she told them.

Two days later, on Friday afternoon, Angus bolted out the school gates under the hot sun. Angus had never run all the way home from school before. Doing so made him almost pass out. Sucking in gasps of air and ignoring the awful feeling of sweat dripping down his spine, he waved to Olivia, who was waiting in her parked car outside his house.

Olivia looked at herself in the rear-view mirror for the umpteenth time and got out of the car. She was wearing a black skirt and white blouse. She had done her makeup and tied her blonde hair into a tight bun.

"You look very nice," Angus said between breaths.

Olivia straightened her skirt. "Is this what you had in mind?"

Angus opened the front gate for Olivia. "I had nothing in mind; that's why I asked Rachael to help you. I am not the person to ask for an opinion on fashion, but you do look very nice."

Angus unlocked the house and they went into the kitchen.

"Are the other two coming?" Olivia asked.

Angus couldn't contain his excitement. "They're both on their way!"

Rachael and Lucas, seeing no advantage in running to Angus's house, walked together from school, debating together about what would be the ultimate milkshake recipe. The two students had very little in common, but it turned out milkshakes were a topic that Rachael and Lucas shared an energetic passion for.

By the time they arrived at Angus's house, Angus had constructed their mission control on the kitchen bench. It consisted of his laptop, his phone, and a couple snacks. His mum wasn't expected home for another two hours, meaning there was little chance of their mission being compromised. Olivia sat on a bench stool sipping a bottle of water, tapping the heel of her stiletto on the tile floor.

"Wow," Lucas said involuntarily when he saw the woman. "You look...really good!"

"Thanks," Olivia said without a smile.

"Your hair looks professional," Lucas added.

"You're as smooth as sandpaper," Angus said to Lucas.

Rachael looked across mission control, once again silently marvelling at the effort Angus had gone to. She wished she was as passionate and dedicated to something as him.

"Is this the earpiece?" Lucas asked, picking up clear-plastic box. He squinted inside the box. "It's so small I can't even see it!"

"The packaging is empty," Angus said, pointing to the tiny, cream-coloured earpiece next to the box he was attempting to pair via Bluetooth with Olivia's phone. He had purchased two from the local electronics store at only $12 each, and tested one of them the night before, going as far as to shake his head vigorously to ensure it wouldn't fall out. It sat snug and worked perfectly. It made him wonder how many other people were also covertly using earpieces in day-to-day life.

Once it was paired and confirmed to be working, Olivia put the earpiece in her ear and placed her phone in her handbag.

Angus also gave her a box of Inkdas and a small flyer he had hastily designed and printed the night before.

"Now remember, if everything goes to plan, you just need to repeat whatever we tell you to say," Angus said.

"And if it doesn't go to plan?" Olivia asked.

Angus smiled hopefully and handed her another handful of Inkdas. "You'll do great."

Olivia put the earpiece in, got in her car and drove away.

While they waited for her to make the two-minute drive to their school, the three students settled in at mission control. Angus pulled up a map of the school from the internet for no reason. Rachael sat at the bench to his right. She was nervous, probably more nervous than Olivia, but tried not to show it. She unwrapped some sliced carrots she hadn't eaten at lunch and mindlessly crunched on them. Lucas sat to Angus's left, oblivious to the nerves of his peers. He had a game open on his phone and was tapping away at colourful fruits flying across the screen.

Angus's phone was connected to Olivia's and set to speaker phone so all three could hear what was going on. They could hear Olivia's car driving down the road.

"Can we get a 'testing one, two, three'?" Angus asked, moving his mouth closer to the phone. Muffled by the rev of the engine, they could hear Olivia faintly say, "Testing, one, two, three."

"We can barely hear you," Angus said. "Make sure when you're in Mrs Campbell's office, you put your phone on the desk or somewhere closer to your voices."

Angus got up and went to the pantry to look for more food.

Being nervous made him hungry.

Olivia drove her car onto the school grounds. Although it was approaching 4:30pm, there were still a few students waiting for their parents to pick them up.

She scrutinized the signs as her car crawled through the car park. "Which building is it?"

"The office building is the big grey one," Rachael explained, seeing that Angus was preoccupied with opening a box of chocolates. "You should see a sign above it that says 'Office'."

Olivia spotted the building and put the phone back into her bag. When she'd parked, she sat in the car taking deep breaths.

"Is everything okay?" Angus asked loudly, worried that the silence meant the phones had lost connection.

"Yes," Olivia snapped back. She got out of her car and walked across the car park to the office. A 20-something-year-old mother dressed in track pants and a baggy jumper was on her way out of the office, shepherding a flock of shouting, jumpy primary school-aged children. The two women met eyes, and both noticed the contrast in how they were dressed. Olivia felt very out of place, dressed immaculately in business attire with heavy makeup. Inside the office, she came upon tired teachers who were glad the day was over, tired parents who were dreading that the school day was over, and tired students who were grumpy, but excited that they could finally go home.

Olivia approached the front reception desk, putting on a giant smile. "Hello, I'm here to see Mrs Campbell—"

"To the right," the office lady said abruptly.

Olivia followed the corridor around to the right until she reached another desk. It was here where she found Mr Tilley. That afternoon, Mr Tilley had 500 school newsletters in front of him that needed to be folded and prepared for distribution. The expensive folding machine in the print room had broken down, meaning the job was left to the person at the bottom of the food chain. Mr Tilley's head was down low, completely focused on his one important task: folding paper.

Olivia approached the desk, gripping her handbag tightly. "Hello?"

Mr Tilley jerked back in fright, hitting his knees on the desk's underside, which caused Olivia to jump back as well.

"I'm sorry! I didn't mean to frighten you," Olivia said.

Mission control, only hearing a bang and apology from Olivia, exchanged quizzical glances.

Mr Tilley picked up a stapler he had knocked onto the floor, subtly looking the woman over. She clearly wasn't a teacher or parent. "No, I'm sorry. Can I help you?"

"Yes. I'm here to see Mrs Campbell. I called and made an appointment for four-thirty."

Mr Tilley powered on his computer monitor and began searching through Mrs Campbell's calendar.

Every second of silence made Angus antsy. "What's going on?" he asked into the phone.

"She can't answer you," Rachael said. "People will think she's crazy if she starts describing everything that's going on around her."

"It's so muffled," Angus complained. He leaned into his

phone. "Can you hold your phone outside of your bag so we can hear what's going on?"

They heard scuffling before the atmospheric noise of staff members talking in the distance became clearer.

Olivia held the phone down by her side as casually as possible, the microphone pointed towards Mr Tilley.

"Four-thirty? Olivia from Inkdas?" Mr Tilley asked.

She nodded.

He got up from his desk and walked briskly to Mrs Campbell's door. He gave two knocks on the door. The door whipped open, causing Mr Tilley to jump back again. Mrs Campbell stood in the doorway, hand on the door knob and eyebrows raised.

"Your four-thirty appointment is here," Mr Tilley said.

Mrs Campbell leaned out and looked Olivia up and down. She glanced at a wall clock. "I'll see her in three minutes."

She retreated back into her office and closed the door.

Mr Tilley signalled for Olivia to take a seat.

Olivia, now aware the clock was ticking for her first task, didn't sit down.

"That looks like a lot of folding," Olivia said as Mr Tilley sat down at his desk.

"What's he folding?" Angus asked.

"What are you folding?" Olivia repeated.

"The school's weekly newsletter," Mr Tilley explained. "I need to fold them all before tomorrow morning."

"That's a bit rough," Olivia said, not sure how to stand in a way that looked natural.

Mr Tilley shrugged. "It's part of the job."

"What do you do outside of work?"

Mr Tilley appeared taken aback by the questioning, but Olivia was watching the time; she wasn't thinking about subtlety.

"Well, on weekends I do archery."

"Archery? That's very cool." Olivia smiled.

Mr Tilley blushed. "And I also do art. I like painting."

"Painting? That's very creative," Olivia said. "What sorts of things do you paint?"

"Well, you know," Mr Tilley said, looking at his sketch-book, "portraits, landscape, animals."

"That's very quaint," Olivia said. She was waiting for someone in mission control to give her an idea of how to steer the conversation.

It was Lucas who delivered. Without taking his focus from his game, he leaned over Angus's phone. "Ask him if he likes to draw using pens."

"Do you draw using pencils and pens as well?" Olivia parroted.

Mr Tilley thought about it for a moment. "Pencils, definitely, but rarely pens. Not unless I'm just doodling."

"Tell him he should use Inkdas for drawing," Lucas said, finally pausing his game.

Angus shook his head. "I'm sure she could work that out for herself."

"I'm trying to help here," Lucas said defensively.

Olivia tilted her head to one side, trying to listen to what was being said in her ear.

"Are you okay?" Mr Tilley asked.

Olivia laughed it off. "Yes, I'm fine. I think I just had a buzzing fly in my ear. It was quite annoying."

Rachael reached over and pressed the mute button on Angus's phone. "Let's keep it muted unless we have something actually productive to say."

"Then you like to sketch?" Olivia continued.

"Well, yes. I do scribbles here and there. I find it enjoyable," Mr Tilley said. Olivia saw him glance again at his sketchpad.

"Are those some of your sketches?" Olivia asked. "Could I see?"

Mr Tilley hesitated. "I don't know. I don't really show other people."

Olivia saw she only had one minute left until 4:30. "Please?"

Mr Tilley reluctantly picked up his sketchbook. "They're just scribbles, really. Little doodles here and there between work."

He flicked through the pages and arrived at one he was happy to show. The drawing was lines on a page that could resemble a vase of flowers, but only if those flowers had first been through a garbage disposal unit.

"Oh wow," Olivia exclaimed in genuine surprise. "I really like your style. It's very... quaint."

"Thanks," he said proudly. "I'm still learning."

Olivia took an Inkda out of her bag and placed it on the desk. "Have you ever heard of an Inkda?"

"Yes, I think I have," Mr Tilley lied to his art admirer.

"Well I think this pen and your art would be a perfect

match." She smiled. "It's a gift from me to you."

Mr Tilley was smitten and didn't pay much attention to the pen. "Thank you, that's very kind." He looked around his desk for something to give in return. "Did you want a mint?"

Olivia shook her head.

Mr Tilley suddenly whipped the sketchbook off the desk and into a drawer. With a transformed disposition, he signalled over Olivia's shoulder. "Mrs Campbell will see you now."

Olivia turned and was greeted by the principal who had the friendliest of smiles.

"Hello. My name is Rosalyn," Mrs Campbell said. "I am sorry to keep you waiting."

Olivia reshuffled the phone to her other hand and shook the woman's hand. "Hello, Rosalyn. My name is Olivia."

"Rosalyn?" Lucas repeated. "I didn't know her name was Rosalyn."

"Pretty old school," Angus said.

"I really like your school. It's so pretty and old!" Olivia repeated.

"You think so?" Mrs Campbell look around. "This building is quite new. It was built five years ago with a government grant."

Back in mission control, Rachael had snatched the phone away from the boys and placed it in front of her, giving them a stern look.

Olivia laughed nervously. "My apologies—I mean steeped in history."

"Oh, so you know a lot about our school, then?" Mrs

Campbell asked proudly.

"Only from what I've read online," Olivia said. "I always research clients beforehand so I can create solutions that fit their needs."

Angus gave a clap of excitement. "That was a good line."

"Can I get you anything? Tea? Coffee? Water?" Mrs Campbell asked.

Olivia realised how dry her throat was. "A glass of water would be really nice, thank you."

Mrs Campbell led Olivia inside her office and went out again to fetch a bottle.

Checking the coast was clear, Olivia positioned her phone on the principal's desk to give those back at Angus's house the best chance of hearing the conversation.

She leaned into the phone. "You guys need to shut up unless you're saying something helpful. It's too confusing otherwise."

Rachael unmuted the phone. "I'm sorry, Olivia. I've taken control of the phone now. I'll filter the boys."

"Thank you," Olivia said quickly. She heard footsteps, and Mrs Campbell returned with a plastic bottle of water, which she placed on the desk for her guest.

The principal sat down in her desk chair and took a sip from a mug of tea, her eyes watching Olivia carefully.

Olivia smiled back, waiting for someone, anyone, to say something.

"Is the line dead?" Lucas asked.

"No," Angus said. "I think she's giving Olivia the classic silent treatment."

"I understand you are here from a stationery company?" Mrs Campbell finally asked.

"That's right," Olivia said. "I am head of sales at Inkdas, a new start-up making a strong impact in the stationery and office supply markets."

Mrs Campbell furrowed her brow. "Inkda?"

"Yes, that's right. Inkda."

"Where have I seen that brand before?" Mrs Campbell asked herself aloud.

Angus signalled to Rachael to unmute the phone. "Tell her about our satisfied buyers in the medical profession."

"What are you talking about?" Rachael asked. Angus had never mentioned selling any pens yet except to students at their school.

"Trust me," Angus whispered with a grin.

"We have many satisfied buyers in the medical profession," Olivia repeated to Mrs Campbell. She handed the principal one of the orange Inkda pens from her handbag.

"Ah yes, that's right," Mrs Campbell said. "I saw one of these at my doctor's office last night."

Rachael and Lucas both turned in shock to see Angus at the smuggest they had ever seen him.

"What is she talking about?" Rachael whispered.

Angus, taking the advice from class that a brand consumers are more familiar with will be better liked, decided the best way for Mrs Campbell to believe Inkdas was a big brand was to put the pens in her path as much as possible.

"That's very kind of you," the medical surgery receptionist had said as Angus handed over a box of free pens as a

208

"donation for his appreciation of their great work".

"How did you know Mrs Campbell would be going to the doctor's?" Lucas asked.

"Mr Tilley doesn't do much to hide Mrs Campbell's calendar on his screen," Angus explained proudly.

"And the calendar said exactly which doctor's office Mrs Campbell goes to?" Rachael asked sceptically.

"That's very kind of you," eight out of ten medical receptionists in the local area had said as Angus handed out box after box of pens. It was a gamble that had paid off.

"It's really funny the things you can remember, like a pen at a doctor's office," Mrs Campbell said to Olivia.

"Also say we have started advertising in letterbox drops," Angus said.

Olivia relayed the information.

Mrs Campbell nodded her head. "Yes, I do remember seeing a pamphlet in my letterbox just yesterday. You must be doing very well for such a young company."

"Well, we are a fast-growing company," Olivia said, pretending to understand the lines she was being fed.

"Also mention the North Haven Football Club sponsorship," Angus added casually.

Lucas almost fell off his stool. "You sponsored what now?"

The North Haven Football Club had been quite happy to receive five boxes of free pens.

"Are you a football fan?" Olivia asked Mrs Campbell.

"No, I can't say I am," Mrs Campbell said, confirming Angus's assumption.

"Well, then I'll just quickly add we are also a proud sponsor of the North Raven Football Club."

Angus saw no need to correct her from *Raven* to *Haven*.

"That's all great to hear. I'm very happy for the success of your company," Mrs Campbell said, "but before you get too far into your sales pitch, I must let you know we do already have a stationery supplier.

"Find out who it is," Angus said.

"If I may ask, who is your current supplier?"

"Moving Stationery," Mrs Campbell said.

Angus begin feeding Olivia the main pitch. She silently nodded for a moment as she listened before starting to echo Angus's words. "We love Moving Stationery, but they don't stock our products yet. We're still in discussion with their buyers at this time. But what I'm offering you today is a deal you certainly won't be able to get at Moving Stationery. They need to pay for their staff, rent and utilities. By buying straight from the manufacturer, you'll save hundreds, if not thousands of dollars. And we know what's important to schools: saving money."

"And the success of students," Mrs Campbell added.

"Absolutely," Angus said through Olivia. "Good grades and successful students are essential for schools. And for both these reasons, Inkdas are exactly what your school needs."

Mrs Campbell scribbled her name on a piece of scrap paper with the Inkda. "How exactly is a pen going to give my students better grades?"

"Well, one of the big things preventing good grades *is* the use of low-quality pens—"

"Is it?" Mrs Campbell interrupted.

210

"The time a student spends getting a low-quality ballpoint pen to work properly and write exactly what they want is wasted time," Olivia parroted. "Our pens are fountain pens, which write faster and smoother, meaning it's far easier for the students to get the material out of their heads and onto the page."

"But the thing that prevents good grades is the material in their heads, not the writing instrument they use," Mrs Campbell argued.

Olivia bit her bottom lip. Back in mission control, all three students were also growing anxious. Angus put a chocolate in his mouth in the hope of making his mind work faster, searching for a good argument for Inkdas leading to better grades.

"Recommend the school should give pens to the teachers to help them teach better," Lucas suggested, clutching at straws.

"Overall," Olivia said, her heart pounding, "our pens present a better method for both teachers and students to be able to worry less about writing, and more on the teaching and learning."

Mrs Campbell leaned back in her chair, resuming her soul-gazing stare from the start of the meeting.

"I can see you're not convinced," Olivia said loudly enough for the students to hear the desperation in her voice.

Angus put some more pieces of chocolate in his mouth. "What does she care about?" he whispered to himself.

"Should we get Olivia out of there?" Rachael asked nervously.

"I bet you Mrs Campbell knows it's us," Lucas said from the edge of his stool, looking ready to run for the hills. "We're all dead."

"Discipline!" Angus said loudly, only just preventing chocolate from flying out of his mouth.

Olivia had to pretend she was taking a long drink of water from the bottle while listening to Angus spit words rapidly into her ear.

"Is it too hot in here?" Mrs Campbell asked.

Olivia put the water down. "Oh, no. It's fine. I'm just thirsty." She repositioned herself in the chair, getting ready to wrap up the meeting quickly if this final pitch failed. She cleared her throat, which still felt dry despite all the water. "We have done market research, and one of the other aspects of schooling that we think is crucial is discipline."

Mrs Campbell leaned forward.

"As I'm sure you can attest," Olivia continued, "distraction and behavioural issues can occur when students spend too long on one task and get bored or burned out. Inkdas, with their ultra-smooth writing, means students will be able to... enjoyably get their work down and finished before becoming distracted. I realise that a single pen is only a small piece of the puzzle when it comes to educating the next generation of scientists, lawyers and teachers, but a pen is still a piece of the puzzle in reducing their distractions."

Rachael stood up from her stool after hearing Angus's pitch. She couldn't believe Angus thought that would work; it was by far the silliest thing she had ever heard.

"Just wait," Angus said, seeing the disgust on Rachael's

face. He knew his principal, or at least he hoped he did.

"So you're telling me," Mrs Campbell said, "that this pen will result in students being less distracted, which will lead to fewer disciplinary issues?"

"Mm-hm," Olivia mumbled, taking another sip of water with a shaky hand.

Mrs Campbell picked up the Inkda again and re-wrote on the scrap paper several times. She focused her eye on the nib of the pen. "Your pitch interests me, Olivia. It resonates with me. I am always searching for new ways to decrease the distractions of my students. You won't believe the number of distractions kids face these days, with their phones and computers and social media. Especially the students in the older grades; I think these distractions are causing them to feel that they're superior to their teachers. For example, this one boy comes to mind. His name is Angus."

Angus's confidence vanished. He looked at his friends with wide, fear-stricken eyes.

"We banned chocolate bars in the canteen at the start of the term," Mrs Campbell continued, "because the school introduced stricter healthy eating policies. This student, Angus, decides to buy chocolate bars from the supermarket and resell them at recess, in secret, for a profit!"

Olivia couldn't help but laugh.

Mrs Campbell smiled and nodded. "I know. It was incredibly disrespectful to the school, but an absolutely brilliant idea. That boy, Angus, is an incredibly smart boy, but an example of a student that is constantly distracted."

Angus's mouth hung open. His principal, whom he was

213

sure tore her hair out once a week thinking about him, thought he was brilliant.

"She thinks I'm brilliant," he whispered to the others in mission control. The other two were equally dumbfounded.

Mrs Campbell laughed. "In fact, I'd say making pens and selling them around school would be exactly the sort of thing Angus would do."

Olivia froze, worried that moving a muscle would reveal her puppet controller. Angus almost threw up. Unable to see what was going on, he didn't know if the principal was standing there ready to arrest Olivia with a gun or a police squad or the national guard, every muzzle trained on his innocent actress.

"I'm very interested if your pens, these 'Inkdas', will help improve my students' learning," Mrs Campbell said. "What is the price per pen?"

Olivia pulled a pamphlet from her handbag and placed it in front of the principal. "The pens are fifty cents apiece."

It was as if Mrs Campbell had read the training script. "That's about twice the price of our current pens, if I'm not mistaken."

"We are aware of the higher price of our product," Olivia said quickly, "but we are so confident in our pens that we don't feel the need to compete on price alone, but on the quality, which you won't find in any other pen on the market."

"Ask her if she wants to make an order," Angus said impatiently, feeling it would happen now or never.

"Can I put you down for an order of pens?" Olivia asked with a smile.

214

Mrs Campbell smiled, but shook her head. "I love your enthusiasm, but I'll need to think about it."

"Is that a yes or no?" Lucas asked his classmates.

"That sounds like her way of saying no," Rachael said.

"Oh, before I go," Olivia said, placing a box of Inkdas on the desk as she had been instructed, "I'll leave you with a box of samples for you to try out."

"Well, thank you for that, Olivia," Mrs Campbell said. "I'll be sure to try them out. And thank you for coming in. It is always interesting when companies come up with new, innovative products that look to improve the education of my students."

"Be sure to call me with any questions you might have," Olivia said. "My number is on the flyer."

"Yes, I'll call with any questions."

The four accomplices couldn't stop shaking with adrenaline until they fell asleep that night.

LESSON FIVE:
HUMAN RESOURCES

Angus optimistically waited up until 11pm for news from his actress.

He hoped Mrs Campbell was agonising over the decision to order Inkdas, unable to sleep, her fingers poised over the call button to make an order with Olivia. He was also concerned that the police or Department of Fraudulent Student Businesses could kick in his bedroom door at any moment.

He woke up the next morning, a Saturday, feeling surprisingly calm. He decided to let Mrs Campbell be the catalyst for whether to continue with his pen business. If she made an order, he would continue with the venture. If she didn't, he would shut up shop, focus on school, and try to put aside his entrepreneurial tendencies until after graduation. In the second scenario—the doomsday scenario—coming up with new ideas would still be allowed, he just wouldn't allow himself to act upon them.

New ideas struck him most often on the walks to and from school, and occasionally while he was forced to wash dishes after dinner. He had a spreadsheet on his computer of random ideas that he would like to try one day, and the constantly increasing number of ideas was getting close to a hundred.

His new idea, on the walk to school the following Monday morning, was to avoid having any new tempting ideas. This idea led to another idea of a theme park that consisted of sleep pods with different themes, like 'jungle' and 'space'.

"Any news?" Rachael asked quietly as they walked together to the Business and Enterprise classroom for their lesson.

Angus shook his head.

"Any news?" Lucas asked loudly as he met the pair at the classroom.

"Nope," Angus said. "If Olivia calls today with news of an order, I'll give a code word."

"What will the code word be?" Lucas asked.

Angus gave it little thought. "Red onions."

"How are you going to work 'red onions' into a BnE discussion?" Lucas asked.

"Wouldn't it be easier to just give a thumbs-up?" Rachael suggested.

"A thumbs-up would be too obvious," Angus said. "I'll just casually mention what I had for dinner last night."

"So I'll ask, 'What did you have for dinner last night?'" Lucas said. "and you'll say..."

"Red onions," Angus said.

Lucas's face lit up. "So we made a sale?!"

Angus rolled his eyes. "No, that's just the example of the code word."

"So how will we know if it's the code word or you talking about what you had for dinner last night?" Lucas asked.

"I didn't have red onions for dinner last night," Angus said. "So if I mention I had red onions for dinner last night, you can guarantee it's the code word."

"What did you actually have for dinner last night?" Lucas asked.

"Irrelevant."

"Was it red onions?" Rachael asked.

Angus sighed. "Yes, red onions might have been in the recipe. Change of plans: there will be no code word. I'll just nod my head if I see any notifications on my phone from Olivia."

Mr Redding wasn't in the open classroom yet. Angus and Lucas got out their laptops and opened their shared planning spreadsheet for their movie theatre project. Angus turned his head around to ask Rachael how the movie theatre flyer designs were coming along.

"Oh, hello," he said, seeing Rachael had seated herself a few chairs down in the front row. "I see you've joined us in the superior row."

Rachael shrugged. "A bit easier to talk this way."

"Good morning," Mrs Campbell said in the open doorway.

It wasn't merely the fact that Mrs Campbell had entered the classroom that made all three students nearly pass out. It had become an expectation that Mrs Campbell would pop in and out of their schooling days randomly and without prejudice, as if a final reminder to the Year 12s of her existence in their lives. What gravely concerned all three students was the fact that Mrs Campbell came into the classroom holding the box of sample Inkdas she had been given on Friday afternoon.

Angus wanted to immediately confess all and take the blame onto himself, but his body stopped working. Lucas wanted Angus to confess all and take the blame. Rachael saw her career dreams disappear in a puff of expulsion and thirty long years of child care employment.

"Is Mr Redding here yet?" Mrs Campbell asked, oblivious to the internal torment of her students.

Rachael shook her head.

Mrs Campbell looked up at the clock on the back wall and frowned. "Well, while we wait for him, how is the sun safety campaign coming along?"

None of the students could speak.

"Have you made any progress?" the principal restated. She moved to the front of the classroom and casually placed the box of Inkdas on Angus's desk. She searched the faces of the students one after the other. "I assume from your silence that you haven't made sufficient progress."

"We have made progress," Rachael said quietly.

"Oh good," Mrs Campbell said. "And what have you come up with?"

Angus wondered if Mrs Campbell was the most sadistic, evil principal on Earth. He felt like the box of pens on his desk was the same as a smoking gun being placed in front of a murderer, and Mrs Campbell was waiting to see if the guilty would crack under the pressure. But something gave Angus a glimmer of hope that Mrs Campbell was oblivious to their business: she wasn't giving any of the students her accusatory stare Angus had received all those weeks ago for his chocolate business. She appeared to be in quite a good mood.

Angus took a deep breath and cleared his throat. "For the sun safety campaign, we're going to do a presentation in assembly, then hang posters around the school so the students will see them when they leave the auditorium."

Mrs Campbell nodded approvingly. "Can I see the flyer?"

Rachael, giving caveats that the design was still a work in progress, opened a poster design on her computer. The poster read, *The sun will kill you. Wear a hat.* in thick white text against a blue, cloudy sky. Rachael had created a very basic consequence chart and placed it as small as she dared at the bottom of the poster.

The three students had discussed at great length what tagline they would use, and Lucas had convinced them to take an assertive approach.

Mrs Campbell leaned in to look at the poster on the laptop. "It's interesting. It maybe could use a little more colour."

"We haven't finished the design," Angus said in defense of Rachael's work.

"And don't forget to add that the students should seek shelter. And put on sunscreen," Mrs Campbell said. "And I see you've included a consequence chart at the bottom. Well done. But yes, more colour would really help it stand out."

Rachael patiently wrote the suggestions down in her notebook.

"I think you are all doing an excellent job," Mrs Campbell said. "I will just need you to send me the script for your presentation, and I will make sure time is allotted for you at assembly this week."

She picked up the box of pens, and all three students resumed their silent panicking. "Now, I have a question for the three of you."

She opened the box and took out three Inkdas, handing them one by one to the students. When Angus received a pen, he did his best to pretend he had never seen any writing instrument before in his life.

"I had a very nice lady from a new stationery company come and visit me on Friday night with a compelling sales pitch. Since you three students are doing business and Enterprise, I would like your opinion on these pens. Give them a scribble and tell me what you think."

Angus, taking a leap of faith that Mrs Campbell was unaware of who she was handing the pens to, uncapped the Inkda and wrote *the end of the world* in the back of his notebook.

Lucas, feeling even more faith in his principal's ignorance, gave the pen a big scribble in the back of his book. "It's incredible!" he announced. "I really love it. It feels really good in my hand and it writes really smoothly. I could see me using this pen every day!"

The other three in the classroom looked at Lucas with surprise. Lucas, realising he might have laid it on too thick, put his head down and continued scribbling.

"So, you like it?" Mrs Campbell asked.

Lucas shrugged his shoulder. "Yeah, they're all right."

"And what do you think, Angus?"

"Well, a pen's a pen," Angus said. He wrote *the end of the world* again on the page, as if undecided. "It is pretty good. How much is the company charging for it?"

"I think about fifty cents each."

"Fifty cents?" Angus repeated, raising his eyebrows. "That's really cheap. I'm pretty sure they cost more than that at the store."

"You've seen them in stores?" Mrs Campbell asked. "The saleswoman said the pens were yet to be sold in retail stores."

Angus swallowed his misstep. "I haven't seen these specific pens in stores, but pens are expensive. Even a basic pen can cost at least a dollar at Moving Stationery."

"These pens look like they could easily be worth three or four dollars," Rachael added to support Angus's rambling.

"Welcome, Mr Redding," Mrs Campbell said as the BnE teacher entered the classroom. Angus thought he saw a twinge of concern on the teacher's face as he noticed his boss already present. Mrs Campbell held up the box of pens. "I saw that you were not here yet and took the opportunity to use your students as a focus group for some pens we are looking into ordering for next year."

Angus had to cover his mouth to hide his smile at the notion.

"I apologise. I was just printing out some readings." Mr Redding squeezed past Mrs Campbell to dump his belongings onto the teacher's desk. "Can I see one of the pens?"

Mrs Campbell handed him a pen. Asking Lucas's

permission, Mr Redding leaned over the desk and wrote a word with the Inkda on the boy's scrap paper. The word was *fail*. Lucas was horrified.

"Sorry, just practicing for one of my Year 11 students," Mr Redding said with a wink. "This situation offers a good case-in-point of your homework readings from a few weeks back. What considerations would the school need to make before switching to a different supplier for their stationery?"

Angus knew the answer was, "Will switching suppliers give a better return on investment?" but he wasn't interested in saying anything that could steer Mrs Campbell away from the sale.

"Will switching suppliers give a better return on investment?" Lucas said proudly.

"Yes. Well done, Lucas," Mr Redding said. "What is the other important consideration when choosing suppliers?"

"Ethics," Rachael said.

Mr Redding nodded. "Correct. Even if this pen could give a better ROI for the school, if the new supplier is unethical, it's not going to be good for the wider community in the long run."

"Well, in actual fact, switching to these pens won't offer a better return on investment," Mrs Campbell said. "They're more expensive."

Angus bit his lip hard.

"If it's not giving a better ROI, in my opinion it's not worth switching." Mr Redding connected his laptop to the projector.

"Yes, but not all returns on investments are financial," Angus added while stretching his arms, trying to appear as nonchalant as he could.

"What do you mean?" Mrs Campbell asked.

Angus and Rachael looked to each other. Angus pleaded with his eyes for her help. Rachael silently pleaded not to look to her for help.

"I believe," Rachael said, "that Angus is talking about... For example, if you're a company that allows staff to go home early every Friday, you might lose money because less work is completed, but your staff is happier, and that makes them give better service."

Mr Redding looked quite proud of his students. "That's very true. A return on investment can be in something other than profits. But what we're talking about here is pens. These new pens are going to do the exact same thing as any other pen the school buys."

"Actually," Mrs Campbell said, "the saleswoman said these pens had a number of features such as an ergonomic grip, longer-lasting ink and smoother writing, which will allegedly help students focus better on their work."

Mr Redding visibly cringed hearing the sales pitch, but ultimately didn't continue arguing with his principal. "Well, they sound like good pens, then."

Mrs Campbell nodded and held out her hand to Lucas.

"I thought you said we can keep the pens," he said.

"I said no such thing." Mrs Campbell seemed disgusted that Lucas had suggested as much. "You received your allotted stationery at the start of the year. If you need additional stationery, you need to go to the office and fill out a stationery request form."

The students handed their pens back, and Mrs Campbell left the classroom without another word.

As soon as she was gone, Mr Redding put his Inkda on Lucas's desk. "Early Christmas present."

Angus was relieved, to say the least. He didn't know whether the past five minutes had convinced Mrs Campbell to make an order, but at least he and his friends hadn't been found out.

"By the way," Mr Redding said, "I hope you are all prepared for both your sun safety presentation and the movie theatre. Is everything going according to plan? Do you want me to check over anything?"

"We'll be putting up flyers for the movie theatre tomorrow," Rachael said.

"And our assembly presentation is all set for the sun safety campaign," Lucas added.

"Good work," Mr Redding said. "We must get to today's topic: human resources. Before you completely zone out, I know human resources sounds boring, but it's actually incredibly interesting. HR covers a plethora of different functions in a business, from dispute management to internal communications, but it's all about managing people. The theoretics of HR takes a lot from psychology and sociology. To begin, can anyone guess one of the hardest parts of managing people?"

"The conflicts?" Rachael guessed.

"Conflicts can be a problem, but this issue I'm thinking of is probably the cause of many conflicts. Any other guesses?"

Mr Redding looked to Lucas, who was preoccupied by

something on his laptop screen.

After a couple seconds of silence, Lucas sensed something was amiss and looked up to see his teacher staring at him expectantly. "I'm not in any conflicts."

"Good to know," Mr Redding said. "But can you think of what would be one of the hardest parts of managing people?"

"I don't know," Lucas said quickly. He was much more interested in going back to reading pop-science articles.

"I'm surprised, Lucas. This is all about psychology, which is your area of expertise, isn't it?" Mr Redding said. "If you can think of a difficult aspect in managing people, I'll buy you a chocolate bar from the canteen—I mean the shops."

The offer of chocolate got Lucas's synapses firing, but Angus beat him to it. "Motivation."

"Correct. Well done, Angus."

"Dude, I was about to get a free chocolate bar," Lucas complained.

"Do I get a chocolate bar?" Angus asked.

"No," Mr Redding said. "That offer was only for Lucas. Besides, chocolate's bad for you in more ways than one, Angus."

Angus laughed as the teacher wrote *motivation* on the whiteboard.

"Motivation is one of the hardest parts of people management," Mr Redding continued. "Not only is it one of the hardest parts, but it's probably the most crucial aspect of getting work done. To explain, let's use your movie theatre. If you ask another student to help you sell tickets in exchange for a free smoothie, they wouldn't be expected to work anywhere near as hard as you three will in selling tickets. What's their motivation? A free smoothie and a pat on the back. Compare that to your motivation of making real cash and getting a good grade. In your handouts, you'll see Maslow's hierarchy of needs. Maslow, a scientist back in the 1940s, theorised that everyone's needs in life fall into this hierarchy. From the bottom, physiological needs, then safety needs, then needs of love, needs of self-esteem and finally, at the top, needs of self-actualisation. The need for self-actualisation is a fancy term for your need to believe that a job or task is actually worth doing."

He wrote the five needs on the whiteboard. "Let's do a survey. Everyone close your eyes. I'm going to go through Maslow's five needs and ask which of you—show me through raising your hands—finds the given need is being met here at school."

The three students did as they were told and closed their eyes.

"Starting with physiological needs. Who feels that the school meets your basic needs of air to breathe, water to drink, food to eat, shelter from the cold in winter and the heat in the summer?" Mr Redding paused, waiting for all three students to raise their hands.

Lucas did not.

"One of you doesn't think the school is meeting your physiological needs?"

"I've been deprived a chocolate bar," Lucas said dryly. "But besides that, yes."

"Next is the need for safety. Raise your hand if you feel the school meets your need to be safe from physical attacks, financial ruin, and sickness."

All three students slowly raised their hands.

"What about the need for love or social belonging?" Mr Redding asked. "Do you feel the school meets your needs for belonging—for friendships?"

He paused while the students silently considered the question. Angus and Lucas eventually put their hands up, but Rachael couldn't do it. She considered just putting her hand up so she wasn't asked any questions, but Mr Redding moved on before she had the chance.

"Do you feel the school meets your need for self-esteem? Does the school give you positive recognition for the things you do? Do you feel the school builds up your confidence rather than tear you down?"

Rachael always won awards. She didn't feel she had any place to complain about the recognition she received, so put her hand up. Lucas got the grades he wanted, and that was enough recognition for him. Angus created a thumbs-down option.

Mr Redding continued. "And finally, do you think the school meets your need for self-actualisation? That is, does it meet your need to excel at what you do?"

Lucas didn't fully understand the need, but raised his hand anyway. Rachael suddenly considered that maybe Mr Redding would feel personally attacked if she didn't raise her hand, so proceeded to do so. Angus raised his hand, and gave another thumbs-down. He heard Mr Redding laugh.

When the students were told to open their eyes, they could

see Mr Redding had recorded a tally next to each need on the whiteboard. Physiological and safety had three tallies. Needs of love, self-esteem and self-actualisation only had two each.

"That was a very interesting exercise. Thank you all for your honesty. As you can see, of the top three needs, only two of you felt those are being met. Theoretically, that means whoever among you felt several of your needs are not being met is going to be less motivated at school, and that may be reflected in your grades and overall satisfaction."

"I don't agree with that," Angus said defensively.

"That's absolutely fine," Mr Redding said. "Maslow's hierarchy of needs is just one theory among many. But which part do you disagree with?"

"The idea that because I don't feel those top two needs are being met, I'm going to have worse grades."

"I didn't say you," Mr Redding said.

"It's all right," Angus said, looking at his friends. "They would have guessed it was me anyway."

Lucas nodded.

"But let's say I'm super smart," Angus said. "I could be really smart and not feel those needs are being met *and* still have good grades."

"Following that line of thinking," Mr Redding said, sitting down at his desk, "let's say you're the smartest man in the world, and the government gives you a job of multiplying one through a billion by 54.238, without a calculator, one equation at a time. The job is nine hours a day, forty-eight weeks per year, for a prospective fifty years until you can afford to retire. How long do you think you would last in that job?"

"If the pay was good," Angus lied.

"On the other hand," Mr Redding continued, "let's say, as you're the smartest man on Earth, your job is to design the first ever completely self-powered autonomous car that will save the earth from global warming. If you succeed, you are promised limitless wealth and a monopoly in the global car industry. Additionally, your child is born with the inability to use her limbs, so an autonomous vehicle would offer her unprecedented freedom in life. Which of those two jobs do you feel you would work harder and longer at?"

"I don't see how that relates to me here at school. We're stuck here—we don't have a choice," Angus said.

"Many people are stuck in their jobs because life requires them to earn a wage to pay for their livelihood and provide for their families."

"Well, people should choose jobs that they enjoy doing," Angus argued.

"That's connected to self-actualisation. But a job that gives you self-actualisation now may not meet that need in a decade's time."

Angus was spent of arguments. "Well, I'm doing really well in all my classes, so that proves the theory wrong."

"You might be correct that the theory is wrong," Mr Redding said. "But surely you agree that people have needs, and if a workplace meets many of an individual's needs, that worker is going to have much higher job satisfaction and work better because of it."

Angus gasped. He'd felt his phone vibrate in his pocket. He let it vibrate again, making sure it wasn't his imagination.

"Are you alright?" Mr Redding asked.

"Can I go to the bathroom?" Angus asked. "I have a need."

Angus walked briskly from the classroom and down to the toilet block. He didn't dare take his phone out before arriving at the building. On the way, he felt the phone stop vibrating. His brisk walk turned into a jog. He burst into the bathroom and whipped out his phone; the missed caller ID was Olivia. Heart pounding, he called her back.

"Hey, what's up?" Angus asked.

"Well done—you've made the sale," Olivia said.

Angus was speechless.

"Your principal ordered two thousand five hundred pens."

Of all the places to be hearing the news that his plan had worked, talking on the phone in the school bathroom after sneaking out of class was almost exactly where he imagined he would be.

"Thank you so much," Angus said in a shaky voice, overcome with shock and happiness. "You are...a legend!"

"No worries," Olivia replied. "She asked for an invoice. She's given me her email address—"

"Yep, I'll organise all that." Angus paced the bathroom. "I'll pay you as soon as her payment comes through, I promise."

Angus hurried back to the business studies classroom with a smile he couldn't control. Lucas and Rachael, assuming his phone had been the cause of his quick exit, looked to him as he entered the classroom.

He gave a nod of the head, trying to hide his smile behind his hand. "There was a pile of red onions outside—"

The other two raised their eyebrows, understanding it had

been a success.

"What are you talking about?" Mr Redding asked Angus.

"Nothing—it's an inside joke. It was just an enjoyable toilet break," Angus said quickly. His legs were jiggling with excitement.

Mr Redding frowned. "Good to know. We were just talking about how employees possess different types of intelligences, including linguistic and spatial—"

The excitement reached Angus's bladder. He raised his hand. "Sorry, I just need to go to the toilet again. I won't be a moment."

———————

"You did it?" Rachael asked as soon as the three students left the classroom after the bell rang.

"We did it," Angus said. "Mrs Campbell ordered two-and-a-half thousand pens."

"Wait, so does this means I own twenty-five percent of the company?" Lucas asked.

"No, that sale was a joint effort," Angus said. "You have to sell pens as an individual salesman to earn ownership."

"I'm pretty sure that's not what we agreed to," Lucas said, but he was still over the moon that he'd contributed to making the sale.

"I really couldn't have done it without you two," Angus said. He could see from her smile that Rachael was also proud of herself. "I'll pay you as soon as the payment comes through from Mrs Campbell."

She shook her head. "Don't worry about it."

"Why not?"

"I'm happy I could help," she said. "And we'll need the cash to produce better pamphlets."

"So you'll join the company?"

Rachael immediately closed off again, holding her pencil case close to her chest. "I don't know yet—"

"If Rachael doesn't join, can I earn up to fifty percent of the business?" Lucas asked.

Angus ignored him. "Please think about it, Rach."

Rachael was slowly warming to the idea of helping more, but still wasn't convinced that they wouldn't be found out and expelled. "Let's finish next week's Business and Enterprise projects first, and then we can discuss it again."

"Speaking of which," Lucas said, "I've had a completely new idea for the sun safety presentation. Do either of you think the auditorium is flammable?"

SUN SAFETY

The students sat restlessly in the auditorium, row by row, class by class. The only students who liked assemblies were those who disliked schoolwork. Assemblies varied in their content and could consist of anything from a Mrs Campbell lecture on the importance of school-grounds cleanliness, to a talk from a bygone athlete who had competed in the 2000 Sydney Olympic Games. The assemblies anyone would consider fun were few and far between.

A memorable assembly for the Year 12 students was two years ago when a member of the state parliament, Tim Menelaus, came to speak in assembly about leadership. A group of Year 10 students, which Lucas had almost been part of before chickening out, had watched a few too many online videos of political activists, and thought it might be fun to try activism themselves. As soon as the Hon. Menelaus rose to begin his presentation, the group of Year 10s chanted, "If you don't care for the whales, the ecosystem fails!" Upon further investigation by Mrs Campbell, that phrase was found to be the final choice of twenty possible slogans written in the back of one girl's notebook. Mrs Campbell, absolutely livid with anger and embarrassment, would have expelled every single one of the whale advocacy group if the member of parliament hadn't pleaded otherwise. If the Year 10s had done any research whatsoever, they would have found that the Hon. Menelaus was a strong advocate of ecosystem protection laws and didn't need it shouted at him in a school assembly.

Lucas wanted to blow that assembly out of the water with their sun safety presentation. He wanted the students to remember their presentation for years to come.

"This is so over the top," Rachael said nervously as the three Business and Enterprise students waited in the auditorium's foyer for their entrance to the Wednesday assembly. The two boys had to remind her constantly that the presentation had been commissioned by the principal, which made the chance of consequences low. Rachael was sceptical about that and had chosen the most responsible role in their presentation.

Angus, who had been surprised at Lucas's last-minute push for the success of the campaign, shrugged at Rachael's apprehension. "Mrs Campbell said she wanted it to be memorable."

"She never actually said that," Rachael replied.

"She implied it with her eyebrows. It's what she wants," Lucas said, hands deep in his pockets.

Inside the auditorium, the assembly was proceeding as it

always did. A student read the morning notices in a monotone voice. Damien gave a rousing message about a charity casual-clothes day scheduled for the following week. A teacher announced winners for some competitions that were sport related, and a runner-up for a state-wide writing competition that was a money-making scam either preying on schools' need to receive awards, or preying on hopeful parents who wanted to see their children succeed in something.

Then it was Mrs Campbell's turn at the podium.

"Good morning, everyone," she said into the microphone. "I would also like to give my congratulations to Thomas for doing so well in the South Australian poetry awards. Now, as you know, the season has changed to summer quite early this year, which means that it is a requirement that you have your hats on your heads at recess and lunch. I don't know why, but a lot of you seem to be either blatantly forgetting or misplacing your hats. This will not be tolerated, and I have instructed teachers and staff to immediately write up detentions if anyone is seen without a hat." Her voice softened. "This is for your sake. We don't *like* writing out detention slips. We don't *like* keeping you inside at lunch. We want you to be safe in the sun, which means being sun-smart. I have asked the Year 12 Business and Enterprise class to put together a small marketing campaign for sun safety, which they are launching today. Could the Year 12 business class please come up?"

Angus, Lucas and Rachael exchanged final glances as if they were heading on a mission to Mars with an unknown chance of survival. They walked quickly, single file, down the auditorium aisle and onto the wooden stage. The other

236

students murmured while they waited. Mrs Campbell nodded to the three Year 12s and sat down in the front row.

Lucas, hands still in his pockets, coughed loudly into the podium microphone—a signal to his fellow students in the audience to shut up.

"The sun," Lucas began, nodding to the Year 11 student tasked with operating the projector. A slideshow lit up the big screen behind the trio on stage. It was a picture of blue sky with the word *SUN* in yellow text.

"The sun is going to kill you," Lucas continued. There was some quiet laughter around the room.

Angus approached the microphone next. The slide changed to a dot-point list from which he read. "Sun facts: The sun is one hundred and forty-six million kilometres from Earth. The sun is fifteen million degrees Celsius. It takes eight minutes and twenty seconds for the light from the sun to reach Earth. The sun's diameter is big. The sun is going to kill you." Another buzz of laughter came from the audience.

Rachael stepped up to the microphone. "According to Cancer Council Australia, two out of three Australians will be diagnosed with skin cancer before they reach the age of seventy. Every year, skin cancers account for about eighty percent of new cancer diagnoses. The sun is going to kill you." The slide changed to a sunny beach scene. "But you don't have to become another skin cancer statistic. Angus and Lucas are now going to demonstrate this point."

Rachael took a big step to her left away from her classmates. Lucas, unable to hide his grin any longer, reached deeper into his pocket with his left hand. When he pulled his hand out again, it was covered by a very thick glove. It was a move he had been practicing all morning. Angus, although disappointed by Lucas's glee over what was meant to be a serious topic, reached into his own pocket and pulled out a box of matches. At the hint of possible danger, the audience went silent. Anything to do with fire or explosives, especially inside a school, had the students interested and excited. Mrs Campbell and the teachers also became interested, but for a much different reason.

Angus reapproached the microphone, maintaining his seriousness by not looking anyone in the eye, especially Mrs Campbell. "The sun, as I said, is fifteen million degrees hot. A match"—Angus lit the match, ensuring he kept it back from the microphone and wooden podium—"a match is about eight hundred degrees. Far less hot than the sun."

Lucas removed his right hand from his pocket and held both hands out in front of him; one covered in the thick glove, and the other with his sleeve rolled completely up. Angus waved the match over Lucas's arms, watching the kids' reaction as it hovered over the glove-free hand. Most of the students gave no reaction at all, confused by the presentation. Some the older students in the audience, catching on to the absurdity and cheesiness of the premise, continued to laugh.

Angus's enthusiastic movements caused the match to go out in a wisp of smoke. Angus quickly lit a new match and leaned toward the microphone to explain the illustration. "One of Lucas's hands is protected from the match, while the other is exposed. If we place a lit match on the protected hand"—which Angus proceeded to do by dropping the burning match onto the glove—"nothing happens. The match just continues to burn, but Lucas's skin is safe." Angus picked up the match off the glove and hovered it over Lucas's other hand. Lucas gave Angus a quick glance, hoping he wouldn't get carried away.

"This arm, however, has no protection," Angus explained, "and so dropping the match—which obviously I won't do—on his hand would really, really hurt him." The crowd gave a collective laugh, relieved that Angus was not going to drop the match. "And so, I hope you understand what we're trying to—"

A Year 8 girl screamed as Lucas's hand caught fire.

Angus jumped back, still holding the match.

Lucas froze as gasps ran through the audience, his hand burning in front of him.

"Put it out with you glove!" Angus said frantically.

Lucas hit away at the fire with his protected hand, but the flame wouldn't go out.

Rachael ran off stage and returned with the first available fire extinguisher. She ripped out the safety tag and gave Lucas's hand a short burst.

The fire extinguished and Lucas cradled his hand, still in apparent shock along with the hundreds of other people in the assembly.

Mrs Campbell ran onto the stage to check the damage. Lucas ran straight past her and through the nearest exit to find a water source to douse his hand. Angus also left after his friend. Rachael assured Mrs Campbell she would fetch the school nurse and ran out towards the front office.

Angus caught up to Lucas, who was still clutching his hand and walking briskly to one of the drink fountains. "Is your hand okay?" Angus asked with a laugh.

Lucas turned to see if anyone else was following. "My hand's burnt."

Angus stopped laughing. "Wait, you mean for real?"

"Yes, I mean for real!" Lucas snapped. "The gel must have dripped off between my fingers. And Rachael took her time getting the fire extinguisher!"

"To be fair," Angus said, "it was you who told her to wait a moment before getting the extinguisher so it wouldn't look planned."

"She waited at least thirty seconds!"

"It was about five seconds."

They arrived at a drink fountain. Lucas washed the clear fire-retardant gel from his hand. His hand clean of the gel, he kept it under the running water to soothe the burn. "Well, at least it worked. Everyone looked freaked out."

"Yeah." Angus chuckled, still concerned that his friend might have a disfigured hand.

After a couple minutes, Rachael arrived at the drink fountain with Nurse Brianna. Nurse Brianna, who had only been a school nurse since the start of the year, had already seen too many false alarms of scrapes, "sick tummies" and "headaches". Most ailments could be miraculously healed with a ten-minute rest on the infirmary bed or a call to the terminally ill student's parents for permission to give a magical paracetamol tablet. Nurse Brianna didn't expect Rachael to arrive at her office and explain that a boy had burned his hand, but was probably fine because they were using a flame-retardant gel.

"Who in the world gave you kids permission to play with fire? Who was supervising?" Nurse Brianna asked, gently taking Lucas's hand and observing the reddened webs of his fingers.

"Well, I guess the whole high school was supervising," Angus said. "It happened in assembly."

"Lucky for you, these are first-degree burns, nothing more," Nurse Brianna said. "Keep your hand under running water for another twenty minutes and then come to the first-aid room so I can write an incident report."

The three were all relieved at the diagnosis. The nurse returned to the administration building, shaking her head.

Angus's relief turned to panic as he looked at the time on his phone. "We've got less than fifteen minutes to get all the posters up. Are you able to help?"

"She told me to keep my hand under water." Lucas leaned against the drink fountain.

Angus and Rachael had no time to argue. They ran to Lucas's locker and pulled out the two hundred A4 posters they had printed the day before. They armed themselves with packaging tape dispensers and began putting up the posters. Every flat surface in the high school where a poster would stick and stay, they put one. Sweating under the warm morning sun, Angus and Rachael ran across the high school, slapping the posters up haphazardly. Then they ran to the primary school, where they stuck up the remainder of the posters even more haphazardly.

Angus still had a pile of posters left as the classes began returning from the auditorium. Keeping his head low to not draw attention, he walked back over to the high school, where he could already hear the reaction to the campaign. Everyone was solemn but chatty. For all the students and teachers knew, they had just witnessed a teenager lose his hand in a pyrotechnics accident.

The students began gathering around the posters. A cackle of laughter erupted from some Year 10 boys. A gasp of disgust came from a Year 11 girl who had spotted a poster stuck to her locker. A Year 7 teacher ripped a poster from her office door and threw it in the bin.

Angus headed straight for his locker and didn't look anyone in the eye as he retrieved his books for maths. He sensed someone come up next to him but still didn't turn and look.

"I feel like everyone's about to form a lynch mob after me." Rachael gripped her maths books tightly.

"After *us*," Angus corrected. "If there's a lynch mob, it'll be coming after us."

Rachael, by far the most artistic of the three business studies students, had designed the poster using the boys' ideas. She felt like she was stuck up all over the school, and everyone was disgusted with her.

Alan, one of their classmates, arrived at his locker. Seeing a poster stuck on a locker adjacent to his own, he gave a hearty laugh. "Did you guys design this?"

Angus nodded.

"That's hilarious!"

"That's Rachael's design," Angus said.

"Hey, Warren! Did you see the posters?" Alan called to a boy farther down the veranda.

"Yeah. Did you BnE people make them?" Warren called back.

"Yeah—Rachael's design!" Angus called back, relieved the other students liked their design.

"Why are you telling everyone it's my design?" Rachael asked.

"Credit where credit is due."

"This was a bad idea," Rachael said. She regretted caving to the encouragement of her BnE classmates . "Everyone's going to think I'm sick and twisted."

"It's not sick and twisted. Everyone loves it. I wonder if Mrs Campbell has seen it yet."

As if on cue, Angus turned to see Mr Tilley waiting patiently for the crowd of students to clear for him to get through.

"Mrs Campbell would like to see you," Mr Tilley said to Angus.

Angus nodded, not surprised in the least.

Mr Tilley looked at the yellow sticky note on his finger. "And she would also like to see a Rachael Armand. Do you know where she is?"

Mr Tilley didn't know the faces of all the students. Angus turned to Rachael, who had become as white as a sheet. "Have you seen Mrs Campbell's office lately?"

Lucas was already in Mrs Campbell's office, his burnt hand resting in a plastic bowl of water. Mrs Campbell was composing an email in a mood that he couldn't place. She seemed calm. He gave a brave smile as Mr Tilley showed Rachael and Lucas in, following behind them with two extra chairs.

Mrs Campbell stopped typing the email and swivelled in her chair to face the students. Her familiar tactic of staring intently at whomever she was addressing wasn't effective with three people, so she began talking right away. "I really don't know where to start."

"What did you think of the campaign?" Angus asked, somewhat mindlessly. He was still kicked up on adrenaline from that morning's events.

Mrs Campbell picked up a poster she had ripped off one of the walls outside the administration building. She held the crinkled poster out at a distance and scanned it up and down. She sighed and turned the poster around to show the students.

"Who designed it?"

"It was a joint effort," Angus said quickly.

"Can someone please explain it to me?"

Lucas repositioned his hand in the bowl of water, causing some to splash over the side and onto his pants. "Well, as you can see, it's a grave in a cemetery with a hat on top of the gravestone. There are other students gathered around the grave, wearing their hats, paying respect to their fallen classmate. The kid in the grave didn't wear his hat."

Mrs Campbell read the big letters at the top of the poster. "Lost Hat, Lost Life."

"The kid lost his hat, so he lost his life," Angus explained.

244

Mrs Campbell turned back to her computer and searched for an email in her inbox. She turned the monitor to show the students the poster with the title that read *The sun will kill you. Wear a hat.* It was the original design they had sent to Mrs Campbell for her approval.

"Do these," Mrs Campbell asked, holding up the printed poster next to the monitor, "look the same?"

"There was a last-minute design adjustment," Angus explained.

"I don't care if there was a design change," Mrs Campbell said. "You didn't seek approval for this design."

The three students were silent, preparing themselves for the tongue-lashing to come.

"I asked a simple thing: seek my approval for your campaign. What did you do?"

"Decide on a different direction—" Angus said.

"We didn't do what you told us to do," Lucas said loudly over Angus.

"Exactly right," Mrs Campbell said. Her voice remained measured and calm, but her eyes showed otherwise. "You have blatantly disobeyed what I asked of you. All three of you—three very bright teenagers who are almost adults. You couldn't do something so simple as to follow my instructions and email me your poster and script. How do you think your future bosses will tolerate you saying you're going to do one thing, and then just changing your mind and doing another?"

Mrs Campbell waited for a response.

"They won't," Lucas said, looking at his principal with determined focus.

"Exactly right, Lucas," Mrs Campbell said.

"Are you happy with the campaign?" Angus asked in frustration. He'd known changing their plans would make Mrs Campbell angry. He wondered if he had agreed to the changes just for that effect.

"Whether I'm happy with the campaign is completely irrelevant," Mrs Campbell said.

"Are we in trouble?" Rachael asked timidly, holding her laptop and books tightly in her lap.

Mrs Campbell looked at Lucas. "One of you seems to have already got their punishment by playing with matches."

The students dared not breathe, hoping she would let them off with only one out of six hands burned.

"Actions have consequences," Mrs Campbell said, turning her computer monitor back to face her. "I've just been writing an email to let Mr Redding know that you will no longer be allowed to complete your Business and Enterprise assignment as a practical assessment. You may not run the movie theatre."

LESSON SIX:
BUSINESS EXPANSION

Angus, Lucas and Rachael, dumbfounded by their punishment, left Mrs Campbell's office with laptops, textbooks, and a water bowl in their hands.

Lucas felt bitterly disappointed. He had been looking forward to putting his sales skills to the test with the movie theatre project and had even started reading a book on "up-selling techniques", which he had planned to use on their customers.

Rachael was upset that all the hard work she had put into both campaigns was going to waste. She'd thought she understood Business and Enterprise; she wasn't so sure now.

Angus hoped Mr Redding would be able to talk Mrs Campbell out of their punishment—not because it was his dream to run a movie theatre and sell smoothies, but because he knew how hard he and his classmates had worked. He knew Rachael and Lucas had struggled through the Business and Enterprise classes to get to where they were now. Angus considered himself responsible for the downfall by encouraging them to pursue the most provocative ideas for the sun safety campaign.

They didn't talk about it for the rest of the day.

The following morning, a Thursday, when they should have been busy finishing organising the movie theatre, Mr Redding pulled the three BnE students from their homeroom class and confirmed that their practical assessment would be replaced with an extended written business plan. Although they were relieved that the plan would still be for their movie theatre, allowing them to use the information they'd already gathered, the students were still upset.

"It's not fair," Lucas said. "We've put so much work into it!"

Mr Redding nodded. "I know, and I'm sorry, but it's above my pay grade."

"Are there any compromises we could propose, like running the movie theatre without food?" Rachael asked.

"This is the compromise," Mr Redding said. "I don't think you three realise that Mrs Campbell could expel you all for playing with fire inside a building."

"It is a fair compromise," Lucas said quietly.

"Fine," was all Angus said.

The three students returned to the classroom like wounded soldiers. The rest of the class was mulling around, waiting for the bell to ring for the first lesson.

"I guess I'll call and cancel the fruit order," Lucas said.

Angus rested his head on his hand and chewed on the end

of an Inkda.

"Are you alright?" Lucas asked.

"I'm over it."

"Over the assignment?"

"Over everything."

Angus drifted through the rest of the school week. He blocked all thoughts and ideas and dreams from his mind and did his best to fill his head with the schoolwork in front of him. He got annoyed with himself for finishing homework and assignments so quickly, as it meant more time to just sit there and try not thinking about businesses or his future. He even considered doing extra questions for his maths revision, but his despair wasn't *that* great. The boys didn't speak to Rachael for the rest of the week, because no one felt there was anything to talk about.

The following Monday morning, after a weekend of finding old video games he hadn't played all year and playing them until his eyes went red, Angus gathered up his laptop and exercise book and walked slowly, alone, to the business studies classroom. It was an unsuitably sunny morning for how he felt.

He entered to find Mr Redding seated at the teacher's desk, using his laptop.

"Good morning, Angus," Mr Redding said with a smile.

"Morning," Angus replied. "When's the business plan due?"

"I was just thinking about that," Mr Redding said. "I'll extend the due date to Week 1 of next term, so you'll have the holidays to complete it."

Angus nodded. "I'll get it done tonight and hand it up tomorrow."

Lucas arrived and was surprised to see Angus sitting in the second row of desks. Knowing his mate was down in the dumps, Lucas joined him. Rachael, unsure where to sit, put herself in the first row.

"Did one of you want to try the teacher's desk?" Mr Redding smirked. "Good morning, everyone. I was just saying to Angus that, due to the unforeseen circumstances, I've extended the due date of the business plans to Friday, Week 1 of next term. Is everyone okay with that?"

Lucas and Rachael nodded.

"But despite everything, we must push on!" Mr Redding announced, doing his best to create cheer among the gloom. "There is so much more I need to teach you before you enter the real world, where you'll really be playing with fire. By the way, how is your hand, Lucas?"

"That was a cheap shot," Angus said, but without a smile. "I liked that."

Lucas raised his bandaged hand. "It's a hundred percent fine. I'm just wearing the bandage so the other students think it's still badly burned."

Mr Redding opened his bag and pulled out three items. He placed one on each of the students' desks. It was three chocolate bars. None of the students understood what they were being rewarded for.

"You guys made history," Mr Redding announced. "Last week, you created an apparently unprecedented record. Not a single detention was given out for missing hats after your presentation. Your sun safety campaign was a success."

Lucas's mouth dropped open.

Rachael raised her eyebrows. "Really?"

"Really," Mr Redding confirmed. "Well done, you three. Although your methods of execution were dangerous, they were effective. The students received your message loud and clear. Those prizes obviously weren't sanctioned by the school, so don't go waving them around."

Lucas was beyond proud of himself. "We knew it would work! I will say, there was no way the demonstration could have ended badly. I had practised dozens of times putting out the naked flame using the glove. I just pretended not to be able to. And Rachael was pretending to be slow to get the fire extinguisher we placed backstage. She could have had any fire out in two seconds."

"You were still lighting matches inside an auditorium full of school kids," Mr Redding said. "I don't think it would have looked good in the nightly news if you had dropped the match onto the wooden stage. I'm just suggesting that, next time, you run your ideas by a teacher."

Angus stared distantly at the chocolate bar on his desk. The last time he had eaten a Caramilk bar was when he was selling them out of his backpack.

"Let's move on to our second-to-last lesson for the semester, which is about business globalisation." Mr Redding handed out booklets with a large picture of the Earth on the front. "Let's say you've started a successful hot dog business here in Australia. Your profit margins are good, and you

251

feel like you've captured as much of the Australian market as possible. What would the next step be for your business? Rachael?"

"Go global?" she suggested, taking a hint from the title of the booklet.

"Yes, absolutely. But 'going global' is not a straightforward process. There are many ways of going global, and you need to decide the best course of action for your business. Angus, what would you call this successful hot dog business?"

Angus looked up from the chocolate bar, wondering why they were talking about hot dogs. "Spicy Chihuahuas."

"Excellent name. Let's say Spicy Chihuahuas wants to go international and start operating in India. What are some different ways for Spicy Chihuahua to start operating in India?"

"They could just open a new store?" Lucas guessed.

"They could start a franchise," Rachael said. "Licence out the name."

"All correct," Mr Redding said. "But operating in other countries can go beyond just selling products in that country. Spicy Chihuahua may want to start operating in India to take advantage of other benefits in that country, such as cheaper manufacturing or tax benefits. If you look at page 3 in your booklets, you'll see a big list of reasons behind globalisation."

"You're recommending we move a business to another country for taxation purposes and lower labour costs?" Angus asked. "Isn't that unethical?"

Mr Redding shook his head. "No, I'm not recommending anything. I'm simply listing why companies do pursue globalisation. And you're right: Ethics should be a major consideration in globalisation. Are your business activities helping or hindering the global society? But is it a black-and-white ethics issue to move a company's operations to take advantage of lower manufacturing and labour costs?"

"Of course it is," Rachael said. "By moving manufacturing overseas, you're taking away potential jobs for workers here."

"To play devil's advocate, is that a problem?" Mr Redding asked. "Yes, you're taking away a job from someone local, but you're giving the job to someone else. As you can imagine, these are tricky conversations, but the business always needs to act for the advantage of the greater society, not just its own interests."

For the first time that semester, Angus did not enjoy the BnE lesson. He stopped listening to Mr Redding's lecture. His mind wandered from thinking about what he was going to eat for lunch, to wondering if imaginary numbers in math had any purpose beyond confusing school kids. He couldn't wait for the lesson to end so he could continue doing nothing productive for the rest of the day.

———

"How was school?" Cathy asked that afternoon. She watched her son pile up peanut butter and fritz between two pieces of bread.

"Fine," Angus replied.

"Are you okay?"

"Yeah. School's just getting hard."

"Academically or socially?

Angus stopped adding pizza-flavoured Shapes to his plate and considered the question. "Neither."

Cathy had received a call from Mrs Campbell the week prior and had been informed about the incident in assembly, as had Lucas's and Rachael's parents. Thomas had talked Cathy out of punishing Angus any further than the school already had. They could see Angus was working very hard, always at his computer or making calls for this or that business project, and the sun safety campaign had just been a lapse of judgement.

"You've only got a week to go until holidays, and then a couple more weeks until graduation." She gave him an empathetic smile. "Keep your eye on the end goal. You're almost there."

Angus sighed. "The end goal is just a piece of paper saying I graduated high school. I have no idea what the goal is after that."

"There's so much you can do after high school," Cathy said. "You could go to university, study a trade, just start working in a low-skills job or even take a gap year. There are some great humanitarian projects you could join overseas."

Angus did appreciate that his parents never pressured him into any career pathway. His plate full of snacks, he picked it up and began toward his bedroom. "I'll just do uni. It's the easiest option and most likely to get me a good job."

He closed the bedroom door behind him and sat down at his desk.

It was mid-September. If he wanted any chance of getting into a choice university degree, he had to start submitting his degree preferences. Between munches of his afternoon tea, he browsed the websites of local universities. He saw the smiling faces of people not much older than himself. He wondered how they'd been able to choose what they wanted to do for the rest of their lives.

His phone vibrated loudly on his desk; the caller ID read Olivia. Angus had sent the invoice to Mrs Campbell for the Inkdas, transferred the $300 Olivia had earned to her bank account, and had even organised Pentastic Importers to ship the Inkdas directly to the school. He didn't know why Olivia was calling.

Angus answered. "Hello?"

"Hi, this is Olivia," she said quickly. "You need to stop giving people my phone number."

"Is Mrs Campbell calling you?" Angus asked. "Just let her know email is preferred, and then I'll deal with her."

"It's not Mrs Campbell. It's all the other schools," Olivia said heatedly. "We didn't agree that you can hand out my mobile number to new customers!"

Angus frowned. "I'm not sure what you mean. I haven't given your number to anyone."

Olivia sighed. "Well, this afternoon I've received about eight calls from different schools requesting pricing for pens."

Angus couldn't believe what he was hearing. He thoughtlessly picked up and bit down on a paper clip sitting next to his plate of Shapes. He spat the metallic object across his desk.

"Are you there?" Olivia asked.

"Sorry. Yes, I'm here. Exactly how many schools have called you?"

"Exactly eight."

"Did you get their email addresses?"

"Yes, but that's not the point. Please don't give my phone number out."

"I promise, I didn't give your number to anyone else," Angus said. "Mrs Campbell must have given the number out. No one else had it."

"Well she must have put it on a billboard somewhere. I really feel like this is beyond what I signed up for. I only kept taking the calls because you were generous to me in the first place—"

Angus cut her off. "I'll pay you for all your troubles, I promise. Can you please email me the names and contacts you've received? I'll take it from there."

Ten minutes and another handful of Arnott's Shapes later, Angus stared at a new email from Olivia in disbelief. Before him were eight email addresses and phone numbers of staff from eight different schools across the state. He had no idea how they found out about the Inkdas or why they were all suddenly so interested in buying pens. Another email came through from Olivia with two more contacts.

Hands shaking, he called Lucas and skipped the salutations. "I've got ten schools wanting quotes for Inkdas."

Lucas also skipped the greetings. "No you don't."

"I swear—they're right in front of me. All these schools have been ringing Olivia."

"Where did you advertise?"

"I haven't done a thing!" Angus squeaked. "Did Rachael do something?"

"It was the conference on Friday," Rachael said after being

added into the conference call.

"What conference?" Angus asked.

"The school leadership conference for all the private schools in the state," Rachael explained. "Brooke went along with the rest of the prefects. My guess is Mrs Campbell must have gone to supervise and told the other schools about the pens."

Angus laughed nervously, imagining Mrs Campbell talking to the other teachers, selling his product for him. Another email popped up with two more email addresses.

"Two more!" he exclaimed. "What do I do?"

"What do you mean? You send them an email with the pricing pamphlet," Lucas said.

Angus felt overwhelmed. "But what if they all want to buy pens?"

"Then you tell the pen supplier how many to order and where to send—" Lucas paused. "You should be telling *us* what to do. This is your business!"

Angus couldn't think straight. "I need to go for a walk. I'll let you know my decision tomorrow."

"Wait, decision for what?" Lucas asked.

"Whether to keep the business going."

"Why wouldn't you keep the business going?" Lucas asked. "This is all you've talked about for months! I'm sitting here ready to start selling pens and get my thirty-three percent ownership of the company!"

"Sorry, I'll see you both tomorrow. Have a good night."

He hung up the call and looked outside. There was only about half an hour left until sunset. He went to the kitchen where his dad sat at the bench with a coffee, talking to his mum as she prepared dinner.

"Is it all right if I walk to the shops?" Angus asked.

"Dinner is only about half an hour away," Cathy said. "Can't you wait until after we've eaten?"

"I really just need to take a breather. School is getting to me."

"Emotionally or physically?" Tom asked.

"Both," Angus answered. With their permission, he left the house and walked to the shopping centre. By the time he arrived, the sun was only a glimpse over the horizon. Busy people in creased clothing were purchasing dinner ingredients from the supermarket. Tired mothers with children accelerated through the shopping centre to buy rolls from the bakery. Several stores were already shuttered, but the larger stores were still a hive of activity.

Quite habitually, Angus entered Moving Stationery and walked to the pen aisle. He stood in front of the pen display with his hands in his pockets. He didn't know why he felt so reluctant to continue the business. With a few clicks he could send quotes to the schools and potentially make thousands of dollars. Would that make him "officially" a pen salesman? He didn't know if he wanted to be a pen salesman for the rest of his life.

He imagined where the Inkdas would sit in the pen display. Would seeing his pens on the shelf make him feel satisfied?

A bright-purple pen caught his eye. He picked it up and wrote *the end of the world* on the tester paper. The pen wrote in a thick, glossy, vibrant-purple ink.

258

"Did you need a hand?" a man asked.

Angus was about to instinctively say "No, thank you", but turned to see a man in a Moving Stationery uniform who appeared much older than the usual worker.

"Are you the manager?" Angus asked confidently.

"I am the manager," the man said with a smile. "Did you have any questions?"

"How many pens do you sell each day?"

That was not a question the manager was asked often. "Heaps. Why's that?"

"It's for a school project," Angus said. He had learned people generally liked to help kids if a question was for a school project. "Do pens have a big profit margin?"

The manager laughed. "I don't know if I can tell you that much, company policies and all, but selling stationery is important for the business's bottom line."

"I'm actually a pen salesman," Angus blurted out in a shaky voice. He watched for the manager's response.

The manager frowned. "I thought you said you were a student."

"I'm both, I guess."

The manager began walking away. "That's nice. If you need a hand with your selection, I'll send someone to give you assistance."

Angus smiled as he left the store. It was clear to him there was no way he could exist as both a student and a business owner. No one took him seriously. He walked outside the shopping centre and along the exterior on his way home. A man stood outside a closed bank in a dirty jacket. He was staring off into the distance with a coffee cup at his feet. Angus had never given money to a homeless man. His dad had taught him it was better to offer to buy them a meal or whatever they needed rather than just give them money.

At that moment, Angus felt sorrier for himself more than anyone else.

"Hey, you!" a voice called behind him as he walked on. "Hey, Andrew!"

Hearing a name similar to his own, Angus turned around to see a man in a neatly pressed suit waving at him from afar. It was Luke Pilcher, the investor. Pilcher hurried down the line of shops to meet Angus, waving at him the whole way. He was wearing a suit and a large coat.

Angus stood and waited for the man to reach him.

The homeless man looked upon the scene with a puzzled expression before picking up his cup and moving away.

"Andrew!" Pilcher said, shaking the boy's hand.

"Angus."

"Ah, Angus. That's right. How are you going?"

"Fine, thanks. I'm on my way—"

"You'll be happy to know I purchased a new business just this past week! It's a little stationery franchise called Letters. I'm sure you've heard of it."

That was surprising news to Angus, especially after the strong position Pilcher had given about stationery being worthless because of technology. Letters was Moving Stationery's main local competitor in the stationery and office supplies market.

"That's great," Angus said, slowly inching away. "I really

need to go—"

"My investment fund got them incredibly cheap. They were pretty much bankrupt, but that's how business goes. It was essentially a charitable act on my end." Pilcher laughed. "How is your little business coming along?"

Angus stopped moving away. He turned back to face the man. "My 'little' business has had a dozen sales enquiries from large corporations just this afternoon."

"Oh...really?" Pilcher asked in surprise. "So it's growing, then?"

"Yes. Yes, it is growing. And I predict it's going to begin growing quickly, as well. We're forecasting quite a decent profit this quarter."

"Well, that's good to hear. If you want to discuss getting stocked in Letters, I can—"

"Nah, I'm good for the moment. Thanks for the offer." Angus forced a smile.

Pilcher's smile all but disappeared. "That naivety is going to stunt your business's growth. I am offering you a hand of help. You should consider taking it, Angus."

"You've been more help than you realise."

Pilcher nodded his head and walked away muttering to himself, hands deep in his pockets.

Angus walked home with his head held high. He had found a new purpose: Regardless of who was willing to help him, he would prove to the world that he *could* run a student's company and turn out a better man than Luke Pilcher, without the years of experience.

It was just the company part he had to finalise.

SMART NOT HARD

"We're doing it," Angus whispered to Lucas the next morning as they waited for Mr Fletcher to start homeroom.

"Nice! What are we doing?" Lucas asked.

"We're gonna grow the business. We'll sell directly to schools and businesses and get stocked in retailers like Moving Stationery."

Lucas laughed at his friend's excitement. "I knew you weren't going to just walk away."

"Are you on board?"

"You bet I am," Lucas said quietly. "We'll make a killing, and then I won't have to work while I do my first years of uni."

Rachael entered the classroom quickly with a pile of books. She sat down next to Brooke and immediately continued with extension questions in her maths book.

Angus almost skipped over to her desk. "We're doing the business!" he whispered.

"Good for you two," Rachael said without pausing.

Angus sensed something was amiss. "Can you still help us?"

"Nope," Rachael said bluntly. "Sorry."

Angus looked to Brooke, checking with her if he had done something wrong. Brooke nodded her head sadly in Rachael's direction and mouthed, *D.*

"You got another D in maths?" Angus asked gently.

"Angus, I really don't have time to talk."

"Maybe I could help you get your maths grades up in exchange for your help with—"

Rachael looked up from her page. "Please, just let me be. Thank you, but I don't need your help. I just need to focus."

Angus went back to his seat without another word. The rest of the class waiting in the classroom pretended not to have heard the exchange.

"I guess it's just you and me," Lucas said quietly.

Angus wasn't listening.

"So, what's the next step?" Lucas asked. "Are we going to set up an office area or something?"

Angus got up from his chair and walked back to Rachael. "As part owner of the business, we really need your help."

Rachael couldn't believe his persistence. She put down her pen and locked eyes with him. "Angus, I put in my applications for university last week. I need an ATAR of at least 90 to get into my courses. Helping you with your business is not going to give me ATAR points. I hope you and Lucas succeed with the Inkdas, but from now on, I'm focusing on school-work."

Angus didn't want to exasperate the girl any further, so he returned to his seat. He had envisioned the three of them running the business together.

"Why is it crucial that Rachael helps us?" Lucas asked quietly. "I know she's smart, but I'm sure between the two of us we could make the business work."

"Maybe you're right," Angus said. "It's just...that's how I envisioned Inkdas working. You, me and Rachael working together to sell pens, complementing each other's strengths and weaknesses and all that."

A grin crossed Lucas's face. "You know, you could just ask her out."

Angus looked at his friend with contempt. "You're kidding."

Lucas shrugged. "You really seem to always want her around."

Angus did want to have Rachael around, but not once—well, not twice—did it occur to Angus that he'd like to go out with Rachael. He was looking for a business partnership, not a romantic one.

"Getting a girlfriend is for later," Angus said. "Not for when I'm starting a business and finishing Year 12."

"You've finally decided to try to finish Year 12 strong?" Lucas stirred.

Angus took a moment to compose his thoughts. "I think finishing Year 12 with good grades might be helpful."

After recess, a few of the Year 12s had a free lesson in the library. Angus looked over at Rachael. She sat alone at one of the desks in the middle of the study area, doing yet more maths questions. Angus cautiously walked over and sat down in the empty seat next to her. He opened his laptop and typed aimlessly in an empty document. Rachael gave him a look that made him be quieter.

"You're working hard." Angus tapped lightly on his keyboard.

"Thanks," Rachael mumbled. She was already struggling to focus on her work, even before Angus joined her.

"That wasn't a compliment," he said.

"I really don't appreciate snide comments."

"Sorry, wasn't aiming for snide. I'm just trying to help."

"I don't need help."

"I thought the same thing."

Rachael put her pen down and stretched out. She needed a break from the numbers. Every spare moment in the past twenty-four hours had been spent answering math question after math question, and she didn't feel any smarter.

"What did you get on Monday's math test?" she asked.

"B."

"How did you get a B and I got another D?" Rachael asked. "I don't mean that in an offensive way. You're smart."

"I've been wondering the exact same thing," Angus said empathetically.

Rachael tried to swallow her pride. For her whole life, she had never needed to ask anyone's help with her schoolwork. She normally just sat down at her books and worked at question after question until it eventually made sense.

She took a deep breath in and slowly asked, "What's your advice?"

"For what?"

"For maths. You said you wanted to help me."

Angus didn't think Rachael would actually take him up on the offer. He closed his laptop. "Well, uh...you know how you keep doing more and more maths questions?"

"Yeah?"

"Maybe stop."

"Stop doing the maths questions? How am I meant to learn if I don't do the maths questions?"

"Smart, not hard," Angus said.

Rachael looked at him blankly.

"That means instead of worrying about getting fifty questions done a day, just focus on doing, say, five questions, but understand completely what the questions are asking," Angus said. "I've found that in maths, if I understand the basic concepts, I can apply them to most of the problems."

"That's not the problem. I understand the mathematics," Rachael said. She held up her maths exercise book; it was covered in worked-out answers, each neater than the last. "It's all correct and easy when I do the questions on my own time."

"Then what do you think the problem is?"

"I don't know," Rachael said quietly. "Every time I do a test or exam, I second-guess myself. I know the correct answers in my head but struggle to write them down correctly."

"That's just self-doubt."

"*Just* self-doubt?" Rachael said. "Well, if that's what it is, my stupid self-doubt has made me fail two maths tests this term alone. If I do the same on my end-of-year exam, I'll fail the whole subject."

Angus honestly had no idea how to help his friend. He wasn't a psychologist or counsellor. All he knew was how to not care about his schoolwork enough to not doubt his own abilities.

"What's the worst that could happen?" he asked. "What's the worst that could happen if you failed maths?"

"I wouldn't get into uni." The thought caused her throat to catch.

"And what's the worst that could happen if you don't get into uni?"

"I'll get a bad job."

"So, the worst thing that could happen if you fail all of maths is you get a job?"

"A bad job," Rachael corrected.

"And what's the worst job you can think of?"

"Working in a child care centre."

Angus smiled. "I'm sure working in a child care centre isn't that bad. Don't you get free snacks and a sleep?"

"No one expects to find me working in a child care centre," Rachael said. "Everyone expects me to be an engineer or a scientist or accountant. I don't want to let everyone down."

"Look, in my opinion as a certified therapist, you need to ignore this 'everyone'—whoever they are—and follow the path that *you* want to follow."

"I can't follow the path I want to follow if I fail Year 12."

"It sucks to fail a test. Trust me, I know. When I was younger, I would test how long my pet fish could last above water. I always failed to resuscitate them in time."

Rachael smirked.

"Don't let failure be the time to give up," Angus continued. "Everyone fails at something at some point. It's the people who know failure is good, that it's something to learn from, who succeed. I read that in a magazine at a ukulele festival."

Rachael, despite Angus's rambling way of giving advice, understood what he was trying to say. "I'm sorry for this morning."

"All good." Angus smiled.

"Maybe I can help you and Lucas out part-time after I graduate."

"Yeah, maybe." Angus shrugged. "Did you hear what I said this morning? You're a part owner in the business, if you want to be."

Rachael had heard him say that, but had ignored it. "What does that mean?"

"That means if the business becomes profitable, you'll get a third of the profits."

"You want to give me a third of the business?"

"If you want to help out, I do."

"Why?" Rachael asked.

"It's payment where payment is due."

Rachael considered it for a moment, but eventually shook her head. "Thanks for the offer, but no thanks. I still see my future as attending uni, not as a pen salesman."

Angus nodded. "Same."

"Then why are you trying to build up the business?"

Angus looked around to see if anyone was eavesdropping. He leaned in and quietly told her his plan for the business in a single sentence.

It sounded to Rachael like a great idea, which made the decision making even more difficult. "I'll help you one afternoon a week."

"Really?" Angus sat up straight.

Rachael nodded. "But if I'm worried about my grades, I'm out."

"That's fair."

"And in the study week before exams, I'm not available."

"I'm sure we can work with that."

"And if I have an assignment due the next day, I'm not available."

Angus held up a hand. "Rachael, you'll need to talk to our head of finance if you need any more days off."

"Who's head of finance?"

"You are."

There was no time to be idle. As soon as Angus got home that evening, he forwarded the leads email to Lucas.

They spent the last week and a half before the mid-semester break preparing business operations and calling the schools who had requested information. Angus set up a shared spreadsheet so they could keep track of which leads had been contacted.

"Hello, this is Northridge College. Amanda speaking. How may I direct your call?"

Lucas sat on the edge of his bed on the Thursday evening before the last day of the semester. He put on his salesman voice. It was slightly higher-pitched than his normal voice, but very friendly. "Good afternoon, Amanda. This is Lucas from Inkdas. I'm just returning a call from *Richard Jones*. Can I please be put through to him, please?"

"One moment."

Lucas marked Richard Jones in orange on the spreadsheet, indicating he had contacted the prospective customer.

"Hello, this is Richard," the man on the line answered.

Lucas cleared his throat and spoke in an even higher pitch. "Good afternoon, Richard. This is Lucas from Inkdas returning your call. How are you this afternoon?"

"I'm doing very well, thank you," the man said, matching Lucas's joyful demeanour. "Thank you very much for calling back."

"Absolutely. My pleasure!" Lucas replied. "Now, I understand you were interested in getting a quote for an order of our pens?"

"Yes, that's right," Richard Jones said. "I was at a school conference a couple of weeks ago, and one of my friends, Rosalyn Campbell, couldn't stop raving about these pens she had ordered. She practically told everyone she met."

"Oh, that is just too kind of her to say." Lucas worked hard to keep his voice from squeaking. "Yes, Inkdas are selling and selling fast. How about as a next step, I send you some free samples? I'll include a price list in the package, and as soon as you're ready to order, give me a ring, and we'll get as many pens as you need as fast as we can."

Richard Jones sounded over the moon at the good service. Lucas marked the entry for Northridge College as yellow, signifying the client needed to be sent a sample package, and ended the call.

His phone immediately rang again. It was Angus.

"How many did St Andrew's order?"

"Just a thousand," Lucas said proudly, looking at the box coloured green in the shared spreadsheet for St Andrew Primary School.

"A thousand?" Angus replied. "How in the world did you pull that off?"

"Like I said, this selling thing is easy!" Lucas exclaimed. "To be honest, I almost verbatim used a sales script off the internet. But in more important news, I now own fifteen percent of Inkdas!"

"Yes, yes. Well done." Angus laughed. "Have you called Newton Secondary yet?"

Lucas tutted. "Dude, I've was talking to St Andrews for half an hour completing their order. What's the rush?"

"I promised Newton Secondary we would call them tonight," Angus replied. "We need Inkda Pens to be known for our impeccable customer service. Please just remember to mark them orange when you call them."

"Yes, sir!" Lucas replied haughtily. "I expect to be awarded employee of the month. Catch ya tomorrow."

Angus, still in his uniform at his bedroom desk, scrolled through the list of twenty schools—their twenty leads—while he neglected an English report that was due the next day. He couldn't wait for all the time they would have during the mid-semester break to work on the business.

So far, every lead they had contacted had accepted free samples, which Angus expected, because he knew everyone liked free stuff. What he hadn't expected was that every single school so far had ordered pens. The smallest order was just fifty pens. The largest order was now a thousand pens. In just over a week, they had sold four thousand pens. Rachael had over $3,000 in the bank account she had set up for the business, with more payments arriving every couple of days. Angus already considered the business a success, but certainly wasn't going to stop this soon.

Seeing a few schools marked green on the spreadsheet, Angus phoned Pentastic Importers.

"Hello," Doug Fox said gruffly.

"Hey, this is Angus."

There was a moment of silence on the line. "And?"

"This is Angus? I buy pens from you?"

"All of my customers buy pens from me."

"Yes, of course. My brand is the Inkda pens."

Angus heard Doug sigh. "I know who you are, Angus. What do you want?"

Angus prepared himself for what felt like a momentous occasion. This would be the first order he was going to place that would give him excess stock of his product. All his previous orders had been direct-order fulfilments. "I would like to order ten thousand pens, please."

"Is that all for today?" Doug asked. "A fifty-percent deposit needs to be made before the order is processed."

"Well, before I transfer the money, I was wondering if there was a better price you could do on the pens, since it's a big order."

Angus heard Doug laugh for the first time. "It will be

$5,000 for ten thousand pens, plus costs for shipping and handling."

"No discount at all?"

"I'll throw in a bonus pen. That's fifty cents worth of product for you which I can't tax deduct, but probably will anyway."

Angus felt like he had no choice in the matter, and so he placed the order and forwarded the invoice to Rachael over email. Making the orders wasn't the difficult part he had to consider; it was the distribution.

Currently, Pentastic Importers was adding a handling fee and shipping the pens directly to the schools, but Angus knew it would be cheaper to distribute themselves. He knew the day had come—much sooner than he had expected—to tell his parents about the business. It felt like a heavy, dirty burden.

He found his parents sitting in the sun room. His dad had just arrived home from work and was stretched out on the chaise lounge in his dark-blue pants and high-vis collared shirt. His mum was reading on her tablet computer.

"Good afternoon, Angus," Tom said, sitting up as his son entered the room.

Angus slumped down in an armchair. "Hey, how was work?"

"Fine, fine. How was school?"

"Fine, fine." Angus stared at the carpet.

Cathy sensed an announcement was coming. She turned off her tablet.

Angus didn't know where to start, or where to go. "Do you

both remember that pens assignment I was working on?"

"That one where we went to that shady little store in the city?" Cathy asked.

"Yes, that one. Well, it wasn't actually a project for school. It was a personal assignment."

His parents exchanged very concerned glances.

"Don't freak out," Angus said quickly. "I promise it hasn't affected my school grades, but I've started a business."

"What sort of business?" Tom asked.

"Selling drugs," Angus said dryly.

"What?!" Cathy exclaimed.

"That was a joke. I'm selling pens," Angus added quickly. "I've started a business selling pens."

"As in...writing stationery?" Cathy asked.

He nodded. Both of his parents' faces contorted with confusion.

Tom leaned back in his chair. "Sounds interesting. Who will you be selling them to?"

"Well, we've already started selling them."

"How many?" Tom asked.

"A couple of thousand," Angus said as casually as he could.

"A couple of thousand!" Tom exclaimed. "Who in the world needs a couple of thousand pens?"

"It wasn't all to one person. We've sold to a number of businesses so far," Angus explained. He didn't want them to know it was all schools. That would raise questions about secrecy that he didn't want to answer until after he had graduated.

"Who's 'we'?" Cathy asked uncertainly.

274

"Do you remember when Lucas, Rachael and Olivia came over? All of them." He took an Inkda from his pocket and handed it to his mum.

Cathy looked the pen over. "You started a whole business, you and your friends, and you've sold thousands of them, and presumably made..."

"Thousands of dollars," Angus finished her sentence.

"You're meant to be focusing on Year 12," Cathy said.

"My grades have not dropped." Angus said, trying to stay as chipper as he could through the interrogation.

"That's quite impressive," Tom concluded.

"Hang on," Cathy said. "I'm not sure we're ready to support this. Besides the fact that you've lied to us, this does not seem like a good use of your time. You should be focusing on Year 12."

"My grades have not dropped," Angus repeated quietly.

"They might not have dropped yet, but they still might," Cathy said. "Are you willing to risk receiving a high ATAR on this business?"

"I feel like this is what I should do at the moment." Though Angus suddenly felt very unsure about what he was doing.

Cathy looked at her husband.

Tom shrugged back. "I think it's amazing what he's done."

"I think it's amazing, too," Cathy said softly, seeing the eagerness in her son's eyes for their approval.

Relief washed over Angus. He had been keeping it a secret for so many months, he had really started to believe that as soon as people knew, he would be whisked away to prison with a life sentence. "Thanks. It's taken a lot of work."

"What does Inkda mean?" Tom asked.

Angus proudly gave an edited narrative of how he started the business. He explained how the idea came to him as a result of a bet with Lucas; how he market-tested the product with fellow students; how he made the first sale with Olivia's help as a saleswoman to a "local" school principal; how he and his fellow Business and Enterprise classmates were using their newfound skills to create a whole business from scratch. He didn't mention that if Mrs Campbell found out about the business they would most likely be expelled, and that, ironically, it had been her who had sparked the word-of-mouth flame that had enabled the business to grow quicker than Angus's wildest dreams. His parents listened to the story with amazement at their son's audacity.

"...and so now I have about four schools whose orders need to be fulfilled next week, and so I was wondering if, Dad, you could take me in your pickup to get about 5,000 pens from that shady pen shop in the city."

Tom looked to Cathy for permission.

Cathy looked at her son, standing taller than her by almost a foot.

She sighed. "You've got your father's 'I'll just do it' spirit."

"Well if this all goes belly-up, I guess we can blame Dad." Angus smiled.

"Works for me," Cathy said.

Tom frowned. "I'm just the delivery driver, bosses."

THE GLORY DAYS

The teachers had told the Year 12s to use their final two weeks of holidays wisely by finishing assignments and studying for the final exams. Angus had initially created a plan to spend half of each day studying, and the other half working on the business. It was Wednesday of the first week, and his plan was yet to really be put into practice. It was all business from 8am until 8pm.

Angus's brother's old bedroom was officially the home of the pen company for however long their landlords—Angus's parents—allowed them to occupy the space. They set up some foldout tables and Angus put up a whiteboard he had purchased on Gumtree. At the end of every day, Angus would make sure everything in the office was neat and tidy, ready for the next day.

"Look at us," Lucas exclaimed. "Just like the glory days!"

"What are these 'glory days' you're referring to?" Angus asked.

"Back when we were planning our movie theatre business. Don't you remember how young and naïve we were?"

"We are still young and *very* naïve," Rachael said. She had open the last completed order form on her laptop. "Lucas, you've just written '100'. One hundred of what? One hundred pens or one hundred boxes?"

Lucas reached over the table for another handful from the bag of chips. "Who's the order for?"

Rachael read the top of the form. "You've written 'That school near the KFC down south'."

"They wanted a hundred boxes," Lucas said.

"Okay, that's fine, but *who* wants a hundred boxes?" Rachael asked, rewriting the order form. "Which school is near a KFC down south?"

"I think he's talking about Sacred Heart," Angus said, busy reading marketing tips from a shady-looking marketing website. Rachael adjusted the form accordingly and moved the file into the folder labelled *Orders*.

Apart from Lucas's distractedness when it came to filling out forms, the business ran a tidy operation.

It only took a couple of days for Rachael to become addicted to her role as head of finance, and she thrived in it. Angus was very relieved that she took the finance role whole-heartedly, because he didn't know how he would have managed without her. She made sure the correct money was coming in, and the correct money was going out to their supplier. She always brought her homework with her to Angus's house, intending to complete it during spare moments, but there were never spare moments. Angus was constantly coming up with new leads or another idea for marketing the Inkdas.

Lucas, surprising even himself, turned out to be a star salesman. He spent hours researching new sales scripts to try on cold calls, and easily sold enough pens in those first weeks to make him a full partner with the other two. He was honest in his motives—to make money—and had no shame in expressing it.

"Did you know that after 10pm, most businesses have to pay their employees time-and-a-half?" Lucas asked.

"You're not an employee," Angus looked at the time. "And it's not ten yet."

"Yes, but I'm just giving a forewarning that if I need to stay past ten, we'll need to recalculate our sipens."

"Our earnings are called *stipends*, not sipens," Angus said as he scrolled through websites on his laptop.

"I can't stay past ten," Rachael said. "I need to be in bed by 10:30 at the latest or I feel like trash the next morning."

"So does Lucas," Angus said. "But I feel like he would rather get paid an extra five dollars than get a good night's sleep."

"Not true," Lucas said. "I think sleep is vitally important for my health and well-being. And that is why I'm suggesting a bigger stipend after ten to discourage us being up that late."

Angus looked up from the screen. "Well, I was actually thinking of suggesting we pay triple stipend after ten. Would that be okay with you?"

Lucas shifted excitedly in his seat. "That's fine with me. I'll sleep in!"

"How much sugar have you eaten?" Angus asked, looking

at the half-empty bag of M&Ms sitting on the table in front of his friend.

"My role in this business isn't to count things."

"Speaking of counting," Angus said. "Rachael, how many schools have we sold to so far?"

Rachael opened her personal spreadsheet that she didn't allow either boy to touch. "We've sold pens to eleven schools, and have sent samples off to a further twenty."

Angus nodded. "I've just done some research. There are about a hundred independent schools in the state and around a thousand independent schools in the country. That's how many cold calls and sales we need to make."

"What about the government schools?" Rachael asked.

Angus laughed. "Including government schools, we'd be looking at close to ten thousand schools across the country. Even I'll admit that's a lot of cold calls to make."

"Well, we've got time," Lucas said. "As soon as Year 12 is done, we can just cold call all day, every day until we reach them all."

Even if Angus did want to take his time, the thought of making that many calls, even between the three of them, made him feel uneasy. He opened a bookmark in his web browser and turned the laptop around.

Lucas didn't understand why he was being shown the homepage of Moving Stationery's website.

"We need these people," Angus said.

"What do you mean?" Rachael asked.

"I mean Moving Stationery needs to be our next target. If we can get our pens on the shelves there, we've made it.

And when we've made it there, there will be no more need to cold call schools. No need to decide how much of a stipend we get if we work late. No need to argue whether snacks should come out of Lucas's stipend."

Lucas yanked his hand out of the bag of M&Ms. "No one was suggesting that."

"If we can stock Inkdas in Moving Stationery and as many other retailers as we can, then nothing will be able to stop our growth, and then those ten thousand schools will be calling us for orders!"

"I think your enthusiasm is great," Rachael said, "but Moving Stationery is very big. What if we try selling to Letters first? I think they might be easier to get into."

"Nope," Angus said. "We're not supplying to Letters."

"Why not?" Lucas asked. "I thought you said we should be stocked everywhere? Letters is a pretty big franchise."

Angus looked back down at his laptop. "They're not that big, and I don't think they'd be a good fit for the brand."

Lucas laughed nervously. "We're a pen brand. Letters sells pens. How would they not be a 'good fit'?"

"I don't mean to create conflict," Rachael said, "but I'm pretty sure we're all equal partners in this business. You can't just decide we are or are not going to do something and not give an explanation."

"Luke Pilcher owns Letters," Angus said.

Rachael looked to Lucas for guidance on who this person was.

"He was the investor that turned Angus away," Lucas explained.

"So, this is a personal grudge?" Rachael asked.

"No, it's not a personal grudge," Angus said firmly. "Look, I know I don't have the final say anymore, but please just trust me on this. Getting stocked in Letters is a bad idea."

"It sounds like a personal grudge," Lucas said.

"I promise," Angus said slowly, "that if and when we get stocked in Moving Stationery, I'll be open to discussing getting stocked in Letters."

"So, we're trying to eat the main course before sampling the entrée," Lucas said. "You know, you can learn a lot by starting with the entrée at a restaurant. You can learn about the quality of the main course and dessert."

"What's the dessert in this scenario?" Rachael asked.

"Churros," Lucas said. "Dessert is always churros in every scenario. Is anyone else hungry?"

Rachael sighed. She watched Angus avoid their eye contact as he pretended to be engrossed in his computer. "Fine. I'm trusting you, Angus, that you have some scheme up your sleeve and it's not just a personal grudge against this investor. I vote let's start with the main course."

"Burgers!" Lucas said. "Wait, have we moved onto discussing lunch or are we still talking about the business?"

———

"I'm sorry, you'll need to contact our head office," the lady at the Moving Stationery support centre said.

"I'm sorry, you'll need to contact one of our stationery buyers," the receptionist at the Moving Stationery head office said.

"Could you please transfer me to one of your buyers,

please?" Angus asked. Lucas had advised him that saying "please" excessively helped in negotiations.

"Why don't I get your contact details and pass them on?" the receptionist suggested. "If the buyers are interested, they'll contact you."

Angus knew that would go nowhere. "There's not even an email address I can contact directly?"

"No, sorry," the lady said. "Is there anything else I can help you with today?"

"No, that will be fine. Sorry, what was your name?"

"Linda."

"Thank you, Linda. Have a good afternoon."

Angus handed the phone to Lucas and instructed him on what to say and how to say it. Ten minutes later, they called the head office again.

"Moving Stationery, this is Linda speaking. How may I help you?" the receptionist asked cheerfully.

"Hey Linda," Lucas said with a big sigh, as if making the phone call was putting him out immensely. "This is Lucas. Can you put me through to James in buying, please?"

Lucas held the phone away from his mouth and yelled, "Yes! I'm calling James now... It doesn't need to be James? Anyone from buying? Okay... No, they're still putting me through. Please tell the customer to wait a moment! I will be less than thirty seconds. The lovely receptionist is putting me through now!" He held the phone back to his mouth. "Anyone from buying would be fine. Thanks, Linda."

Linda apparently felt it was easier to comply and let her colleagues deal with whoever was on the phone. "Hold one moment."

Lucas excitedly pointed at the mobile. "They're putting me through."

"Pass the phone back," Angus said.

"I can do it."

"No, let me do it!" Angus whispered angrily.

"Stop fighting," Rachael whispered. "Lucas, let Angus do it."

"I'm the best salesman. Why does Angus get to do it?" Lucas complained.

"Because this plan is his idea. If anyone is to ruin the pitch, let it be him."

"Hello, this is Gabby," the lady on the line said.

Lucas begrudgingly passed the phone back to Angus, who put on a big smile. "Hello Gabby, this is Angus from Inkda. How are you doing this afternoon?"

"I'm good thank you, Angus. How are you?" Gabby replied.

"Fine, fine. Thank you for asking, Gabby," Angus said. There was a long pause.

"I'm sorry, I didn't catch where you're from," Gabby said.

"Inkda Pens? We are a local pen brand. We're new in the industry, but you might have seen our products out in the wild. Since releasing our first pen, we've been overwhelmed with demand."

Gabby paused. "No, I don't think I have heard of you. What can I do for you today?"

"Well," Angus started, "to be quite frank and honest and transparent, we're looking for new distribution stations—"

"Channels," Rachael whispered.

Angus coughed. "Distribution channels! Sorry, I must

have television on the mind." He gave a forced cackle of laughter that was met by silence. "We are seeking new distribution channels, and we have identified Moving Stationery as a fantastic outlet for our product."

"Okay," Gabby said. "Please mail some samples, product information, pricing and contact details, and we'll get back to you if we're interested in placing an order."

Angus was not expecting it to be that easy. He was prepared to argue for hours that they were a legitimate business. He wrote down the postal address he was given. "And you'll let me know soonish if you're interested?"

"Unfortunately it's impossible to give a timeline, but we will contact you if we're interested. I hope you have a great afternoon—"

"Before you go," Angus interjected, "what are the factors that Moving Stationery uses when deciding on a new product?"

Rachael shook her head in disbelief that he had asked such an amateur-sounding question.

"It's a whole lot of things," Gabby said. "It's availability of shelf space, customer demand, the brand's marketing power, product price."

Angus thanked the buyer and ended the call. His hopes were dashed. "She wants to see that we have marketing power."

"What's marketing power?" Lucas asked.

"I think it's having the money to spend on marketing," Rachael said. She made a stark realisation before the boys did. "That's the end of that pursuit."

"What do you mean?" Lucas asked. "Surely we can start spending money on marketing? Don't we have a few thousand dollars in the bank?"

"We don't want the school to know that we're behind this company, because we could get expelled," Rachael explained. "In order to have 'marketing power', we would need everyone to know that we're the ones behind Inkdas."

"Not necessarily," Angus said. "You don't see founders of companies being put up on billboards next to their products. You see the product and the brand name. We can spend money on TV, billboards and social media advertising."

"I've already looked at the cost of advertising, and it's very, very expensive," Rachael said. "One billboard alone costs at least five thousand dollars. The only marketing we can afford is cold calling, free social media, word of mouth and publicity. And the only way we can get free publicity is if we, the owners, have a good story to tell."

"We'll just use Olivia again," Angus said. "She can be the face of the company."

"What's Olivia's story?" Rachael challenged.

"Beautiful actress makes thousands selling pens," Lucas suggested.

Rachael looked at her classmates. She hadn't had a decent conversation with either of them before the start of the semester, and here she was conspiring with them as if they had been colleagues together in this business for years. She knew what the solution was, but it didn't sit well. "We are the story. Outing ourselves as the owners of Inkdas is the only story that's going to get us even a hint of publicity."

286

Angus stared into space, reading the invisible title from a newspaper article. "High school students create company and make thousands."

"That's too long of a title," Lucas grumbled. He had come to the same realisation as Rachael. "It would most likely be 'Three students expelled in capitalism crackdown'."

That did not help Rachael's anxiety. She started packing up her laptop. "I can't do it. I'm out."

"What?!" Angus exclaimed.

"If it's the business or the grades, I need to choose grades. I'm sorry," Rachael said sadly. She felt bad that she had led the boys on.

Lucas watched Rachael begin to pack up and wondered what would happen if he stayed. "I'm sorry, Angus, but I'm with Rachael," he said softly. "If it's a choice between publicity and finishing the business... I need the grades for university. I forfeit my ownership."

"Everyone just...wait," Angus said. He took a deep breath in while trying to quickly think of a solution. "No one is forfeiting their ownership. I get it—you're both worried about getting bad grades."

"We're worried about getting expelled," Rachael said. She reluctantly took a box of Inkdas she had in her bag and placed them in the middle of the table.

Angus's biggest nightmare—an even worse one than being expelled—was being realised. He watched the company crumbling before him. "How can you leave after all the work we've done?"

"I don't want to leave," Lucas said. "But...it's just really

287

bad timing, mate."

Angus shook his head. "I know it's because there's a million things going through my head right now, and maybe I'm going through a second bout of puberty that's making me emotional, but to be honest with you both, this feels like a betrayal or something."

Lucas gave an uneasy laugh. "Isn't that a bit melodramatic?"

Angus bit into his thumbnail.

There was a long silence.

"I'm not going to die If I get expelled," Angus said to himself. "I'll have this business to fall back on."

He looked up at his friends and could see neither of them were going to change their minds. He clearly had no choice but to push on alone.

"I'll do it by myself," Angus said. "I can do it all by myself."

That offended Rachael. She put her laptop into its bag and stood up to leave. "I'll email you my spreadsheets when I get home."

Angus just nodded.

"I'll email you the receipts from yesterday's lunch for reimbursement," Lucas said solemnly. "I also have receipts for snacks from... Never mind. I'll cover them."

PUBLICITY

Angus protected his hands in the front pocket of his hoodie; the cold morning winds seemed extra crisp as they blew through the city streets. It didn't feel like summer. He was walking across town from the bus stop to the offices of the state newspaper, *The Vine*.

As he walked, he wondered how his life would change once he went public. Would people recognise him on the street? Would he be ridiculed or praised? Was he being naïve in assuming that he could call himself a success? Would a journalist even take his story?

The receptionist at the front desk of *The Vine* looked up at Angus with the same expression he imagined cleaners had on entering a high school bathroom.

"How can I help you?"

"Hello, my name's Angus," he said calmly. "I've got a story."

"Is that right? What story is that?"

"Are you a journalist?"

"No, but I pass the messages on to the journalists."

Angus was quite tired of receptionists doing their jobs correctly and keeping riff-raff like himself out of businesses. "Would it be possible to speak to a journalist, please? It's a very important—but also highly confidential—story that I would prefer to tell only to a journalist. Would you like a free pen?" He placed an Inkda on the counter and stepped back. He was ready to wait.

The receptionist stared at Angus for a moment, then picked up the phone. "Hello, Gary. There's a lad here who would like to speak to a journo. He says it's a highly confidential story. Is there anyone you could send to the front desk? Thank you."

Within a minute, a middle-aged man came to the reception desk. The man's shirt was coming untucked, his sleeves were rolled up and his tie was loose. Given Angus was the only one in the area, the man made a beeline for him.

They shook hands. "Morning. Gary Wright, supervising editor. What was your name?"

"Angus Newton, Year 12 student and entrepreneur," he replied quietly but confidently.

Gary raised his eyebrows and smiled. "Entrepreneur? That's interesting. I'm told you have a potentially confidential story? Follow me."

Gary led Angus to a meeting room constructed of transparent glass walls looking into the main desk bullpen.

"My story is regarding my entrepreneurship," Angus began. He'd rehearsed what he was going to say on the bus. He produced an Inkda from his pocket and handed it to the journalist. "I am the owner and founder of the Inkda Pen company. I founded it all by myself, from scratch, learning everything I know from my Business and Enterprise classes at school, as well trial as error."

Gary nodded his head thoughtfully, so Angus continued. "The wonderful thing is, not only have I started a business, but my business has become a success. I have sold my product to over fifteen schools. We're talking thousands of pens and thousands of dollars in profit in less than three months."

"Really?"

Angus nodded. He took another pen out and placed it on the meeting room table.

Gary turned his Inkda over in his fingers. "I can definitely see a possible story in what you've achieved. That's very impressive, if what you say is true. And you haven't even finished high school?"

Angus wanted to talk about everything they could put in the story, but he kept his calm, professional disposition and just nodded.

Gary took Angus's phone number and promised that Angus would be called that afternoon.

Yeyaaaah! Angus texted Rachael and Lucas. *Talking to a journalist from The Vine this arvo!!!!*

For an obituary? Lucas replied.

Well done, was Rachael's reply.

Angus had hoped for more enthusiasm from his friends

and felt another pang of disappointment that he couldn't share this victory with them as a company. He texted Lucas again and asked if he wanted to kick the footy in a few hours. He wanted to take his mind off the business for a while.

———————————

The boys met up at the local community oval. The sun had eventually emerged from behind the clouds, and the oval and adjoining playground had a number of school-aged children making noise in celebration of their second week of school holidays. As Angus and Lucas kicked the football to each other and joked about news stories they could make up for the newspaper, they enjoyed knowing that neither harboured bad feelings toward the other. They didn't discuss pens or school.

They were just starting to make bets for who could kick the farthest when Angus's phone started ringing. He would have felt nervous if he hadn't been using all his energy booting the football as far as he could. He answered the call and put the phone on speaker so that Lucas could listen in. They walked to the edge of the oval and sat on the wooden oval barriers.

Ruby, the journalist, sounded very polite and cheerful. "Gary, my supervising editor, gave me your story this morning, and I think it's just brilliant! We should be encouraging young people like yourself to follow their dreams."

"Ha. Tell that to my school," Angus said to get a laugh from Lucas.

"What do you mean by that?" Ruby asked. Angus could hear a keyboard being tapped in the background.

"Well, it's just that—and I don't mean to single out my

school; I have heard from many friends that other schools struggle with this as well—but schools sometimes forget that students are unique. Or they try too much to recognise uniqueness, which just makes everyone un-unique."

"I'm not sure I follow what you mean."

"I'm not really sure, either," Angus said. He was becoming nervous and excited—his optimal recipe for rambling.

"No, it's an interesting direction," Ruby said reassuringly. "From what I understand, you think that schools try to teach all students the same when students are different, but you also don't believe in the theory that every child needs to win a participation prize."

"Yeah, I guess so."

"And starting this pen business is your way of aiming for your own prize? You want to stand out as unique?"

"No, I don't think so."

"Why did you start your business?" Ruby asked.

Angus was thankful they had started talking about things he could easily articulate. "Well, as I learned in Business and Enterprise, I looked for a need and I saw a need."

"And the need you saw was for pens at your school?"

"I saw the need for *better* pens at school."

"I thought schools predominantly use computers these days? Why do you think schools are evidently willing to spend hundreds if not thousands of dollars on pens instead of upgrading technology?"

Angus didn't want the interview to be critical of his business. "We still use pens at school. It is true that computers are used a lot of the time, but that means when someone uses a pen, they want it to be as enjoyable and easy as using a computer."

"Is that your selling point—an enjoyable experience?" Ruby asked.

Angus paused to formulate a response. His hands were beginning to sweat, and it wasn't from kicking the football.

"I'm sorry if I sound blunt. I'm just seeking your opinion," Ruby added.

"You're fine," Angus said. "No, I would not say my selling point is 'buy our pens for an enjoyable experience'. We're selling our pens on the fact that they are a brand new, unique formula of ink that lasts longer than standard water-based inks, and Inkdas also write smoother than a standard ballpoint pen. The design of the pen is really cool, and all our customers so far have loved it." He suddenly knew how politicians must feel when reading scripted answers to tough questions.

"That's really great," Ruby said, typing her notes as she listened. "And how would you say that your school has helped you with this business?"

"My Business and Enterprise teacher, Mr Redding, is really good," Angus said. He quickly added, "Although he hasn't helped me directly, he's been a really good teacher."

"Is there anyone else who has helped you out? Starting and growing a successful business all by yourself is incredible."

Angus looked at Lucas, wondering if he had changed his mind. Lucas shook his head.

"No, not really anyone I can think of."

"Do you think it would be good to interview your teacher, Mr Redding?"

294

"Oh, I think he's on holidays at the moment and quite busy, coming towards the end of the year and all," Angus said. He considered that the newspaper would want to call his school. He had no contingency plan for that besides giving another number and speaking in a funny voice, so he hoped for the best.

"Speaking of the end of the year," Ruby said, "what are your plans for next year? Are you looking for investors to continue building your business?"

"I might do," Angus said. "The business is still in early days, but I can really see Inkdas becoming a very big, important company. From just a regular Year 12 student to CEO in a couple of months." That was the headline Angus hoped to see, and thought it might help to slip it into conversation.

"That's really great." Ruby laughed. "I love your ambition."

Angus's heart was thumping hard by the time Ruby concluded the interview. "Last thing is a photo. I'm going to get in contact with your school to see about setting up a photo of you in a classroom."

Angus realised in that moment that every school-based news article he had seen contained a photo of a group of students smiling awkwardly either in front of a playground or a science classroom.

"I'm not sure I want my photo taken."

"Why not?"

Angus considered saying that he had a black eye or a missing ear. "I'm just very shy," he said slowly.

Lucas let out a loud chuckle, which was met by a kick in his direction from Angus.

Ruby graciously said she would use a photo of the pens he had given at the office that morning, and that the story would be run online and in the daily edition newspaper the next day.

As soon as the call finished, Angus let out a sound he had never made before, something halfway between a cry and a sigh. "What am I doing?" he asked himself aloud. He held his hand to his chest, feeling his heart beat against his ribs. The adrenaline made him feel like he could do a thousand push-ups, but he knew he wasn't that fit, so he picked the next best thing. "I'm going for a run."

Angus ran around the oval as fast as his legs could carry him. He ran around that oval faster than he believed was possible. He wouldn't have been surprised if he had broken the world record.

Lucas remained where he was sitting and silently watched the one-man race. He wondered if he was doing the right thing for his friend.

Angus arrived back to Lucas and collapsed onto the grass. The soft grass felt like a memory foam mattress.

"This better be worth it," Angus panted, his eyes closed.

"I think you just lost a kilo," Lucas said. "I was thinking of joining you for a second lap, but it looks like you've finished for the moment."

Angus took a couple minutes of gasping to catch his breath.

"Why are you doing this?" Lucas asked. "You know, Rachael and I have discussed the possibility that you've gone slightly crazy."

Angus tried propping himself up on his elbows, but all his

energy was drained, so he settled back down in the grass and crossed his feet. "I don't care what other people think."

"Well, that's a load of rubbish; you do care what other people think," Lucas said. "If you didn't, you would have pressured Rachael and me to stay in the business to make the publicity story sound even better. A company of students sounds better than a one-person business."

Angus wasn't listening to Lucas. "I think I'm done with school. I know I don't know everything, but I'm okay with that. The teachers make school sound like the be-all and end-all. But it's not. Heaps of people are successful without a university degree."

"Heaps of people are successful *with* a university degree."

"You and Rachael know what you want to do next year," Angus said. "I have no idea what I'm going to do."

Lucas bounced the football against the grass, thinking about his future plans. He stood up and booted the footy as far as he could. It sailed across the oval and landed near the boundary line on the other side.

"Was that farther than mine?" Angus asked without opening his eyes.

"Probably," Lucas said. "I don't know what I want to do, either."

Angus looked at his friend. "I thought you were going to be my point of call when I need some brain surgery?"

Lucas took a deep breath in. "So did I, up until I started helping you with the business. Now I don't know. I'm obviously a great salesman—"

"Obviously." Angus laughed.

"And so now I wonder if maybe I should pursue being a salesman," Lucas continued. "I looked it up, and salesmen can make serious cash. Maybe I should do a degree in business or management?"

"Then go and do a degree in business or management."

Hearing someone else say it repulsed Lucas. "But all my life the plan was to become a brain surgeon or doctor! I can't change my plans now. I've already put in my uni preferences."

"You can change your uni preferences—"

"No I can't. What does it show if I just change my mind at the last minute over what I'm going to do for the rest of my life? I'm not a flighty person. I don't change my mind on a whim like you—no offense."

"None taken." It was too much effort to take offense. "Wasn't it you who told me that I shouldn't try to cram my life into as short a time as possible?"

"Probably," Lucas said. "But I've already spent the last two years getting ready for medical school. I've even read the text-books they use in first year."

"Make the choices that you want to make, and look up the sunk cost fallacy. That's the idea that it becomes hard to make choices about things you've already invested a lot in, even if choosing to abandon that investment would make you better off, or happier. I am very smart."

"Has school caused a sunk cost fallacy in all of us?" Lucas wondered aloud.

Angus laughed, followed by a coughing fit. "That's too depressing, even for me."

He closed his eyes again.

Angus woke the next morning in his bed with his phone vibrating on his chest. He had fallen asleep watching online videos late into the night before. Bleary eyed, he answered the private number.

"Hello, is this Angus Newton?" a cheery voice asked.

"Yes."

"Hi Angus, this is Ruby from The Vine. I'm just calling to let you know that your story was finished early and is now live on the website."

"It is?" Angus tried to sound awake. "Thanks for letting me know. I'll go check it out now."

"Also, is it okay if I pass your number on to a colleague in our digital media department? She was wondering if you would be interested in doing a video about your business, for online."

Angus couldn't believe it. "Absolutely. That sounds fine."

After the call, Angus ran to the Inkda office and loaded up his laptop. He searched for the news site and found the latest articles:

YEAR 12 STUDENT WRITES HIS FUTURE BY STARTING PEN BUSINESS

Angus Newton had almost finished Year 12 when he founded his own pen company. Using the knowledge from his Business and Economics course, Angus, aged just 17, says he saw a need for high-quality pens in schools, and sought to seize that opportunity. When asked about whether pens were necessary in the current, technology-saturated education environment, Angus said: "It is true that computers are used a lot of the time, but that means when someone uses a pen, they want it to be as enjoyable an experience as using a computer."

The young entrepreneur believes that schools should be encouraging students to take on activities to further their own learning. "Schools sometimes forget that students are unique."

Optimistic for the future, his first product, the 'Inkda' pen, is reportedly being considered as a potential line item at Moving Stationery, Australia's largest office supplies retailer. Gabby Barnes, stationery buyer at Moving Stationery, said she is excited about the prospect of stocking Angus's product. "We have had a preliminary conversation and look forward to continuing the process with Angus. We'd be excited to add another product to the vast range in our 160 stores nationwide, and online store."

Angus says he is proud of where he came from and where he is going with his business: "I can really see Inkdas becoming a very big company. [I've gone] from just a regular Year 12 student to CEO in a couple of months."

THE AVERAGE
EXPULSION MEETING

Earlier that year, Angus had purchased a gorilla suit online for an animal-themed 18th birthday party. He momentarily considered wearing it as a disguise on the first day back to school. He figured the students and teachers would be looking to either congratulate or condemn him for his rise to success and fame over the holidays; instead, they would just see a gorilla wearing a backpack and the school blazer.

Having decided the gorilla suit might get uncomfortable in the heat, Angus loitered around the shopping centre until 8:20am, when he could blend into the crowds of students walking onto the school grounds.

As he walked with his head low onto the school grounds, Angus felt like every student was looking at him—or at least talking about him behind his back. The truth was, very few of the students really cared. Of the students who had seen Angus featured in the newspaper or online article, or the video, or

301

the other online article for the local council, or another click-bait video titled 'How did this student make thousands of dollars in three months?' that had garnered 20,000 views, most just chuckled to themselves and continued with their holiday procrastination activities.

"Morning, famous one," Rachael said as she joined him in the sea of students. It was the first time they had seen each other since she and Lucas had stepped aside from the business.

As soon as she had left Angus's house that day during the holidays, she had regretted her decision. But after a lot of talking to herself in the car, she decided it was for the best, for her future. For the rest of the holidays she worked on her homework and tried not to think about the fun they had in their makeshift office, trying to figure out what things like "import taxes" were and whether they had to pay to them.

Rachael didn't know if Angus was still upset with her on that first Tuesday of Term 4, but Angus was clearly distracted by other worries.

"Have you heard any students talking about me?" Angus asked quietly, his head down.

"No, sorry."

"Don't be sorry. That's good."

"I thought the point of the publicity was to get everyone talking about you and the business."

"The publicity was for the real world," Angus said. "Not for school."

"By the way, thank you for not mentioning me in any of the interviews."

"That was what we agreed to," Angus replied. They reached their lockers. Angus kept an eye out for any approaching teachers while he stowed his belongings.

Rachael opened her locker a couple of doors away. "I'm up to date with all my work, and I feel good about my exams, thanks to your advice."

Angus gave the best smile he could. "That's great."

"I'm sure Mrs Campbell will be fine," Rachael said softly. "I'd feel really bad if she expelled you."

Angus sighed. "It's all good. I'm at peace. If she expels me, I'll get a job or start another business."

"I'm glad you're optimistic," Rachael said. "I don't know what I'd do if I couldn't go to uni."

"At this point, I don't know what I'd do if I *could* go to uni." Angus looked at the girl he'd grown quite fond of over the past couple of months. "Don't worry yourself, Rachael. You'll succeed in whatever you do."

"Angus Newton?" A man's voice called over the drone of students. Angus didn't need to turn to know who it was or what he wanted.

"Well, that's for me," Angus said with a smile. He closed his locker and followed Mr Tilley to the front office with his head held high.

Angus sat on the waiting room chair, watching Mr Tilley try to focus on a task on his computer. The bell for first lesson of the day had rung a few minutes ago and there was still no sign of Mrs Campbell.

"What's your plan for next year?" Angus asked the

303

principal's assistant.

"What do you mean?" Mr Tilley seemed unsure if he should be communicating with the student.

"Are you going to go to art school or continue working here?"

Mr Tilley shrugged. "I'll probably stay here."

"Until when?"

"I'm sorry, I've really..." Mr Tilley trailed off, nodding his head to his computer monitor.

"You should go and do an arts degree, or just create an exhibition."

"I'm planning on doing an arts degree," Mr Tilley said.

"When?"

"When I decide to."

"What's that decision based upon?"

"I need to get a bit more practice first."

"Says who?" Angus said firmly.

"Says lots of people!"

"And who says 'lots of people' are right?" Angus crossed his arms. "Your art is *your* art, man. Create art you think is good."

Mr Tilley looked over at his sketch book, lying open to an abstract sketch of a woman who was most likely Mrs Campbell, and smiled. But he shook his head and turned back to the computer.

Mrs Campbell opened her office door without warning and stepped out. She looked down at Angus.

Angus slowly turned his head to look up at his principal. He gave her a thin-lipped smile.

"Angus," was how she greeted him. She signalled him inside with a wave of her hand.

Angus entered the office and sat down in the visitor's chair. He wondered if she would let him take the chair out with him as a souvenir.

Mrs Campbell, after requesting of Mr Tilley that their meeting not be disturbed, came in and closed the door behind her.

Angus looked at the clock on the wall, wondering how long the average expulsion meeting required. Mrs Campbell's office chair squeaked as she sat down. Angus didn't know what was going to come next, and it appeared that Mrs Campbell was still deciding herself. Along with her signature silent glare, she held her mouth agape, seemingly formulating what she was going to say. Angus didn't see her as the type to drag a meeting out with monologuing or preaching, and that thought kept him calm.

"Before I finished high school, I worked for a fast food restaurant in the middle of the city," Mrs Campbell said. Angus began to worry. He knew very little about his principal's history, and frankly preferred it that way.

"The restaurant was very busy," she continued. "There was a constant line of customers and orders, and we would be lucky to get a five minute break in a seven hour shift.

"I had a manager. Her name was Paula and, up to that point in my life, she was the most horrible person I had ever met. She would swear at us. She would tell us workers how worthless we were and make us feel no more important than the tiles on the wall. Being only fifteen years old, I did not feel like I had any power to make a stand against Paula." She looked at Angus. "Have you ever had to work for anyone like Paula?"

Angus, caught off guard by the question, shrugged his shoulders.

Mrs Campbell continued. "One day one of my work friends, George, snapped. Mid-way through a Saturday lunch rush, Paula was hurling abuse at us for being too slow. George hit his spatula against the bench and yelled 'Paula, stop. We are people. Just stop'. Paula, clearly not used to being talked back to, did stop. She immediately left the store saying she was feeling ill and we never saw her again."

Angus was in the dark as to what the story had to do with him.

Mrs Campbell smiled. "How were your holidays?"

The boy swallowed to ease his dry throat and wished Mrs Campbell had offered him water. "They've been really good. I've been preparing for my exams."

"And how is your family? Is your dad still a builder?"

"Yes, they're all fine," Angus said. "Dad's still a builder. My brother Quinten got married late last year."

"Ah yes, Quinten." Mrs Campbell nodded. "He was always very studious. I'm so happy for him. So, everything's fine at home?"

Angus nodded.

Mrs Campbell opened her desk's top drawer. Angus smiled when he saw two of his distinctly orange Inkda pens amongst the assortment of stationery, but quickly hid his smile away. Mrs Campbell reached farther still into her drawer and pulled out another object. It was a chocolate bar. She placed it on her desk. "Do you remember us having a conversation at the start of last term about chocolate? I'm sure you do. And I am sure you will remember the conversation we had halfway through last term, when you promised me you had ceased selling things at school."

Angus nodded. "I remember both those conversations."

Mrs Campbell picked up an Inkda from the drawer and placed it next to the chocolate bar. "Then I hope you can explain to me, Angus, how your product turned from chocolate to writing instruments, and you thought that the situation had somehow changed?"

Angus's foolish dream that Mrs Campbell somehow hadn't read the news or seen the online videos or hadn't remembered being asked to comment on the story by a monthly education magazine were dashed as he looked at the two objects that had changed the course of his year, and probably his life.

"Firstly, the pens were sold outside the school grounds—" He stopped as Mrs Campbell quickly sucked in air and her cheeks flushed.

"Don't you dare try and take me for a fool by speaking in technicalities, Angus Newton," Mrs Campbell hissed. "Don't you dare try to treat me as anything but your principal."

Angus met her stare, his arms crossed tightly. "Okay, fine. I'll explain it: I saw a need in the school for better pens. I made better pens and now I have sold lots of better pens. None of what I have done has negatively affected my grades or negatively affected anyone else and so, quite frankly and with the utmost respect possible, none of this has anything to do with you, and you can't do anything to stop me from running my business."

"Why are you frustrated?"

"Why am I frustrated? Because you're not treating me like an adult!" Angus said. "Some of us in Year 12 are actually adults. We have lives outside of school, jobs to go to, businesses to run, and you act like school is the sun which life revolves around or the only road one can take to succeed in life. Some of us are planning to take different roads than academics, and I'm pretty sure we're going to survive."

"And what road are you taking?"

"I don't know yet," Angus admitted. "But it's my road, and I'm quite happy on it."

"And this road. You paved it yourself, did you?"

"Sure did."

"With no help from anyone else?"

"There have been people who have helped me along the way," Angus said, thinking of Rachael and Lucas.

"Who has helped you build this road?"

"Various people."

"Your family? Have they helped you?"

"Absolutely they have. My parents are proud of my business."

"What about your friends?" Mrs Campbell asked. "Have Lucas and Rachael helped you build your road?"

"Who my friends are that have helped me is irrelevant. This is about me."

"What about your teachers? Has Mr Redding helped you build your road? Has Mr Fletcher helped build your road?"

"No teacher has helped me directly with my business, if that's what you're inferring."

Mrs Campbell leaned forward, her hands in her lap. Her voice softened. "Have I helped you build your road, Angus?"

"No," Angus replied without a moment's hesitation.

"Have I prevented you from building your road?"

"I feel like you're about to try as hard as you can to tear up all the road I've built so far."

The principal picked up a daily edition of *The Vine*, an edition which was very familiar to Angus, and turned to page 4. She read the article aloud. "The young entrepreneur believes that schools should be encouraging students to take on activities to further their own learning. 'Schools sometimes forget that students are unique'."

She placed the newspaper down on the desk and Angus saw something on Mrs Campbell's face he had never seen before: disappointment.

"Do you know why I got into the education system?"

Angus shook his head, staring down at the desk.

"I wanted to find a way to care for people. I considered becoming a nurse, but after a year of study, I changed courses and became a teacher. For twenty years I worked in a classroom, and for the past nine years I have worked as a principal. I have seen kids lose parents to cancer. I have seen kids lose themselves to their own insecurities. I have seen kids flourish, graduate and succeed at the highest level in their fields. I have seen students marry other students and start families. And you tell a newspaper you think this school forgets students are unique?" Her eyes searched Angus. "I

309

can see you want to tell me I'm wrong."

"As you say," Angus said calmly. "All of those people you mention had lives that are very different from each other, and yet in the classroom they're all the same. It's either a letter between A and D, if letters are given anymore in place of vague 'satisfactory' comments, or the student is told to repeat the grade. Or, even worse, students are now diagnosed with whatever the latest fashionable problem is. My friend's little brother was diagnosed with dysgraphia because he's a messy writer. If I was in primary school now, I'd probably be diagnosed with the worst case of dysgraphia since the cavemen!"

"Dysgraphia is a real condition," Mrs Campbell said. "We diagnose people with those conditions so that we can individualise their learning paths because we acknowledge that they *are* unique."

"So the only way to get unique attention at school is to have a problem?"

Mrs Campbell sighed. "Lay it out for me, Angus. What do you want me to do? How should the school change? How do you want to be recognised for being unique? Because you've certainly being recognised out there in the media, and you've recognised this school as one that doesn't support students. What can I do to help and encourage the next student who doesn't think school is worth the effort and time I put into it?"

"I don't know," Angus said, exasperated. "I don't know anything. I don't know what I'm doing next year. I hardly know what I'm doing right now. How are students supposed to know what to do with their futures? How are we supposed to know what our purpose is in life? Do you expect me to go to

310

university and complete a Ph.D. in education to understand what school is trying to teach me?"

Mrs Campbell closed her eyes and leaned back in her chair. Angus knew he had stepped too far, but it felt like a burden had been lifted. There was no question he would be expelled now.

"You are dismissed," Mrs Campbell finally said.

Angus stood up. "You'll have to explain it to my parents."

"Explain what?"

"Why I'm expelled."

"I never said you are expelled."

He stumbled over the leg of the chair. "I'm not?"

"No. Please close the door on your way out," Mrs Campbell said, logging into her computer.

Angus had been so ready to be expelled that the opposite seemed absurd to him. "Why not?"

Mrs Campbell picked up the Inkda. "Because I like these."

Angus left the office and closed the door behind him, wondering what he had just been through. Mr Tilley, pretending to have not heard the raised voices, was still working studiously at his computer.

Angus paused in front of the principal's assistant. "Hey, Matthew."

Mr Tilley looked up.

"Get together enough artwork for a gallery and find a venue. I'll cover the costs."

Mr Tilley didn't reply apart from a reluctant nod of his head.

Angus left the office building with his head swimming,

trying to make sense of the meeting. He knew he owed everything to his friends for helping him. He didn't even realise some of the things Rachael and Lucas did until they were gone from the company. He knew he owed it to his family and teachers, for everything they did for him, whether they knew it or not. He couldn't help but chuckle out loud when he felt he even owed some of the business's success to Mrs Campbell when she—

He froze in the middle of the courtyard, the realisation hitting him like a bucket of sunscreen to the face. Angus spun around and marched back into the office building. He returned to Mrs Campbell's office door and knocked sharply.

"Come in," Mrs Campbell's muffled voice called.

Angus opened the door. "You knew."

"From the morning I drove past and saw you standing outside the retirement village," Mrs Campbell said calmly.

"No one knew," Angus said in disbelief.

"I made an enquiry of one of your customers."

"It was all you. You told all the other schools about my pens, even though you knew."

"I have no idea how you convinced that young lady to be a saleswoman for your company, and I have no idea how the pens ended up in my doctor's office, but I suspect there is a conversation on privacy we need to have."

LESSON SEVEN: THE BUSINESS LIFE CYCLE

Rachael hadn't been able to focus on her schoolwork for the past half-hour. All she could think about was Angus being led out of the school by Mrs Campbell, possibly in handcuffs—she wasn't sure how expulsion worked—and told to never return. She didn't know if it was guilt or stupidity or courage, but she raised her hand while the English teacher was explaining the primary themes of *Macbeth* and asked if she could go to the front office.

When Rachael appeared next to Angus in the doorway of Mrs Campbell's office, he couldn't tell whether she was on the brink of laughing or crying. "I helped Angus with the business," Rachael announced to Mrs Campbell with a shaky voice.

"She knows everything," Angus said.

Rachael's courage dissipated. She leaned herself against the doorframe.

"It turns out our principal is possibly a psychic," Angus said.

Rachael wanted to plead her case. She wanted to get on her knees and beg for Mrs Campbell's forgiveness, but seeing Angus standing with such coolness after he had presumably been expelled gave her confidence. She nodded, feeling defeated, thinking through the next stages of her day: how she would explain it all to her parents; how many retail stores she should send her resume to.

"Mrs Campbell also explained that they're pressing charges on all three of us," Angus said dryly.

"I said no such thing," Mrs Campbell said quickly, before Rachael could comprehend what he'd said and faint. "Angus, that's not helpful. Rachael, I am aware of your contribution to this Inkda business, but there will be no punishments. I hope this whole situation will provide a lifetime of learning to reflect upon for the three of you."

"We're not expelled?" Rachael asked.

"Nope," Angus said. "Mrs Campbell likes our product."

Rachael chose laughter over tears. "But that can't be right."

Angus began closing the office door. He said to Mrs Campbell, "We're going to go back to class before Rachael changes your mind."

———

Mr Redding stood at the front of the Business and Enterprise classroom and stared at his three students with a big grin. "You all started a company?!" He shook his head in disbelief. "That's insane! Not to pat my own back, but that makes me a pretty good teacher."

The students laughed.

"You definitely helped," Angus said.

Mr Redding put his things down. "The amount I've taught you would be good enough to write a basic business proposal. But to actually go out and start a business? You did that on your own. And you somehow managed to keep it a secret for months? Just incredible. I take my hat off to all of you."

"And apparently we're not getting expelled!" Lucas exclaimed happily. Although Angus hadn't gone into much detail about the meeting, all Lucas cared about knowing was whether he needing to start packing his locker. Lucas still didn't plan on going near Mrs Campbell for a while, just in case she changed her mind.

"I unfortunately can't give you a grade for your pen business, because I need some good ol' written evidence I can send in for adjudication." Mr Redding said. "So please don't forget that your business plans for the movie theatre are still due by Friday. I have already received two out of three. Just waiting on the public relations manager."

"Have you even started?" Lucas asked Angus.

"Yes, I've started," Angus said defensively. His "start" was writing all the headings at the top of the pages.

Mr Redding brought up a presentation on the screen titled *The Business Life Cycle*. "Even though you're all apparently business experts, we must move on to one of our final topics. The business life cycle is one of the last topics because it neatly summarises everything that has been covered in this course. Every business goes through the five phases we're exploring today." The slide changed to a graph showing the five phases. Mr Redding looked to Angus. "Can I use the pen company as an example?"

Angus nodded.

"Excellent. So, as I said, there are five phases in the business life cycle. The first phase is the launch phase. This is when the business actually releases its product. In the case of your pen company, in this phase you would have seen very few sales and probably a loss in revenue. Is that correct?"

"More or less," Angus said. "I had to pay for a saleswoman, an initial order of product and Lucas's shockingly unhealthy eating habits."

"Geniuses have to eat," Lucas said.

Angus quickly added, "But I will say we asked the clients to pay for the product upfront, so we weren't making losses for long at all."

"In an accounting sense, even if the customer paid you a million dollars upfront, that money is not yours until the customer receives their product. Something could go wrong with the order, and if you've spent the customer's money and then need to refund them, you'd be as stuffed as a Christmas turkey. But it sounds like you moved quite quickly from the launch phase to the next stage, which is the growth phase. In this phase your sales would have risen dramatically, resulting in the beginnings of modest profits and increased cash reserves. Would that be correct?"

"Yep," Angus said proudly.

"Good," Mr Redding said. "Enjoy it while it lasts or get ready to change."

"What do you mean?" Angus asked.

"Do you have a growth plan?"

"Yes, I have a plan," Angus said.

"What's your plan?"

"We have some ideas for distribution and that," Angus said vaguely. "But what would happen if we don't keep growing?"

"You'll hit the next phase, which is the shake-out phase. That's when sales won't rise as quickly, and you're going to start seeing competitors bring out competing products. Have you secured the patent for your product?"

Angus was silent, not exactly sure what "securing the patent" meant. He looked to Rachael, who shrugged.

"Who produces the pens?" Mr Redding asked.

"A factory in...China, I think. I order them from a local pen supplier," Angus said with growing concern.

"So, I could go to that pen supplier and ask for my own batch of the exact same pens?"

"My logo is unique," Angus said innocently.

Mr Redding winced. "You better hope none of the big brands find your supplier."

"Why?"

"They'll undercut you on price and overshoot you on marketing power, advertising and distribution. If I were you, I'd call your pen supplier and start working out who owns the patent. Otherwise you're going to hit the next phase quickly, which is 'maturity'. Your profits will start to decline, and it's up to you to either reinvent the business or release a new product and hope the business cycle starts again. If you can't restart the cycle, then you'll be in the decline phase. That's when your profit, sales and cash all decline into oblivion.

You'll have to sell whatever assets the business has, settle all debts, and find a different adventure to pursue."

Lucas looked anxiously at Angus. "Are we in the maturity phase?"

"No. No, we're fine. We'll be fine."

"We can't beat the big brands," Lucas said.

"Just leave it with me."

"Leave it with you?" Lucas snapped. "You didn't secure the patent for the one product our whole business revolves around. Not to mention you got that original order of pens very quickly. That means the manufacturer is somewhere local."

"Just trust me and stop freaking out," Angus said, embarrassed they were arguing in front of Mr Redding. "I have a plan."

"What plan?"

"You haven't told him the plan?" Rachael asked.

Angus hadn't told Lucas his idea because he didn't know if he was convinced it was a good idea himself.

"We're building up the business to sell it off," Angus said.

"You're suggesting we give up?" Lucas asked. He couldn't believe Angus would be willing to walk away from the business he'd built.

"It's not giving up," Angus said. "Businesses aim to be bought out all the time. It's a very common strategy."

The three students looked at Mr Redding in unison for confirmation.

"It is a common strategy," he said.

"But I don't want to sell out," Lucas said. "I want to be a salesman. I want to manage a sales team and teach them everything I know. I'm good at it, and now you're telling me I can't do it?"

Rachael smiled. "You are a good salesman."

"Thanks," Lucas mumbled.

"There are other sales jobs out there, but if we did manage to sell, you wouldn't have to work all year. Maybe even a couple of years," Angus said.

That piqued Lucas's interest. "How much are we talking here?"

"We could maybe sell the business for fifty thousand dollars. Maybe more," Angus said. He was hesitant to say how much he really thought he could sell the company for with Mr Redding present, but it was a much higher price.

"All three of us have to be on board, but that's what I propose," Angus said.

Lucas looked to Rachael.

"I'm happy with that plan," she said. It was the reason she had agreed to help when Angus had originally told her the plan before mid-semester break.

Lucas restlessly tapped his pen on the desk. His decision was between a lot of money now—more than he ever expected to see in his bank account at one time—or doing what he loved. It had taken him weeks to come to terms with not wanting to go to medical school anymore and instead wanting to be a salesman.

"I don't know." He sighed. "I don't know."

The next day, Angus found himself back in the usual daily school routine, as if life would continue like that forever. He leaned against the bench in the Year 12 common room, waiting for his cheese toastie to finish cooking on the communal sandwich press.

"Are you a millionaire?" Alan asked, not asking permission to add his own sandwich to the press.

"Pretty close," Angus said dryly. By this point, all the students in his year had seen or heard about Angus's growing pen company. Just that morning, with Mrs Campbell's permission, a television crew from a national morning show had come to the school to do a live puff piece on the pen business. Bits of anti-shine makeup powder were still coming off Angus's face.

"Did you hear that?" Alan called to some boys playing games on their laptops. "Angus is a millionaire!"

Lucas, sitting on one of the couches, laughed out loud at the lie.

Angus smiled. "I'm not a millionaire. I have exactly nine hundred and ninety-nine thousand, nine hundred and ninety-eight dollars in my bank account. I only need two more dollars, and then I'll be a millionaire."

"Did you hear that?" Alan called out in amazement to the other boys. "Angus needs just two dollars and he'll be a millionaire!"

"I've got two dollars on me," Damien said enthusiastically. He took a coin from his pocket and tossed it to Angus.

"You're a millionaire now!" Alan declared. The dozen students present displayed a mixture of amazement and pretending not to be amazed that they were in the presence of a millionaire.

Rachael entered the common room with her garden salad lunch. "He's not a millionaire."

"No, he is!" Alan insisted. "Damien just gave him two dollars."

Angus flicked the coin back to Damien. "I was kidding. I'm nowhere near a millionaire. I have about a twentieth of that."

"Can I get a job working for your company?" Leah asked. "I've got a year's experience as a dental assistant."

"How is a year's experience at a dentist applicable to working for a pen company?" Alan scoffed.

"It's better work experience than working in a fast food restaurant," Leah fired back.

"Hey, you need to thank me," Alan said. "It's people like me working to keep dentist clinics in business."

"I'm serious, Angus. Do you have any jobs available? I have no idea what I'm gonna do next year," Leah said.

Angus shook his head. "Sorry, I can't promise anything. But I'll let you know If anything comes up."

"Can I get a job as well?" Alan asked.

"I'll let everyone know if there are any job opportunities that come up, but don't count on it."

"Man, you're in such a good position," Damien said.

Angus rescued his burning cheese toastie and singed his finger as he transported it to a plastic plate. "I'm not rich—I promise."

"No," Damien said, "I mean you've got this ability to build up a business and start giving people jobs. Is your business planning on doing any philanthropy?"

"I've considered it."

"Well, let me know if you need a hand with that sort of thing. I could help you work out a sustainability plan," Damien said excitedly as he unwrapped his ham sandwich. "You wouldn't have to pay me, though. It would just be great practice."

"Thanks, man. I'll give you a call when we get to that stage."

Angus stood behind Rachael's couch.

"Are you two dating yet?" Lucas asked.

"Are me and who dating?" Angus replied.

Lucas frowned. "You and Rachael."

Rachael had a look of complete bewilderment.

Angus looked at her equally as baffled.

"You know I've been asking for your help because of your skills," Angus said to Rachael. "Not because I—"

"Well, that's what I've been assuming," Rachael said.

"Ah, a classic friend zone." Lucas laughed.

"Why does there need to be... No, that's now what's happening at all," Angus said. He glanced at Rachael with a quizzical expression to triple-check that he hadn't missed any signs.

She shook her head. "Not everything needs to lead to a guy and girl hooking up."

Lucas leaned back on his couch with his hands up defensively. "Okay, okay. I'm sorry."

Brooke, who was sitting at one of the desks, also chimed in. "Everyone thought you two were practically engaged and preparing the honeymoon."

"Who thought that?" Angus asked.

Brooke laughed. "Everyone."

Angus didn't believe it. He looked around the room and spotted Abigail by her lonesome on the other side of the room with her headphones in. He briskly moved over to her and signalled for her to remove her headphones.

"Hey, Abby. Did you hear about me and Rachael—"

Abigail's eyes lit up. "So it's true? That's so exciting!"

Angus returned to the couches, shaking his head. "Not once this year have I thought about dating anyone at school," he lied.

"Same for me," Rachael lied.

With the excitement of the television production that morning, Angus had been unable to talk to Rachael or Lucas in private all day. He got their attention and nodded towards the door. They walked outside into the courtyard.

"What's up?" Rachael asked, stabbing a cherry tomato onto her fork as they walked through the courtyard. Angus looked down at the steam rising from his toastie, unsure if he wanted to give them the news.

"I've received an offer for the pen company."

Lucas paused mid-crunch of a chip.

"Do you remember that guy I met at the café? Luke Pilcher?" Angus asked. "He called me out of the blue last night. He said he wants to buy the business."

"All of it?" Lucas asked

Angus nodded. "He wants a hundred percent of the business for a hundred thousand."

Rachael could sense Angus's reluctance. "That's really good, isn't it? How much is the business worth?"

Angus shrugged. "I have no idea. Mr Redding hasn't taught us how to value a business, and all the advice online is confusing."

"Did you say yes to Pilcher?" Lucas asked.

"No. I wanted to find out if you both were definitely on board."

There was a long moment of silence as they all considered what they were doing.

"It's strange," Rachael said. "I have no interest in working in sales or retail. I never have and doubt I ever will. But I've really enjoyed working with you two. It'll be sad once it's over."

"Yeah, it's been fun." Angus smiled.

"When I first met you in business studies, I thought you were just an impulsive teen chasing easy money to buy a car or something," Rachael admitted.

"I still am an impulsive teen looking for easy money," Angus said dejectedly.

Rachael shook her head. "You've changed."

"Thanks," Angus said. "I'm trying."

"If you think the deal is good, I'm on board," Rachael said. "I believe you'll do the right thing."

They looked to Lucas.

"I guess if I've already changed my life plans once, there's no harm in changing them again." He reluctantly nodded his head. "Let's do it."

Angus surreptitiously pulled out his phone and messaged

Luke Pilcher. *Let's negotiate.*

"Angus!" Mrs Campbell said as she walked past. "I hope you're using that phone to find the hat that is supposed to be on your head. You've just ruined the school's no-hat detention streak."

Lucas laughed as Angus scrambled away to his locker. "All good things must come to an end."

"That reminds me, Lucas. We haven't had a little chat about this semester yet," Mrs Campbell said. "I'll have Mr Tilley organise a meeting."

Lucas wasn't laughing anymore, especially when Rachael dryly added, "She'll want to let you know about the charges they're pressing."

THE OFFER

Luke Pilcher sounded very keen to get together as soon as possible, so they agreed to meet first thing the next morning.

Angus didn't get a wink of sleep that night. He spent half of the night on the internet, looking up negotiation tactics and case studies on the sales and mergers of other businesses. He spent the other half of the night restlessly wondering what would happen if he couldn't sell the business. Would he be stuck selling pens for the rest of his life? Deep down he knew the three of them could only take the business so far without a lot more help. It certainly didn't help his confidence when all the news stories about Inkda focused on the fact that he was just a Year 12 boy, so young and naïve. Keeping true to his word, Rachael and Lucas's involvement was still a secret to the public.

The next morning, he entered the shopping centre in his full school uniform and sat on a bench outside Café Olka.

Like their previous morning meeting, the shopping mall was quiet. '80s pop music played in the distance over the speaker system.

He was looking at funny pictures on his phone to distract himself from the meeting when Luke Pilcher appeared as if from nowhere. "Good morning, young Angus!"

"Morning." Angus put his phone away. He hoped he didn't look as nervous as he felt.

Pilcher, dressed in a black suit and looking like he had recently visited a barber, led the way to a table in Café Olka by a window that overlooked the near-empty carpark.

"Good morning!" the waitress called, not forgetting the face of the man who had given her $500 for a muffin recipe.

"Ah, good morning!" Pilcher called back. "Can I get some toast? Five pieces should do. Butter and sugar, please. What will you have, Angus?"

"I'm fine."

"Nothing for the boy!" Pilcher called, taking his seat. He looked at Angus with a grin that made Angus's skin crawl. "How are your school assignments going? You must be almost near your exams."

Pilcher was acting like they were old friends. Angus did not feel that way at all, but knew that the old man held the power in this meeting.

"Pretty much all done," Angus said. "I graduate next week."

"Ah, good for you! I remember my graduation," Pilcher said. "How the years fly. Don't let your years fly by, Angus. You can't get them back when they're gone."

"I don't intend to," Angus said shortly. He crossed his arms. "I've thought about the offer you've given for my business."

Pilcher was staring at something out the window. Angus turned to see a woman in a dirty jumper and trackpants searching in one of the carpark bins.

"I wonder what she did with her years," Pilcher said.

"I'm not sure." Angus had let himself believe this meeting would be short and to the point. He kicked himself for not knowing better.

"I do wonder why some of us turn out rich and success-ful, and yet others turn out like...that." Like a light had been switched, Pilcher's demeanour turned from contemplative to excited. "I bought a new car yesterday! It's one of those hybrid electrical-petrol cars. Really expensive, but I care about the environment. I'd be happy for you to take it for a test run."

"No thanks."

Pilcher clicked his fingers. "You probably can't drive yet. When do you get your learner's permit?"

Angus couldn't take the condescension. "Are you trying to talk down to me?"

Pilcher acted surprised. "What do you mean?"

"I know I'm young. I'm very aware of that fact," Angus said. "But as you also know, me and my associates have started a company that is about to be stocked nationally in the largest office supplies chain in the country."

"I do know all that, and I think it's wonderful. That's why we're here today. I think you've done a wonderful job." He looked around. "I think this café has done a wonderful job."

"Please don't change the subject."

Pilcher took a deep breath. His smile faded. "You have a lot to learn, especially about business meetings and courtesy. I can see you're...antsy, so let's set niceties aside for the moment. You'd like to discuss my offer? Let's discuss it, then. Do you accept?"

"What was the offer again?" Angus just wanted to hear the man say it.

"A hundred thousand, in cash, for a hundred percent ownership of the Inkda brand and all its assets."

The numbers meant little to Angus; the sale wasn't for filling his own pockets with money. But as his final act as the founder of Inkda Pens, he wasn't going to accept without seeing how far he could push the negotiations.

He pulled a packet of salt from the table's condiments holder and flicked it absentmindedly. "I've talked with my advisors, and they recommend I ask for five hundred thousand."

If Pilcher's blank stare was meant to worry the boy, it failed. Angus stared back, unmoveable. Pilcher lowered his voice. "You want me to treat you like an adult, and then you say something like that? What you propose is ridiculous and downright stupid."

"I'm happy to hear a counter-offer," Angus said.

"My offer is one hundred thousand. I'm sure that's more than your parents earn in a whole year."

"Probably," Angus said, "but my parents didn't create a highly successful pen company, either."

"Your 'highly successful' pen company has brought in how

much revenue? The numbers you emailed me were what, about sixty thousand dollars?"

"Fifty-five thousand actually," Angus corrected. "Fifty-five thousand dollars in four months. With no paid advertising and three little kids running the show."

The waitress brought over five pieces of toast with five pats of butter and five sachets of sugar. Angus and Pilcher patiently waited for the waitress to move away again.

"You know I could walk out of here right now and you'd never hear from me again," Pilcher threatened.

"Then who would eat your toast?"

"I could buy this whole café, this whole shopping centre, with a snap of my fingers!" Pilcher hissed.

"But you're still sitting there, informing me of how rich you are," Angus said. "That leads me to believe that you really want to buy my pen company. My asking price stands at five hundred thousand dollars."

The foot traffic in the shopping centre was slowly increasing with a handful of early morning shoppers. An elderly man sat at another table on the other side of the café.

Pilcher took his time spreading a thick layer of butter on every piece of toast. He ripped open the packets of sugar and poured the contents evenly over the buttered toast, creating a stack that would make any dietician faint.

"I'm not here to play games," Pilcher finally said.

"Neither am I. What's your counter-offer?" Angus's confidence was building, almost to where he wondered if *he* had the upper hand in this negotiation.

Pilcher finished pouring sugar on the last slice. "I'll go up to two hundred thousand."

"Four hundred."

"Two hundred."

"Four hundred."

Pilcher clanged his knife down against his plate. "Boy, you don't know a thing about business!"

An epiphany hit Angus so vividly that it made him laugh. "You're the first person who has ever said that to me. Everyone has told me how young I am. Everyone has told me that I should focus on my school grades now and start a business later—that I should just listen, learn and not 'do', and there would be some magical point in my life when I would suddenly know how to do whatever I do. But, as it turns out, at no point until now has anyone *ever* said to me 'you don't know anything about business'. And it just happens to come from the man who's trying to buy my business. I feel like I know enough about business to know you're trying to stuff me over by undervaluing Inkdas, and I know that I have nothing to lose from leaving you to eat your sugary toast in peace. With all respect, sir."

Angus, feeling as strong as the day he made his first pen sale, put his schoolbag on his lap to show how serious he was about leaving.

Pilcher's expression was once again unreadable as he looked at the boy, a slice of toast in his hand, the sugar sparkling under the fluorescent lights.

Angus stared back into the old man's eyes.

"Who's your lawyer?" Pilcher asked.

"Why? Are you going to sue me?"

"No. We need to draw up a sale of business contract."

"Oh," Angus said, feeling silly. "So, you agree to four hundred thousand?"

"I do."

This was not the outcome Angus was expecting. He had been fully willing to go down to one hundred thousand and one dollar. He also didn't have a lawyer, but now seemed like a great time to invest in one. "I'll get my lawyer to give you a call."

Angus put his bag back down at his feet. He felt it decent enough to sit with the man who was about to pay him close to half a million dollars, if only for a few minutes longer.

"How's the toast?"

"Getting cold," Pilcher said. He relaxed back into his chair. "What are you going to do with all the money?"

"I haven't decided," Angus lied.

Pilcher wiped sugar off his mouth. "Can I give you a word of advice?"

"Sure." Angus didn't feel like he was talking to a wealthy businessman anymore. Pilcher looked like a lonely old man.

"I see bits of me in you," Pilcher said. "Don't turn out like me. It's never enough."

"Sugar or money?" Angus asked.

Pilcher smiled. "Today I'll say money and tomorrow I'll say sugar. From my experience, good things last far shorter than you realise."

Angus nodded. "I know. This business was just a practice run. If I can create a successful business in a matter of months, I'm sure I can do it all again."

"And if lightning doesn't strike twice?"

Angus shrugged. "I'll recruit more people and umbrellas."

With the start of the school day approaching, Angus excused himself and left the meeting.

He pulled out his phone and composed a short email to his classmate, Damien:

I have a job for you.

THIRTEEN YEARS
AND *THEN* FOREVER

Angus woke up and stared at the wall. Waking up felt the same. His bed felt the same. His bedroom walls looked the same.

The previous night's Year 12 graduation ceremony had made a big deal about his cohort of students and all their accomplishments, but no more than the big deal made about every graduating year. The students all promised to keep in touch, some of the girls suggested a big five-year reunion, but everyone knew neither of those things were going to happen. The only thing all fifty graduating students had in common was that they had gone through Year 12 together. Some students had applied for the same degrees at university, and some were real friends and would continue to see each other, but they were all aware that thirteen years had ended, and nothing would ever be the same. That thought made Angus smile.

Angus got out of bed and went to his computer. He searched the news sites for 'Inkdas' to see if there were any new articles. The latest relevant article was from a week ago, simply stating that the Inkdas brand had been acquired by Pilcher Holdings Ltd. for an undisclosed sum.

A few hours later, Angus, Rachael and Lucas sat around the table in their former office. What was at one time Inkdas' bustling command centre had been returned to a spare bedroom. All brand designs and customer leads were carefully taken off the cork boards and categorized, and the USBs of invoice and receipt files were boxed up to be sent to the new owner, as required by the sale of business agreement.

"My lawyer said we can't start another stationery company for a minimum for two years," Angus explained.

"Which lawyer?" Lucas asked.

"First person I found searching for 'local business lawyer' online," Angus said. "They're expensive. Cost about a thousand dollars in the end."

"Claim it on tax," Rachael said.

"What do you mean?" Angus asked.

Rachael looked with concern at the two boys. "You do know we need to pay tax on the earnings from the sale of the business?"

"Are you telling me I have to get an accountant now as well?" Lucas groaned.

"If you don't want to go to prison for tax evasion," Rachael said.

"Speaking of the sale," Angus said, "I saw the money has come though."

Lucas lit up. "How much was it? How much do I get?"

"Minus the amount paid to the lawyer, each of us get a hundred and thirty-three thousand," Rachael said.

"I know. I just wanted to hear you say it," Lucas said dreamily. "Have you sent it to me yet?"

"I transferred it this morning," Rachael said. "I had to call the bank and do all sorts of verifications. They said it will take about two days to transfer."

"As soon as it arrives, I'm going to go and invest in some shares," Lucas said, leaning back in his chair.

Angus laughed. "Good to see you're happy about the outcome. You're not still having doubts about whether we should have sold?"

"Nope. I'm sticking with the decision," Lucas said. "Also, I've made another decision: I'm not going to uni."

"You're sure you don't want to be a doctor?" Angus asked. "You won the merit award for biology last night."

"I know," Lucas said proudly. "But I'm going to get a job in sales somewhere. Maybe some company somewhere is looking for a top biology student to sell their cars or...fish."

"You want to be a fish salesman?" Angus asked.

"I can learn to swim."

Rachael raised an eyebrow. "Wait, are you selling *to* fish, or—"

Angus shook his head to tell her not to worry about trying to understand.

"What is Miss Dux doing with her money?" Lucas asked.

Rachael, proud recipient of the school's dux award, knew exactly what she was going to do. "I'm paying off my parents' mortgage, and then paying my uni fees upfront. There's a big discount if you pay upfront. I'm even thinking of applying for a university overseas. There is a great engineering program at the University of Oxford."

"A couple of weeks ago you were worried you wouldn't be able to get into any university," Angus said.

Rachael smiled. "I feel like I can do it. What about you? Have you decided what you're doing with your share?"

"I'm still considering the options." It was true Angus was considering the options in the sense that he and Damien were discussing the best charitable recipients for his share of the money—a job which Damien vehemently refused compensation for.

The three former students sat quietly for a few minutes, only the crunch of Lucas's pizza-flavoured Shapes breaking the silence. None of them wanted to say anything that would indicate it was time to leave.

"So, is this it? Was this past semester the glory days?" Lucas asked.

"I guess so," Angus said. "We made a really good team."

Rachael took a deep breath. "I want to say thank you, both of you, for helping me this semester. I've never felt so appreciated."

"We should be thanking you!" Lucas said. "This business would have crashed and burned long ago if you didn't agree to help out."

Rachael smiled. "This was definitely the best way to finish school."

"Let me know if you need a job reference," Angus said.

"Oh, good," Lucas said. "Because I've already applied to a number of places and put you both down as references on my resume. If you get a call, please pretend you love me."

"We will keep in touch," Angus promised both his former business associates and current friends. "And not like how everyone promised last night."

They all nodded in agreement. And with that, it felt like the right time to go their separate ways.

Angus hugged Rachael at the front door. He didn't want to say anything sappy or emotional. Rachael wished Angus would say something sappy and emotional, but he didn't.

Lucas couldn't help but laugh at his two friends. "You two will get there eventually."

Neither Angus or Rachael said anything to shut Lucas down. That is, until he added: "So, should I keep some money spare for a suit this year? Any decisions on the bridal party yet?"

"Thanks, Lucas," Angus said quickly.

Rachael got into her ten-year-old hatchback and drove away. Lucas put his headphones in and walked away down the street. Angus watched them disappear and went back inside the dark, quiet house. He stood in the hallway and sighed, wondering what to do next. He had all the freedom and time in the world, which he immediately found to be quite a nuisance. Experience told him eating food was always a good option for filling one's time, but seeing as it was late morning, he couldn't decide between eating a big late breakfast or a big early lunch.

Angus meandered to the kitchen, opened the fridge,

then the freezer, then the pantry. Nothing interesting. He spotted one of his mum's dessert recipe books open on the bench. He had never really tried baking a cake or pie before and wondered if that could be a fun project to undertake. He flicked from page to page, looking at the colourful pictures and recipes of lamingtons, muffins, slices and tarts. All the recipes looked easy to follow.

"If I can start a business, I can make a chocolate-caramel slice," he decided.

And that was when he felt an urge. He resisted it as much as he could, but the more he resisted it, the more he thought about it. And the more he thought about it, the better he thought the idea was. It wasn't long before Angus considered his idea a stroke of genius. He grabbed his phone and group-messaged Rachael and Lucas.

Come back ASAP. I've just had a new idea...

www.ingramcontent.com/pod-product-compliance
Lightning Source LLC
Chambersburg PA
CBHW030557180626
46816CB00005B/1577